NOW OR NEVER

IRIS BOYS: BOOK ONE

LUCY SMOKE

Dedicated to Now or Never's first reader, Caitlyn Kale. Thank you for being such a good friend and a passionate reader. Also, now you can tell your mom that you're in a book!

ACKNOWLEDGMENTS

A major thank you to everyone who made this book possible. As always, thank you to my closest friends Desiree LaFreniere, Elizabeth Deyoung, and Ashley Isom.

To my author tribe, you ladies have been the most wonderful and encouraging group and I could not do what I do without having you in my life. Well, I probably could, but it wouldn't be nearly as fun.

To my amazing editor, Kristen. Keep razzing me and maybe I'll get better.

To all of my friends and supporters, especially the friends who let me message them in the middle of the night with my ideas and rants. You understand just what it's like to be in my head and not the fun part with the voices and the characters and the stories. Thank you for pushing me beyond and thank you for believing in me.

PROLOGUE

The sand sliding between my thighs woke me; the grimy, grainy feel of each sharp, cold quartz particle as they stuck to my wet skin, my clothes, and every crevice. I groaned under a pounding drum that beat against the inside of my skull. I pressed my palm to my forehead as if that could ease the pain.

The air was chilled despite the place and the season, but the ocean at night was always like that. A few yards away, my best friend snored, curled up in her sleeping bag. Why we both thought a night on the beach would be the best graduation celebration was beyond me. It was a little early since neither of us had actually graduated or finished exams, but I had learned to take the good moments when I could get them. The sand between my toes and fingers cemented the choice we had made.

I pushed dried strands of brown hair out of my face and peeked around, noting that everything was less blurry without a few bottles of alcohol running through my system. The ocean was beautiful; a sight I rarely came to see even though I lived less than an hour away. The waves crashing against the sandy hills of shells and minuscule rocks reminded me of being rocked back and forth as a young child after having nightmares. Lately, my mom rarely even acknowledged me, unless something was wrong – and something was always wrong.

The brief feeling of peace was quickly and easily washed away. I shouldn't have taken the night off, I thought. We needed the money. Guilt crept in even as my headache faded. I sat up and looked over at the empty beer bottles scattered around. I had never been much of a drinker. I didn't even like beer, but after a few, I hadn't cared. The taste had gone away after the fourth or fifth bottle. At least, for me it had. It took Erika several more and a few loud complaints before she had raised the neck of her bottle up without flinching.

With no real sleeping bag, I had spread a sheet out on the ground with a somewhat scratchy blanket that Erika had loaned me to sleep on. It was covered in sand, so I grabbed the blankets and moved several feet away to shake them out before rolling them up together and striding back towards Erika's sleeping form.

Staring at the ocean, so dark that it matched the sky and seemed to go on forever, I thought of all the ways things could have been different for me. Life could have been worse. It could have been better. I would have liked for it to have been better, but what was the use bemoaning something that never even was.

I scanned the old watch my brother had passed down to me. It told me that the sun would be up in another two hours or so. Water flicked over my skin as I began to gather my belongings and put them in my satchel. I nudged Erika awake and she moaned, rolling over and mumbling something about five more minutes. I ignored her and continued to nudge until she was well and truly awake.

"You have the internal alarm clock of an old lady," she accused, stretching. I shuddered as the bones in her joints cracked with a loud audacity that always seemed to surprise me.

"We're gonna be late for school," I said.

I didn't really care if we were late for school or not. With only a few weeks left until graduation, the last thing I cared about was tardiness. I did, however, need to get back to change and check on my mom. Erika grumbled, but thankfully began to pack her things before we headed back to the hotel parking lot that we had snuck into. Luckily, no parking violation waited on the windshield of her parents' rusted pick-up truck. We climbed into the cab, her behind the wheel and me in the passenger side, and settled in for the drive back.

Nearly forty-five minutes later she pulled into Pendergrass Circle, stopping in front of the yellow-paneled, brown-roofed duplex that I lived in with my mom. I waved Erika off as I shut the front door and headed straight to my room. It seemed that almost as soon as I sat down on my sagging mattress, the house phone began to ring. I jumped up and ran for the hall to grab it before the noise woke Mom up.

"Hello?"

"Why do you sound out of breath?" I sighed at the sound of Michael's voice.

"Well, it's 7 am here, so I didn't want the phone to wake Mom up. Where are you?"

My brother, Michael, had been given a full ride to a private college in upstate New York right out of high school. Four years and a bachelor's degree in business management later, he was indoctrinated as a recruiter for a company in the Big Apple itself. A part of me envied him the detachment he felt from our mom. There had been nothing but anger and bitterness between them when he had packed what little he had here, and left. It was nice to have my own room, but I still missed him.

"I'm in Seattle right now, but I should be heading back to New York in another few hours. I'm waiting for a flight. How is she? Any better?"

Michael only called every once in a while, never asking to speak to her, and I didn't blame him. She had accused him of stealing from her and thrown him out of the house several times before he turned eighteen. It was only later that we learned she had severe bipolar disorder and now, with the tumor in her brain, her moods were worse. Even with the medication doctors gave her to help counteract them, the cancer only ate up more of the kind loving mom she had been when we were young.

"Nothing's changed," I said. "Everything's the same as always."

"Okay." An extended silence hung between us.

"Is there anything else?" I asked.

"You graduate in a few weeks, don't you?"

"Yea." Like I could forget that school would be well and truly over and I could finally enter the working world full time. "Do you...I mean, are you...coming?"

"I don't know if I'll be able to make it. I'll be sure to send a gift or something."

"No," I said. "You don't have to do that."

"I gotta go, Harlow. I'm about to board."

"Okay, be safe."

"Bye."

I set the phone back in the cradle and walked towards my room, pausing to glance in on my mom. Her face was tilted towards the only window in her bedroom, the covers drawn to her chest as she breathed slowly. She looked so different from me, light blonde and gray strands spilling over her pillow. If she turned and opened her eyes, I would see pale, blue eyes that weren't anything like my brown ones. They were pretty, but painful to look at sometimes when she screamed and cried at me. Sometimes, I wish I could trade my brown eyes for her blue ones because maybe then, when I looked in the mirror I would be reminded of a younger version of my mom instead of a replica of a dad I hadn't known for very long.

I closed the door and crept back to my room, quickly dressing for school and heading out to catch the bus.

CHAPTER 1

"Hey darl'n, let me get some of that sweet ass over here!" The rolling, deep, southern twang grated through my ears like the shards of glass I was piling into the dustpan near the front door. Even Joanna, the only other waitress on shift, rolled her eyes from across the room and sent me a sympathetic glance. I groaned inwardly as I looked over my shoulder. The spokesman, along with an identically dressed sidekick, slid into a booth in my section. I realized with disgust that it was, in fact, my ass they were drooling over as I bent down to shuffle and pick up the clinking pieces of glass I had dropped.

After trashing the shattered bits, I returned from the kitchen just as the front door chimed and another man ducked in. His head swung low automatically in deference to his height. I looked him over, my eyes trailing up and up, and as he paused, the two redneck truckers began hollering for me again.

"Give me one moment and I'll be right with you," I

assured the giant. He nodded and simply took a seat at the counter.

I flicked him an apologetic glance once more before hurrying through the nearly empty dining room towards the two truckers. They grew progressively louder until I reached them and then their catcalls and whistles abruptly came to an end. I held back the urge to pull the hem of my starched uniform lower and my neckline higher.

"What can I get you, gentlemen?" The last word choked out of me as I gazed down at the greasy men with their balding heads hidden by fish-logo ball caps. Gentlemen, they certainly were not.

"Well, hey there, Miss," The man on the right paused and leaned forward, squinting his eyes to read my name tag, "Harlow." He grinned like he'd found the secret to the universe in my name, and my panties would drop for him at any moment.

Fat. Chance.

My eyes rolled as I imagined how good it would feel to pour an entire pot of freshly-brewed, hot coffee on them. The waste of perfectly good coffee would be worth the looks on their faces. Their attention was unnerving. I could have been wearing a parka and thick jeans and I would have still felt exposed around these guys.

"Two coffees, and we'll have the special if that special includes you."

Did that line really work on girls? It took concentration to keep my disgust from showing. I really hoped they were good tippers, but by the look of them – dirty, ripped jeans and wife beaters that may have once, long ago, been white – I didn't have high hopes.

"It doesn't," I said with a straight face, "but two coffees, coming right up."

They chuckled as I walked away and I prayed that the skirt of my uniform hadn't ridden up.

The giant had taken up a seat at the end of the counter and Joanna was at the back of her section, on the border of the convenience store entrance that shared our building. She giggled shamelessly, flirting with her newest boyfriend: Mark or Jim or Bobby, I couldn't remember. He had been in the restaurant every night this week.

I sighed and decided that the two guys in my section weren't in any hurry and could wait a bit longer. I drifted to the tall stranger, pulling out my notepad to take his order.

"Are you ready to order?"

Sharp blue eyes centered on my face and I froze. He looked down at me, as someone with his height couldn't help but do. He must have been six and a half feet tall. As he stared, though, it didn't feel like he was ogling me the way most guys who came to Alex's Diner did. No, he appeared to be analyzing me, and by the time he turned back to his menu, I was sure he knew everything about me; how many times I forgot someone's take-out order, how uncomfortable I was with the guys at my back watching my every move, and how absolutely, bone-deep exhausted I was.

"Yea, I'd like a glass of sweet tea and the number two special." He glanced back at me as he closed his menu and returned it to its holder behind one of the little condiment baskets that lined the counter. "And if you could grab a cup of coffee and a slice of apple pie too, that would be great." He smiled, a line of straight teeth beaming back at me.

"Okay, sure. No problem."

I shoved my pen and pad back into my apron without writing anything down and rushed to the back. I filled three mugs, imprinted with the Alex's Diner logo, with hot, black coffee and loaded two little bowls with creamers. I paused when I reached the counter again, placing the tray of drinks down to fill a glass with sweet iced-tea. I'd argued with Joanna not to make it an hour before, but was thankful now that she hadn't listened.

I rushed back to the giant. Even sitting down, he towered over me. I guessed that he had sat at the bar because it was the only place in the diner where he wouldn't have had to cram his legs under the table. As it was, his large boots reached the floor quite easily, leaving enough room for him to bend his knees. A twinge of jealousy reminded me of how I always looked like a child, swinging my legs back and forth on those stools.

I placed the tea in front of him and the cup of coffee next to it, with one of the bowls of creamers next to one of the condiment baskets. He flashed me a subdued, distracted smile as he perused his cell phone. The truckers had managed to calm down, I realized as I dropped off their coffees and creamers, engrossed in an animated conversation about a fishing trip one had gone on recently. When neither of them glanced at me, I thankfully hurried away.

As I dropped off the tray, the door chimed again and I couldn't believe how many customers were arriving so late on a Thursday night. Maybe I would actually make enough this week to afford the minimum payment on my mom's latest hospital bill.

I watched as a slender boy, about my age, strode in, his eyes wandering over the worn tile and 50s style counter. He stood out in the room with his dark hair slicked back, wearing slacks and a white button-up under a gray cardigan. My eyebrows rose when he sat directly next to the giant, picked up the cup of coffee and drank.

I approached slowly. "Hi?" They both looked up, a pair of bright, blue eyes and a pair of tornado-gray eyes, both intensely focused on me. "Um, can I get you anything?"

I paused at the end of the counter, directing my attention to the newcomer. He looked me over in the same way that the blue-eyed giant had, analyzing me in one moment, before turning away.

"You ordered pie, right?" the gray eyed stranger asked, and the giant nodded. He looked back at me. "Then I'm good."

"Alright then. Well, if you do need something, my name's Harlow, just call."

He nodded once.

I rushed back to the kitchen, hoping Joanna would take any new tables that came. I didn't want to leave the safety of the back until I absolutely had to. The two at the counter made me feel like a layer of skin was stripped away every time they looked at me.

Carl, the cook, wasn't in the mood to talk. I sat on a wooden stool next to one of the metal prep counters where a radio played 90s hip hop quietly. I counted the beats to three and a half songs before Carl dinged what I called the "order up" bell. No one ever actually said "order up" anymore, but sometimes I liked to imagine that Alex's Diner was truly back in the 50s and things were easier and people were different.

It gave me something to think about, other than bills, school, and work. I cut a fresh slice of apple pie and squirted a dollop of whipped cream on top before taking both plates out into the dining room.

Sitting in the back, I had convinced myself that the two guys at the counter weren't as potent as they had seemed the first time around. However, when I set their plates down and they both looked at me again, I knew I had been outright lying to myself. I tried to smile as I picked up a pot of coffee and filled the gray-eyed customer's mug. I moved back towards the truckers in my section, filling their mugs as well.

"Are you always working this late?" the giant asked as I passed around the counter.

Startled, I almost dropped the half-empty pot on my foot. Looking over my shoulder, both he and his friend had focused on me once again. His friend was actively shoveling pie between his lips as if it were going out of style while still wholly focused on me. I sighed, reminding myself that these were just boys like anyone else. No matter that they seemed far too observant; they were just like any other customers. I placed the pot back on the coffee maker's warming plate and leaned a hip against the counter.

"I'm usually only here this late when no one else can work," I admitted.

"Don't you have school?" The question came from gray-eyes. "You're like what? Fifteen?"

I bristled. "Actually, I'm eighteen. What are you – twelve?" I immediately wanted to slap a hand over my mouth, surprised that I had spoken my thoughts aloud. I glanced over at them and hoped that they didn't take offense.

Please have a sense of humor, I begged silently. The giant's low, baritone laugh sounded like rumbling thunder and it grew louder as his friend's dumbstruck face just stared back at me. Relief slid through me.

"That was beautiful." The giant swiped large fingers under his eyes and looked between us before refocusing on me. "I like you, Harlow. My name's Knix and this is my friend, Marvin, and no, he's not twelve. Although he acts like it sometimes."

I expected Marvin to take offense at his friends nettling, but he simply picked up his coffee cup and took another sip before returning to his pie. Knix held out a hand the size of a bear paw for me to shake and I took it in greeting, watching as my own hand disappeared in his grip.

"Nice to meet you."

"So tell me, Harlow," Knix said. "About how many times a week would you say no one else can work this late?" He released my hand, but followed me with his eyes as I shifted against the counter, wrapping my arms around my middle and pressing my palms to my sides.

"Is there a reason you want to know?" If he wanted to know if we were hiring for late shifts, I'd tell him, but if he was trying to find out my work schedule, well, it didn't matter how pretty he was, that was creepy.

"Curiosity."

I watched him with one brow raised. I hoped he was just looking for a job; feeling me out to see if I would offer up the information.

"There's usually no one else working night shifts but Joanna." I nodded to the other server as she giggled with Mark-Jim-Bob in the corner. "And I work Mondays through Thursdays. Most people have other jobs, or kids, or school." I moved away to wipe down a section of the counter closer to the other end.

"Don't *you* have school?"

I paused and turned to look at Marvin who had asked the question and caught him staring back at me. "Yea."

Marvin nodded once, as though he had expected my answer, and then continued to eat the last two bites of his pie.

"Do you want more?" I asked.

He paused as if considering before shaking his head. "Not today, Sunshine." He shifted on his stool, pulling out a buzzing cell phone. He swiped a long finger across the screen before nudging Knix to stand. Knix drained the last of his tea as Marvin straightened the collar of his white, pressed shirt and threw a bill on the counter before motioning for Knix to follow. "Keep the change."

Knix turned back and left me with another of his stunning smiles as they both disappeared into the gas station's entrance to leave out of the left side of the building. I waited for them to disappear completely before I began cleaning up their plates. My eyes widened as I spotted Ben Franklin's face on the hundred-dollar bill that Marvin had left.

Keep the change? I calculated in my head how much of a tip he'd left me, wondering if he'd accidentally left the wrong bill. A twenty-dollar bill would have left me with almost a seventy percent tip.

I don't know if Marvin knew exactly what he was giving me when he left it, but it was the break I needed. My relief followed me even as I left the diner at 6 am. I now had nearly enough to cover my mom's next medical bill. I smiled as I stuffed the cash in my purse.

The walk home wasn't all that long, especially so early in the morning – thirty minutes give or take. Despite that, exhaustion weighed on my eyelids. I knew the bus for school would be hitting my neighborhood in less than two hours and I needed to shower off the smell of diner grease before I could get ready.

I strode alongside the highway that ran under I-77, taking the fastest route home. I shivered in the early morning chill, but watched as the sky began to brighten, sharpening into a light blue. Cars whizzed past, some honking, but most ignored me.

As I drew closer to my street – where the duplex I lived in was sequestered in the very back – I noticed a scrap of gray and black fur wiggling out of one of the ditches that lined the pavement. I watched as it lifted its head. Emerald-green eyes met mine and flashed with fear just before the little kitten meowed and ran straight for the road.

A blue pick-up truck, blaring rap, sped up from the opposite direction just as the cat reached that side of the road. I gasped and lurched forward as the kitten raised its head and stared at the headlights speeding toward it. I thought only deer did that, but I didn't stop to criticize the idiocy of the animal. Instead, I threw myself across the road, snatching the cat into my arms as the truck's horn blared.

A scream caught in my throat as I hunched my shoulders and dropped into a roll that landed me in the ditch, out of the truck's way. I heard fleeting curses from the truck's rolled down windows as the driver zoomed past, not even bothering to slow down. I threw my head back, letting it thud against the wet dirt and shuddered in a deep breath as the cat lifted its ears and belly-crawled up my chest. I lifted it to look at the creature and noticed she was missing a part of her ear. Knowing that she was unharmed, I closed my eyes and willed my heart to stop galloping inside my ribs. It felt as if it was attempting to run a marathon straight through my chest. One hand drifted up to pat the cat on the head as she squirmed and purred against me.

"Yea, yea, you're welcome."

I struggled up and my purse strap dug painfully into my shoulder, but a dark BMW that screeched to a halt on the side of the road closest to me distracted me as I finally pushed myself to sitting. The passenger door opened and one of the guys from earlier, Marvin, stepped out. Eyes wild, he slid down into the ditch until he stood over me.

"Are you okay?" His naturally deep voice had risen as he glared down at me, now wearing a blue button-down and black slacks. I didn't have a moment to question the change in clothes. He reached down, wrapping his hands around my upper arms, and hauled me up the steep incline.

"Yea, I'm fine. How did you—"

"Then what the fuck were you thinking?!" I blinked as he yelled. "You could have fucking died." The kitten in my arms hissed at him.

Marvin glared at the cat until she curled closer to me, her hissing fading to discontented growls. "Is that thing yours?"

I looked down at the kitten as she clawed at my dirty uniform. "No?" Technically, I had never seen the cat before, but now she kind of felt like mine with the way she clutched at me in front of him – and I *had* saved her.

"No?" He looked even more outraged. "Then why the fuck would you jump across the road to save the mangy thing?!" His nostrils flared as he raged, and stood straighter.

"Just because she isn't mine doesn't mean she deserved to die!" I snapped.

He shoved his long fingers through his perfect hair,

mussing it up as he spun and strode back towards his car before pausing and pacing in my direction again. Reaching me, he grabbed my elbow, yanking me as I stumbled along behind him.

"Come on, we're taking you home."

"What?" I stopped. "No!" He rounded on me once again.

"What the fuck do you fucking mean 'no'? You just almost killed yourself to save a stupid cat that isn't even yours!"

"I don't even know you!" I screamed back. I would have been perfectly fine, and it wasn't any of his business.

"What's my name?" he demanded, knowing that I knew the answer.

"Just because I know your name doesn't mean I trust you." It had only been mentioned once and I had only met him a few hours ago. Why would he even still be in the area?

Someone knocked on the blackened glass from the driver's side of the BMW, causing both of us to turn our heads. Marvin's gaze narrowed on the glass, but he didn't walk over, and instead turned back to me with a frustrated huff.

"It's just a ride. You can't be walking too far; you've got school soon, right? Why the fuck would you stay up all night working?"

I pulled out of his grip, cradling the cat against my chest. I really couldn't afford to keep the poor thing, but looking down at those gem-colored eyes, she wasn't exactly convincing me to put her down and leave her.

"Listen, Marvin, I–"

"Marv," he offered absentmindedly as he scrubbed another hand down his face.

"Marv," I corrected. "I'll be fine. I promise, but you're right, I do have to get home. The sooner you leave, the sooner I can get going."

He glared at me, angry. "No more heroic antics." I nodded. He looked at the cat in my arms, reaching forward and passed one hand – many times the size of her head – over her fur. "Take care of that damn thing."

My head bobbed once more as he looked at me, staring hard before he cursed again and headed back to the BMW. He got in, slammed the door, and the beautiful car pulled away.

I released a pent-up sigh of relief. I almost thought he might have forced me into his car and even though he seemed genuine, he was a bit scary. I stared down at the cat, and rubbed her mangled ear as she purred.

"Well, guess you're coming home with me." She meowed back. "But what should I name you?" She blinked up at me. "Cleo? You kind of look like an Egyptian Mau." Nails sank into my arm as Cleo climbed to my shoulder. "Okay, Cleo it is. Remember, though, you are definitely an outside cat, Babe. I can't afford a litterbox."

She seemed to find no problem with that and proceeded to paw and claw at me as I continued my walk home. Every now and then, I felt like Marv would pop out from behind a corner and follow me to make sure I didn't do anything else. It was confusing, what did he care? He didn't even know me. Some people could be unpredictable.

My duplex came into view a good twenty minutes later and I was already behind schedule. I reached for the keys inside of my soaked and dirty purse and unlocked the front door, pushing it open to a stale smelling hallway. Cleo scratched at me to be let down. When I released her, her nails clicked across the worn, wood flooring into the linoleum tiled kitchen.

Pictures of my mom and I had been packed away when she had been diagnosed with cancer almost a full year ago. She said that she hated the way they made her feel – like our younger selves were watching and judging us. If I didn't know any better, I might have agreed with her.

The quiet of the house told me that she wasn't awake yet. I strode into the living room to find that Cleo had wandered back from the kitchen and was already napping on the threadbare couch. Lucky cat. Tip-toeing down the hall, I emptied my purse of the cash I had earned and carted it back to the kitchen. An old miniature box of cereal sat in the very back of the nearly empty pantry. Unfolding the top, I dropped the wad of bills into the cardboard piggy bank and stuffed the box back into the furthest reaches of the cabinet, hoping my mom wouldn't care to look in it.

When I was younger, and my mom still had a car, and before she'd been laid off from one of her many jobs, she would go on shopping raids. I'd come home from school to find myself with new clothes, and shoes, and no food in the refrigerator. About five months ago, my mom had found my stash of cash that I kept in my room and convinced old Mrs. Grace to drive her to the store. She had spent almost two hundred dollars on clothes and knickknacks, and as a result, I had to shut off our house phone because I couldn't pay the bill. It hadn't been turned back on until I managed to get the funds saved up again. We were still suffering from that setback and the medical bills and the cost of her prescriptions were piling up – but I needed Michael to call every once in a while. I needed to know I wasn't completely alone with her.

Running later than usual, I skipped a deep soak and instead rushed through a five-minute shower, throwing on a pair of old jeans and a faded, green v-neck, before pulling my thick hair into a hairband at the nape of my neck. I poked my head into my mom's room, listening as she snored lightly, and left a glass of tap water next to her pills and a plastic wrapped sandwich from the diner.

"Don't pee on or tear up anything." I pointed at a sleepy, grumbling Cleo as I shrugged my backpack on and left, locking the front door behind me.

CHAPTER 2

I could hear the muted sounds of people talking like I was underwater. I kept rising to the surface only to shy away and sink farther into the depths that promised a comfortable reprieve. Only when a high-pitched bell sounded and my head jerked up from my desk in alarm, did I realize that I'd fallen asleep mid-class. The students around me began piling their books into their bags and filing quickly out of the room.

My AP English teacher, Mrs. Williamson, paused by my desk, a frown on her face. I stiffened, afraid she had caught me sleeping. I smiled pleadingly up at her hoping she wouldn't see fit to give me an after-school suspension that I not only couldn't get a ride home from, but didn't have time for because I had an impending shift at the diner. Instead, she handed me a yellow scrap of paper.

"The front office called for you," she said. I looked at the paper that asked me to report to the front office by 1:20 pm.

My eyes rose to the clock hanging above Mrs. Williamson's whiteboard as it clicked just past 1:17 pm. I snatched up my backpack, my arms loaded down with binders and books, as I ran from the room.

I passed through the stragglers left behind in the hallways as they headed for their next class, and hoped this didn't have anything to do with the ever-growing list of detentions I kept receiving for falling asleep in class. It was almost the end of the year. Surely the administrators wouldn't do anything about it *now*. It wouldn't look good on my transcripts if I *did* decide to apply to the local community colleges. At the moment, I wasn't really sure what my plans were.

I opened the front office as the clock there flipped to 1:22 pm. Mrs. Donovan, the principal's secretary, looked up and smiled warmly, giving me some relief as I approached her desk.

"Hi, Mrs. D, I um..." I handed the yellow paper over. "I was told to come here." She took the pass and checked one of the little boxes on the side.

"Alright, Dear. It'll be the third door on your left."

"Am I in trouble?" I asked. Mrs. D looked surprised by my question, her thin, blonde brows rising above eyes stroked with thick lines of eyeshadow, further reassuring me that I had nothing to worry about.

"Of course not, Dear. Go on back now."

I nodded and followed her directions down the hall to the right of her desk. There was a plaque on the third door on the left that read: *Conference Room*. I hesitated briefly about knocking before I lightly tapped my knuckles on the door and eased it open.

The blinds on the pair of windows at the end of the long room were drawn up, allowing natural light to flood the otherwise bland room. A man in a navy suit stood against the glass directly across from the door, staring out at the outdoor amphitheater next to the student parking lot. During lunch, it would be filled with students as they ate and gossiped.

When the man didn't acknowledge or even seem to notice my entrance, I waited a beat before coughing lightly to alert him. His profile, outlined by the light, didn't move except for the corner of his lips that twitched. Finally, he turned and raised an eyebrow in my direction, rich, coffee-colored eyes meeting mine with a smile.

"Ms. Hampton, welcome."

When his whole body twisted away from the window, leaving it open for the sunlight to stream in and warm the rest of the sparsely decorated room, he seemed bigger – wider. There was, in fact, only one real piece of furniture in the room, a long wooden conference table with various chairs – some mismatching – crowded around its edges.

He came forward, approaching as I fidgeted with the books and papers in my arms. "Here, let me take that for you." I resisted the urge to jerk away in surprise as he took my books from me and placed them gently on the table before reaching to slide my backpack strap down my arm. He set it on the floor. "Have a seat."

We both sat at the end of the table farthest from the window. I focused on him instead – and my confusion.

"Where's Principal Buchanan?" I asked.

Instead of answering, he simply smiled and sat back. I didn't recognize him as anyone I knew from the school – a teacher, one of the many assistant vice principals, or counselors. Even if I had, he didn't look old enough to be in any of those positions. He didn't look the type to be hired on at a high school either. His hair might have been shoulder length, but I couldn't tell because he had it all pulled back in a ponytail. It left his entire face on display, the width of his jaw line, the frame of his cheeks. I imagined that he was of Native American heritage with those high sharp cheekbones.

"Ms. Hampton," he began, "you don't know me, but my name is Bellamy Woodstone." He paused, his eyes zeroing in on my arm. I looked down, groaning inwardly at the huge purple bruise the size of a child's hand peeking out from my t-shirt sleeve. It must have come from the ditch this morning. My eyes drooped at the reminder of my lack of sleep. I reached up, tugging my sleeve a little lower.

"Okay?" I blinked, waiting. "Is there something I can do for you, Mr. Woodstone?"

His eyes refocused onto my face. "You can call me Bellamy," he said. "I'd like to call you Harlow, if that's alright with you?" I nodded and was rewarded with another dazzling smile. "Wonderful. Now, I'm sure you're wondering why you've been called down here – I can assure you, you're not in any trouble."

"Then why–"

"Because I needed to speak with you alone about the options for your future." He reached back, towards the table, picking up a manila folder I hadn't seen before.

"According to your guidance counselor here, your GPA is almost a 4.0, correct?"

"It's a 3.7," I said. Confusion rolled through my mind. "Is that what you called me down here to talk about? Reaching a 4.0?" I had been trying, but between the diner and my mom, studying had taken a backseat.

He glanced up from the folder. "No, a 3.7 is actually quite high, much higher than most of your peers. You're in the top fifteen percent of your class, if not the top ten percent. No, I called you down here to discuss why you haven't applied to a college. With your grades, you are almost guaranteed at least some financial aid or academic scholarships." He flipped a page. "And I see that you actually won some school wide awards on writing – so the entrance essays shouldn't have been a problem. Your transcripts reflect nothing more than detentions every now and then. What were those detentions for?" He looked up from his folder, those severe, almond eyes watching me.

"I, um...they were for sleeping in class," I said, staring at my lap.

"Hmmm." He didn't sound upset as he continued to flip through my file. "Why did you stop gymnastics?" My head snapped up.

"I haven't done gymnastics in years," I replied. "That's still in there?"

He smiled conspiratorially. "This is my own personal file of you. Some of this came from your high school transcripts, but for the group I represent and what we would like to ask of you, we decided to go much further back."

"Are you a college recruiter?" It was the only explanation that made sense. What could someone else want with me?

"Well," he tilted his head to the side, "you could say that I am a recruiter of sorts, but you still didn't answer my question."

"I lost interest," I said, a complete and utter lie. I had loved gymnastics, but it had been around the time my brother had gone away to college and I had to choose between gymnastics or a job. I had chosen the job.

"Hmmm," he said again.

"If you're not a college recruiter, who are you?"

"I never said I wasn't a college recruiter," he replied easily. "Perhaps I am your ticket into college. Would you be willing to answer a few questions for me, if that were the case?"

"Even if you are," I replied, "it's too late in the year for me to get into college. I graduate in two weeks. I'll have to wait for the Spring semester." If I could even afford it then.

"What would it hurt to answer a few of my questions?" He closed the folder and set it aside before folding his hands over his lap.

I fidgeted. "I guess it's fine. I mean, I don't have anything to hide."

Did only people who actually had something to hide say that? I asked myself. It wasn't like I was hiding anything, I just wasn't too keen on telling people things, especially about my mom.

"We'll start with the real reason that you quit gymnastics. You had quite a few awards. Only the dedicated go all the way to the state championships."

"I didn't win."

He waved his hand. "Whether you won or not doesn't matter. What does matter is that you were good enough. You could have tried for nationals the next year, but you didn't."

I shrugged. I didn't know what he wanted me to say.

"Alright, then, what about college? Do you want to go to college?"

"I don't know." I paused, the words to explain flickering through my mind. "It might not be possible for me right now."

"You're not sure if you want to go to college?"

I tried to be as honest as possible. "College sounds interesting, but I don't know what I would want to study and it's kind of a moot point right now. The deadlines have passed."

"What if it wasn't a moot point?"

"I'm pretty sure it is."

Bellamy closed his eyes, inhaling and exhaling a deep breath. After a moment, he reopened his eyes and leaned forward, his torso straining under the light blue and white checkered dress shirt.

"Do you want to know what I think?" He didn't even wait for me to respond. "I think that you have the whole world in front of you, but you aren't sure what to do with it. From what I've been told, you're a brave girl, capable of doing brave things."

"What have you heard?" I narrowed my gaze at him.

Instead of answering, he reached into his pocket and removed a black card. I took it from him. On the back, in silver lettering, was a phone number, and on the front was a name scribbled out in fancy cursive writing.

"Iris?" I read aloud. Arching my brows, I carefully put the card on the conference table between us. He smiled as though he had expected my reaction.

"It's not going to bite you," he teased.

I pursed my lips and frowned. "You never said what you wanted to ask me or what you're here for."

"I'm here because I'm interested in a girl that would risk her life for an animal. I'm interested in knowing why a candidate for the gymnastics state championships quit when she could have been ready for the Olympics in another ten years. I want to find out what makes her tick."

When my mouth sagged open in shock, Bellamy grinned. He stood and straightened the lapels of his suit jacket. Though he looked perfectly at home in the suit, the length of his hair and the slight smudge under his chin – something I noticed only now that he was towering over me – told me he wasn't as business oriented as his surface appearance made him seem.

"How did you–"

"Ms. Hampton," he interrupted, reverting back to my last name. "I hope I've intrigued you." He braced a wide palm on the table and leaned over me. His breath ruffled my hair. "I suggest when you get tired of saving kittens, you give us a call."

"W-what?" I trembled as my heart raced. Not for a second did I think he hadn't noticed.

"That number will reach someone on my team at all hours." He stood straight and strode to the door. "I look forward to hearing from you."

When the door closed behind him, I half expected someone to pop out from under the table and yell, "Surprise!" *Was this a joke?* I held my breath. Minutes passed and another bell rang over the school's loudspeakers, letting me know that I'd missed a full period of class. I stood and made my way into the office hallway. Mrs. Donovan smiled at me again as I passed.

"How'd it go, Dear?"

I blinked at her. "Uh, fine," I said.

"Well, then, you best be getting to your next class."

I nodded once, before stuffing the black business card into my back pocket. For the rest of the day, that card burned a hole through both my jeans and my mind. I contemplated calling and also just throwing the damn thing away. To be honest, it all felt like a very elaborately played prank. But how had he known about Cleo? Did he know the guys from the diner? Was I being stalked?

That particular thought came to me as I climbed into my regular bus and found a seat to crash in on the ride home. My head turned, watching. Students filtered onto the bus en masse just before we rolled out of the school's bus lot. No one appeared to pay me much attention. Several students, that usually sat in the back with me, joked and laughed, getting quieter as more people exited at their designated stops. Erika waved from a window seat in the middle. I waved back and watched as she edged out of her seat and slunk back towards me. I raised my legs and let her scoot past to sit next to the window.

"Ugh," she groaned. "I'm so tired." She leaned against the glass and closed her eyes. I nudged her to keep her awake and she grunted, slapping a hand out at me with her ten and counting bracelets dangling on her arm.

"Go away," she mumbled.

"Can't," I teased. "There's nowhere else for me to sit." Her eyes opened just a smidge.

"I should kick you to curb, you know. Then I'd have more time to spend with my new boyfriend."

"You got a boyfriend?"

"Mmmhmm." Her eyes sparkled with mischief and I pursed my lips.

"I have a favor to ask." I needed to ask now before I chickened out and decided not to go.

"I'm not going to hide your illegitimate child. No one would believe it was mine anyway." True, we looked too different for anyone to mistake us even for sisters. While I had dozens of freckles across the bridge of my nose and across my cheeks and particularly dark eyes, her skin was smooth and unblemished and her eyes were a brilliant blue.

"You're in luck, I'm not pregnant," I replied. "It has to do with graduation. Are you walking?"

She groaned and sat up. "Why are we even friends?" she complained. "You never let me sleep. Yea, I'm walking at graduation. Are you?"

"Maybe," I hinted. "If you could give me a ride."

Her eyes widened. "I thought you were saving up money to buy your neighbors old clunker." I winced, thinking of why that was no longer an option. I hadn't told Erika that Mom had found my cash stash or where and how she had spent it.

"She decided to keep it," I lied. "Can you give me a ride?"

"I guess," she replied. "My dad and I can pick you up. Is your mom coming?"

"I don't know yet. Probably not, though. If she did, would it be a problem?"

"No problem," she said. "But we'd all have to squeeze into the truck. My parents sold their sedan because they figured my dad could just drop my mom off at work and they would invest the money or something like that."

"Is she going to be at graduation?" Erika's mom was an airplane flight attendant. She spent several days – sometimes up to two weeks – flying across the country before she got downtime. According to Erika, the pay was good and she got benefits as well as free flights. It was Erika's dream job and she was going straight to the academy after high school.

"No, she's got to work and because she took off for my eighteenth birthday, they aren't letting her get out of this one. She feels bad, but I don't mind. We'll plan better for when I get out of the travel academy or college. I've applied to both, but haven't decided yet."

"Oh?" I nodded my head as she began talking about her summer plans and all the places she would see if she got a job as a travel attendant. When we pulled up to her stop, she hugged me tight before squeezing out into the aisle.

"I'll talk to you more tomorrow, Harlow!"

I watched and smiled as Erika waved, bouncing off the bus with her hair swaying behind her. We had been talking about graduation for so long, I forgot to ask her about her new boyfriend. When the bus stopped at the end of my street several minutes later, I squeezed through the last of the students to get off, thanking Mr. Jon, the bus driver, and waving goodbye as I did. The walk through my neighborhood was easier during warm days.

During the winter, when I had walked back from work and it was still dark out, my imagination had driven me to picture shadows behind every brick or yellow, panel-covered building. There were approximately thirty houses on the street, ending at a cul-de-sac with my house just before that little half circle. The neighbors were older and quiet, and they kept to themselves for the most part.

As I approached my front door, a white paper fluttered under the welcome mat. I untucked it and read through the note with a sigh. The older neighbor who regularly took my mom to her doctor appointments had left a reminder that she would be by next Sunday to pick my mom up and that her grandchildren would need a babysitter that day since they would both be at the hospital for at least a few hours. I would have to ask if

Joanna or one of the other servers could trade shifts with me since I was already scheduled to work.

"Mom, I'm home," I called out as I shut the door behind me. Softly clicking nails warned me of Cleo's approach. A gray and black bundle of fur attacked my feet, spinning circles around each limb.

"Where have you been?!" My mom's high-pitched screech had my shoulders slumping as I marched past Cleo towards the hallway. I arrived at the door of her bedroom and hesitated.

"I've been at school; did you have a good day?" Looking at the disastrous room, the clothes streaming from the closet, littering the floor, I knew the answer. My mom sat like a pale, regal queen on her pillows and blankets, her eyeglasses perched on her nose as she stared over the mound of random objects pulled from throughout the house that cluttered in a circle around her. She wore a light-pink scarf tied around her brittle and quickly thinning gray hair.

"How can anyone have a good day when I've been home all day, in this mess, while you've been out doing whatever it is you teenagers do? Now, tell me the truth, where have you been?"

I sighed, wading my way through the overturned boxes. "Did you eat anything today?" I asked. She waved her hand at me, eyes unfocused.

"As if you care!" I spied the half-eaten sandwich on her bed that I had left her this morning. At least she had tried it. "Where were you?"

"At school," I repeated, bending down to help her to her feet. I guided her over to her bed and pushed her knickknacks to the floor. I would have to clean up when I got home from work later.

"I don't know why you lie to me," she grumbled. "You're just like your brother."

I ducked out of the room and ran for a fresh glass of water, replacing it for the empty one on her nightstand. A quick glance at the old, grandfather clock at the end of the hall told me I needed to hurry and get ready for work.

"I'm sorry, Mom," I said. "I promise I'll clean up when I get back from work." I headed for my room in a hurry, stripping off my shirt as I went. I listened to her as she fumbled to get out of the bed.

"Don't you turn away from me, young lady!" Her footsteps shuffled over the various shirts and pants before her feet slapped on the wooden, hallway floor.

My room held nothing but a few mixed furniture pieces that I had owned since before I hit puberty. A double bed took up most of the room, my newest accessory, with the mattress sagging in the middle. I stepped around it, stripping out of the rest of my school clothes. A dull, pink and gray dresser was shoved up against the wall next to the doorway with books and papers strewn across the surface. I reached inside one drawer, looking for the apron I knew I had just washed the day before.

The books were old, library-owned hardbacks that had been given away at the end of the year to make room for newer editions. I was lucky enough to have grabbed some of the better, well-kept volumes. The papers ranged from old bills to school supplies. I found a scrunchie and tugged it over my wrist before I finally managed to find my apron.

The same uniform I had on that morning was slung across the back of a chair sitting at the corner of my bed in front of my closet. I ignored it because it was stained with dirt and mud from this morning's adventures. Pulling my only extra uniform from my closet, I yanked the dress over my head, doing up the buttons on the front before grabbing my purse and shoving my apron inside.

"Did you hear me?" Mom stopped at my bedroom door, her small, feeble body blocking my exit. I looked down at her. I wanted to wait until she moved, but I just didn't have the time.

"Yes ma'am," I said. "And I would love to stay, but I really do have to get moving or I'm going to be late." Placing my hands on her shoulders, I gently urged her to the side. She slapped my hands away.

"Don't touch me," she snapped. "Answer my question. Where have you been?"

"Mom," I said, crouching down to tie my non-slip sneakers. "I don't know what you want me to say. I did answer you. I've been at school all day and I can't stay. I just came home to get changed and make you something to eat." I moved towards the kitchen.

"I haven't seen you since yesterday, Harlow Nicole Hampton. School is not an overnight event."

She stood in the doorway as I pilfered through our nearly empty fridge and came up with a small styrofoam cup filled with soup from the diner. I stuffed it in our microwave, pressing buttons to heat it up before I sighed and steeled myself against my mom's wrath. She stood, her pale face flushed in anger, arms crossed. My limbs seemed to sink even more, their weight increasing as I stood beneath her glare. My lack of sleep built rocks on my eyelids until I leaned back and let them close with a sigh.

"Work ran late again last night," I said slowly. "I came home this morning and set up a snack for you on your nightstand next to your meds." I opened my eyes. "Did you take them?"

"What I do with myself is none of your business." She inhaled, her eyes going wide and wild. "I have had more than enough of you sneaking out at night to go wherever you please. No more excuses, I'm tired of your lying."

She stepped forward as the microwave beeped, but I ignored it, remaining still as though she were a hungry animal waiting to pounce. "You will clean this house spotless and you will remain in your room until I say you are allowed to leave. Is that understood?"

I hesitated, my hand reaching for the handle on the microwave as I watched her. My neck bunched under the tension in my skin – looking at her hurt. Pulling the steaming cup from the appliance, I set it on the counter and reached for a clean spoon in the drawer to the left of me.

"Okay," I replied. "I'll clean as soon as I get back from work. For now, why don't you have some of the chicken noodle soup from the diner?" I peeked back at her as something glinted from the corner of my eye and quick movement had me backing up into the corner I had trapped myself in.

Her mouth gaping with fury, her eyes straining, she hefted one of her old, heavy glasses from the counter collection and threw it at me. Instinct made me duck, my arms shooting up to cradle my head and protect it as the glass cracked against the cabinet where my head had previously been. It shattered, spilling pieces of glass that rained down on my shoulders.

"Liar!" Spittle flew from her mouth as she screamed and cursed.

I remained where I was, bent over, head down, eyes wide. My shoulders shook with a hot rush of adrenaline and exhaustion quickly followed. My knees trembled as I forced them to hold their position. Her ranting trailed off as I stood there unmoving. Her eyes dimmed, and she began mumbling about her head hurting.

"Don't leave this house," she snapped once more before turning away. I listened and waited for the quiet snick of her bedroom door closing before I finally released a long held, pent up breath. My hands shook as I slowly stood and surveyed the damage. As the clock chimed in the hallway, I knew I was going to be late for work.

CHAPTER 3

Pieces of glass littered the ground and I bent, picking up the larger, jagged shards to throw away before gathering the rest with a broom and dust pan. Ignoring the black hole in my stomach that made my skin clammy and cold, and my chest vibrate with the tempo of my heart, I tried to take calming breaths as I finished cleaning. Cleo meowed from the doorway as I stepped over the debris on the floor.

"Hey pretty girl," I whispered, "stay right there."

She sat and continued to meow as I cleaned up the glass on the floor and counter. Though my stomach growled, I sighed at the soup and picked out the pieces of glass that had managed to make it into the cup. After making sure I had removed all of the glass from the soup, I redeposited it back into the refrigerator. We were low enough as it was on food. I rummaged through the drawers and found some prepacked deli ham. I grabbed a knife, sliced it up into bits, and dropped the chunks into a small plastic dish. Along with a bowl of water, I placed the offering on the floor by the entrance to the laundry room.

"Okay, you can come eat now." I gestured the cat closer. "Sorry about that. She's just not feeling well today."

Even as the hallway clock chimed again, I sat and scratched Cleo behind the ears. She licked her whiskers and meowed back at me. Rubbing the cat kept my fingers from shaking, but I felt like I could still feel the air above my head whistling as the glass grazed my hair before splintering into what seemed like a million pieces.

When Cleo was done eating, I gave her one last kitty kiss goodbye and headed for the door, purse in hand. I paused before I left, head tilted toward the hallway. I rushed back to my room and dug through my crumpled jeans, plucking the business card from the pocket and shoved it into my bag.

My purse was actually a satchel sewn together with bits and pieces of cloth. I had fallen in love with the design the first time I saw almost an exact replica hanging in Erika's closet and as a birthday gift last year, she had made me my own. It thumped and rattled against my leg with the tin of nearly empty mints hitting an old paperback from a library give away I had received a couple months back. I kept meaning to read it, but with so much to do, I hadn't had the time.

Alex's Diner came into view and the gas station to the side of it. The Carpo Express gas station was lit up like a Christmas tree even though the sun had yet to set. A couple of Hispanic kids hung out by the ice machine on the corner of the building. Two older boys spoke in Spanish next to a short, young girl with big, round cheeks and a dirty, white t-shirt that didn't quite fit. She smiled and waved as I walked past and I did the same.

Joanna was flirting with a five top of guys – five guys ranging in age from early 20's to late 30s – as I opened the door. The sound of Carl's hip-hop station from the kitchen had quickly become a soothing ambiance in these past few months and I was thankful for the familiar sound today as it calmed some of my frayed nerves. A tall, middle-aged man with a short crop of hair wiped down the counter, throwing a dish towel over his shoulder.

"Afternoon, Harlow."

"Hi, Alex."

The owner of the diner rarely ever came in to actually work the diner. From my few conversations with him, I knew that he owned a few other businesses and properties that kept him busy, but every now and then, he would get an urge to sink into some mindless work and would pop in to act as a jack of all trades – server, kitchen hand, and busboy. He said doing so made sure he never forgot what all of his employees did every day. I appreciated that in a boss. I appreciated him in more ways than he could possibly ever imagine just for giving me my job – even though I was inexperienced when I had first started.

"Have a good day at school?" he asked.

"Just like any other."

I moved towards the back of the kitchen where he had installed mini lockers to place our belongings in. I set my satchel and keys inside, pulling the black card from Bellamy out, and absentmindedly slipping it into the pouch of my apron.

"Are you eating dinner here tonight?"

Alex always offered to let his workers eat before a

shift. He was just that kind of guy, the nice, I'll-take-good-care-of-your-daughter-ma'am kind of guy, even at his age. Had he been fifteen years younger, I might have found him incredibly attractive. It was the way he held himself, with such confidence that made him seem so dependable, but with Alex, he didn't just look the part, he acted the part every day. His kind of self-assurance wasn't something I possessed, but I hoped with time it might rub off on me.

"No, I'm not hungry, but thanks for the offer." Even the five dollars spent on a burger and fries could be put to better use. Yet, as the words slipped out of my mouth, my stomach growled in response. I pivoted as quickly as I could, hoping he hadn't heard.

"Eat, Harlow. It's on the house." His big hand came down on my head and rubbed.

"I'm fine. It's okay. I just forgot to grab a snack at home. I'll just eat some crackers when I'm not busy. Besides, I'm late. I should probably clock in and get to work. Sorry," I prattled until his hand fell off of my head and he turned me around to look at him.

"I want you to grab a menu and order anything you want. From the adult menu, not the kid's menu – because I know you would." His eyes burned into me. "When was the last time you ate an actual meal?"

"I heated up some soup before coming to work." Not for myself, but it was true and even though I hadn't eaten it, the statement wasn't technically a lie.

He harrumphed, wandering back towards the kitchen. "Well, you're gonna eat something here. Go on. Get to it."

"Yes, sir." I smiled as my shoes scuffed across the linoleum tiled floor out into the dining area where we kept the menus. I sat at the counter and looked through the cheapest selection of meals for adults.

After a few minutes, Alex came back. "Alright, Harlow. What are you getting?"

"Oh, I'll get it." I moved to hop off the stool when he slapped a hand on the counter in front of me.

"You sit right there, young lady," he snapped. From him, the 'young lady' comment didn't sound menacing; accusing still, but in a playful way. "Tell me what you want."

"Um...okay." I looked back at the menu, the decision I had made previously faltering in my mind. "Can I get the double stacked chicken club?"

"You got it. With fries?" He was punching his fingers at the POS system that logged all of our orders before I even nodded in answer.

As I waited at the counter, I was given a rare opportunity for quiet observation without a million thoughts running through my mind. As dinner time drew closer, more people filtered through the doors. Some were single regulars who took up space in Joanna's section. Others were families of three or four, with kids hanging from their parents' arms.

"Hey there." The deep, reverberating tone that sounded almost musical had me turning my head to a pair of familiar blue eyes. The giant from the night before slid onto a bar stool next to me.

"Hi." I smiled.

"Taking a break, Little Bit?" I tilted my head at the pet name, shrugging. Some southern guys simply liked referring to every girl they met as something sweet or cute.

"Sort of," I hedged as Alex re-entered from the back

with a plate holding an overstuffed sandwich and a pile of steaming fries. My mouth watered immediately.

"Ahhh, waiting on food then," Knix determined as Alex set the plate down in front of me.

I nodded, reaching for a handful of fries. I shoved them in my mouth before he could ask another question and he laughed. The heat and saltiness of the food was enough to wake me up a bit and energize me. My fragile nerves were a thing of the past.

"Haven't seen you 'round here much, Knix." Alex's friendly comment had me tilting my head to watch their exchange while I ate. "Where have you been hiding?"

"I was actually here last night with Marv."

Thinking of Marv reminded me of that morning; how abrupt and irrationally upset he had been. Normal people weren't like that – they didn't really care about strangers or about me.

Not wanting to eavesdrop, I tuned Alex and Knix's friendly banter out. Soon enough my food was gone, my stomach full and happily silenced.

"He said something about running into Little Bit, here," I heard inadvertently and paused as I wiped my mouth on a napkin. I tipped my head in their direction, and brushed strands of my hair out of my face. "–said he saw her dodging traffic early this morning." Alex's gaze found mine. He grinned. I could tell he didn't believe it for a second.

"I would never play in traffic," I said.

Alex's sharp eyes watched us.

"That's not what Marv said," Knix contended. "He told me you nearly gave him a heart attack."

I slid off my stool. "Well, I'm obviously fine, and I won't be dodging cars anymore. I promise."

I turned and strode through the back, wiping down

and washing the dishes I had used before putting them in their respective places. As soon as I reentered the dining area, a large table of rowdy football players from my school came bustling in. They looked around and spotted my empty section, then took it upon themselves to pull three tables together to suit them all. Joanna's lips pinched down as she watched them sit. I could tell she was torn between wanting to take the table because they were all fairly good-looking guys, or not because they likely wouldn't tip very well for the amount of work they would be. I tied my apron around my waist and headed in their direction.

"What can I get you guys to drink?" I asked, pulling out a notepad and pen.

The guy who had initiated the table setup raised a fist for the group to quiet. It was surprising that the rest of his rather loud group actually listened, their roar lowering from yelling across the table to talking normally. They were still loud – so many voices talking at once – but no longer deafening.

"I'll get a sweet tea," he said before bending his head to the rest. Coke. Sweet Tea. Sweet Tea. Water. Water. Water. Water. Lemonade. I nodded after each drink order to let them know I had written it down, though they could plainly see as I hastily scribbled over my notepad.

"Alright, I'll be right back with that."

I spun on my heels as a low whistle rose above the murmurs. I heard an embarrassed groan from the boy who seemed to be calling the shots and my eyes met Knix's as his head lifted, inclining in my direction. Heat flared once again over my cheeks, this time with a rush of angry embarrassment. I glanced at Alex and flinched as he paused behind the counter, his shoulders tensing. I took a breath before continuing towards the soda fountain.

"Come on guys," someone choked out, "don't." It was a quieter voice, not the same as the group's leader.

Instead, the guy who sat at the head of the table tilted his head and glanced at me from the corner of his eyes.

I tempered my reaction and decided to ignore the strangled hiss and the following chuckles from the others, pretending as though I hadn't heard the whistle at all. Alex smiled in approval as I passed him even though his shoulders remained stiff. I punched in their drink orders and grabbed Joanna as she finished folding the pile of napkins in the corner of the kitchen near the non-refrigerated condiments.

"Would you mind helping me take out the drinks?" I asked. I was always hesitant to ask other servers for help, but with my current streak of poor luck – Mom's episode, late to work, rowdy party – I really didn't feel like accidentally dumping tea over someone's lap.

She sighed heavily. "Fine, but only because those guys are cute."

I pursed my lips, but didn't argue. Joanna followed me out, holding her tray of drinks, and stood behind me. She waited for me to hand out the drinks from my tray before I was able to point to where each of the drinks on her tray belonged. Joanna dipped low and placed each drink on the table in front of the guys, presenting her rounded chest for their perusal. Many eyes followed her as she traipsed around the table, coming to a stop next to me.

"Do you need anything else, Honey?" she asked, sweetly. I closed my eyes, refusing to let them roll as I took a deep breath.

"No, I'm good, Joanna. Thank you." She frowned slightly, but tilted her head towards the table.

"Alright, no problem. If you boys need anything, you let me know." More than two or three bobbed their heads, eyes wide, as they followed her retreating rear end.

"Do you know what you want to eat?" I asked, redirecting their otherwise engaged attentions. For several minutes I stood there, writing down simple and complicated orders. Burgers, Salads, arguments about carbohydrates. *Who knew guys could be just as concerned about their weight as girls?*

No other customers entered the diner as I waited for the group's orders to be finished. Knix and Alex talked quietly at the counter and Joanna flirted back and forth with the customers in her section. As I entered the food orders, I remembered something.

"Hey, Alex?" Alex paused, mid-sentence, and looked away from Knix. I ran my fingers over the edge of the counter. "Sorry, didn't mean to interrupt." I glanced back at Knix. "I just wanted to let you know, I can't work this Sunday."

"You can't?" He cocked his head to the side. "I thought you were usually free on Sundays."

"I am," I blurted. "I mean, I was – I am usually – but the lady who takes my mom in for her appointments needs a babysitter that day and she's only willing to help me out if I can babysit when she needs me. Do you mind? I can find someone to cover the shift if you need–"

He waved his hand in front of my face, cutting me off. "No. No. It's fine. Don't worry about it." Alex stepped across the aisle to the drink dispenser to refill a glass with Sweet Tea before returning to set it down in front of Knix.

"I'm gonna head back and see if Carl needs any help. Harlow, stay here and watch the counter for me, will you?" I shuffled over to take his place in front of Knix as he pivoted towards the kitchen.

"Nice guy."

"Who? Alex?" *Of course he meant Alex. Who else could he mean?* I mentally slapped myself upside the head while trying to control the blush I could feel spreading up my neck and across my cheeks again.

Knix chuckled. "Yea, Alex. I've known him for quite a while."

"I've never seen you in here before, not until last night," I said. "How did you meet?"

"We work for the same organization."

"You're into real estate?" That was the only other specific work that I knew Alex did, but for some reason, looking at Knix – his height, his width, his stark appearance – he didn't strike me as the real estate type.

"Not exactly." He leaned forward and raised his glass to his lips.

My eyes followed as a bead of condensation slipped slowly down the outside. Before I could ask another question one of the football players called me over.

I didn't get a second more to myself until well after Knix had paid Alex his tab and left. Between running food, bussing tables with Alex, and seating customers, my break came well after the sun had set. I glanced up as a strike of bright light flashed across the windows. A few seconds later, a crack and thunder rolled through. I sighed.

"Do you want a lift home?" I paused as Alex locked the door to his back office, set in the corner of the kitchen, with two blind covered windows looking into the area.

I hefted my satchel over my shoulder. My eyes were drooping, my neck hurt, and I was more than ready to crawl into bed. Not only that, but I really didn't want to walk home in the rain tonight. "If it wouldn't be too much trouble," I relented.

Alex smiled and patted the top of my head as he passed by. "Not at all, Squirt. Let's go."

He led me outside to his truck, opening the door for me, and even assisting me into the cab as the rain poured down. A thirty-minute walk took much less time in a truck, and when Alex's headlights flashed over my mailbox, I unbuckled my seatbelt, said a hurried goodbye, and practically sprinted for my front door. He waited patiently until I had the door unlocked before backing up and turning out of the driveway.

The house smelled like dust and dollar store hand soap. I passed my mom's room without much fanfare, the light sounds of snoring from beneath her door telling me that she was oblivious to the rocking rainfall outside. Falling face first into my bed, I struggled to reach up and make sure my alarm clock was set for an hour before the bus would arrive in the morning and then sank into blissful sleep.

The baking heat of the school's outdoor courtyard was only a prediction of the oncoming summer. The polarizing, damp, humidity had escalated so badly within past weeks, it had driven most of the usual courtyard inhabitants indoors. Even though there had been a sparse few summer showers the night before, the sun beat down on the remainder of the outside occupants, hot and angry.

"Come on," Erika urged. "Let's go inside, where there's *air-conditioning.*"

"It's too loud." I pushed her through the glass doors, out into the sweltering heat. She groaned as I led her over to a stone bench, half secluded behind a pillar and under a bit of shade. Erika grumbled a few half-hearted protests as she settled and pulled out her lunch, swinging her legs and enjoying the resulting breeze over her skin.

"I heard something in gym class," she said as I pulled out a half-sized portion of a deli ham and cheese sand-wich from my bag.

"Uh huh." I flipped the page of Stephen Chbosky's *The Perks of Being a Wallflower.*

"Are you even paying attention?" Erika's voice grew closer.

"Uh huh." I marked off a section that I was considering using in my final senior English paper. Something hard hit my shoulder, jerking me forward and I dropped the book in a puddle of rainwater under the bench.

"Erika!" I reached for the book.

"What? I'm sorry." I rolled my eyes and picked the book up, shaking out the now soggy pages. "You weren't listening."

"Listening to what?" When she didn't answer, I looked up and she was giving me her 'I told you so' look. "Okay, I wasn't listening. What were you saying?"

"I said I heard something in gym class today."

"Surprise. Surprise," I replied. "I assume it had something to do with how many jumping jacks Coach Davis wanted you to do. Oh, wait, you have selective hearing so it must have been something more gossip worthy."

"No—well, yes—but that's not what I'm talking about." She leaned in close. "I heard that a certain someone caught the eye of one of the football players."

"Congrats, Babe, I'm happy for you." I continued to shake out my book, hoping that it wouldn't take too long to dry. I was almost to the end and really needed to start on that paper if it was going to be finished by the deadline.

"I'm talking about *you!*"

In her excitement, Erika jabbed me again and the book fell right back into the puddle. I looked at her, but her expectant face was so enthusiastic, I didn't have the heart to be irritated. I sighed, picked the book back up, and placed it, pages up, on the bench next to me, scooting it as far away from Erika and the puddle as possible.

"Well?" she prompted.

"Well, what?" I asked.

"Who is it? Did he ask you out? I can't believe you didn't tell me."

"I have absolutely no idea what you're talking about." I didn't even know any of the football players. "Besides, what would be the point in dating now? Everyone is going off to college in a few months."

Erika frowned. "You could too, if you wanted. You're smart enough."

I laughed, smiling at her to defuse some of her solemnity. "I don't have the money. Besides, it's too late to be considered for the fall semester." I stood, and stretched my arms over my head just as the bell rang for our last class of the day.

"Well, it's never too late to get a boyfriend," she informed me with a tilt of her chin. "Having a boyfriend is great."

"Speaking of," I said, "you never told me about him – your boyfriend."

Erika's eyes lit up. "Oh, Harlow. He's so sweet. I was a little nervous when he started talking to me because he's a few years older than me, but he is so nice. I've been misplacing some of my stuff – I can't find that necklace my Mom gave me for my sweet sixteen and he offered to get me something even nicer. Isn't that just the sweetest thing you've ever heard?!"

It sounded odd to me for a new boyfriend to offer to buy her nice jewelry, but I didn't say anything. "He sounds pretty cool," I replied.

"He is," she gushed on. "I can't wait for you to meet him."

"We should probably get to class," I suggested as the warning bell rang. Turning, I slung my bag over my shoulder and picked up Chbosky's book. "And don't listen to every rumor you hear."

Erika pouted as I waved goodbye, and disappeared into the masses of students collecting in the hallways. As the end of the school year drew nearer, more and more students skipped classes, fooled around in hallways, and gave off a general "I don't care" attitude. I managed to squeeze through to my classroom and take my seat well before the late bell rang. I leaned back, cracking my neck and set my drenched paperback to the side. The girl to my left scowled at the wet mark it left on my desk and scooted away.

Halfway through a dreary PowerPoint and monotonous lecture, a piece of lined paper flicked onto the desk in front of me. I jerked up, looking at it before glancing around to see who had put it there. The same girl shot me a disgusted look.

"Just read it," she mouthed before rolling her eyes and turning away. I unfolded the note.

I thought you were pretty cool yesterday. We should hang out sometime. –G

Beneath the scribbled sentence was a phone number. I looked up, even more confused. I saw him, the guy who was among the football team party that had sat in my section at the diner – the one the others had all deferred to. He smiled my way and tilted his head, indicating that the note in my hands was, in fact, from him. I blinked. He couldn't mean me. This note was obviously meant for someone else. I felt so embarrassed. I had read someone else's note. I turned to hand it to the person on my right, but the seat was empty. I forgot that it had sat empty since the last change of seating arrangements. I stared ahead, because the only other girl in my immediate area had been the one to shove it on my desk.

I stared at the note and when the bell rang, signaling the end of class, I jumped because football boy was standing right there. He hovered at the front of my desk, smiling down at me.

"Hey." He had a great smile with impeccably white, straight teeth. Most people didn't have teeth that perfect.

"Hi." I tried to swallow around my dry throat.

"You got my note." He shifted as a couple of students in my row passed him on their way out the door, a couple stopping to slap him on the shoulder. I needed to leave as well or I would miss my bus.

"Yea, I did." I stood and hesitated for a second, my right hand lingering over the note. "Here." I handed the note back and brushed past him. "I'm sorry, but I'm busy."

I scurried to the classroom door, hoping to make it out and away before he could stop me. Unfortunately, I hit a block just outside the doorway. A crowd of students all congregated, some yelling and screaming as two guys broke into a fight. An elbow jabbed into my side and I gasped as I toppled over – right back into football guy.

"Fight! Fight! Fight!" Students jeered and cawed at each other, waving their arms in the air and shaking their heads as they watched.

I frowned as the smaller of the two boys, a freshman

with a crop of curly, blond hair was shoved, face first, into the hall lockers. Blood spurted from his nose.

"Well, if you won't take my number, can I have yours?" Football guy asked. "Name's Grayson, by the way."

My head pivoted in his direction. I had forgotten that he was the only thing holding me off the ground. He didn't seem to mind because his smile hadn't faded.

"Um..."

"Come on! Take him down, Thomas!" someone yelled.

I flinched when the freshman's face came away from the lockers only to be slammed back into the metal door repeatedly. *Where is the teacher?* The crowd of students propagated, breeding unrest and hormone fueled anger. *Do they even know the kid they are condemning?* I wondered.

"If you give me your number, then there's no pressure for you to call me, now is there?" Football boy tilted his head. "It's all on me to call you."

What was he talking about? Couldn't he see that a poor kid was being hurt?

"Aren't you going to do something about this?" I gestured to the fight.

He was a football player, a jock. Despite what TV shows might have people believe, they were fairly nice guys from what I had experienced. A little rowdy, like some had been last night, but they left good tips. Acting juvenile didn't make them bad. He looked up, surveying the circle of angry and yelling students, the fight, as if it was the first time he had noticed it, and back down at me. "Why?"

"Why?" I blinked. "What do you mean, why? Because

that poor kid is getting the crap beat out of him. That's why."

He looked back to the fight again. "If I stop it, will you give me your number?"

I shook my head. "You're bargaining with me?"

The freshman's face made it to the floor as the other, much larger, guy–Thomas–jerked the kid down and began pounding into him. The freshman curled inward, trying to escape the blows.

"Get him! Come on, you can do better than that!"

I couldn't take it anymore. Someone had to do something. I twisted away from football guy, dropping my backpack at his feet, and dove for the freshman. Many students froze the moment I broke the circle as if I had just disturbed a very powerful spell.

The yells and the taunts grew quiet until the guy beating up the freshman looked up, blood on his knuckles. Confusion covered his face as though he didn't understand why no one was cheering him on anymore. I stood over him, panting in anger.

"Get off!" I grabbed the back of his shirt, my hands closing around the neckline, and jerked. He frowned as his shirt stretched, but he didn't move. He batted my hand away as though I were a pesky fly. I glared at him as the freshman peeked at me through his arms.

"This ain't got nothing to do with you, bitch," Thomas snapped, twisting back to his target. The freshman whimpered and covered himself up again.

"Stop it!" I snapped, pulling my arm back.

My punch landed on Thomas' shoulder and I gasped in pain when my thumb crunched under the rest of my fingers. It was tight and I curled and uncurled my fist, trying to relieve the pain. Thomas bent his head back and looked at me again.

He stared. I gritted my teeth and decided that the best course of action was to brazen my way through. The air in the circle was no longer charged with the threat of anger. It was finally empty of noise.

I straightened my shoulders, cradling my wounded fist. "Get off of him," I repeated.

When people began to back up as he stood, I realized just how large this guy really was – or maybe I had always been two feet tall. At least, it felt like I was as I stood next to him. The freshman got to his knees, taking the opportunity to scamper out between the legs of the onlookers.

"What's going on here?" The authoritative voice that sounded nearby caused many of the students in the circle to dash away.

I almost groaned – half in relief, half in frustration. After all of the action had ended and the victim had disappeared, someone finally showed up. Life wasn't fair. I glanced over my shoulder to see who it was.

No. The world could not possibly be that cruel. Bellamy held his position, his back straight, shoulders back, eyes intent on me and Thomas, as he stood next to Principal Wiggins.

"I asked you students a question." Principal Wiggins stopped in front of me, and Thomas shifted back as if he was getting ready to run.

The rest of the remaining students – save for football guy, who watched on with mild interest as he leaned against the doorway of a classroom – dispersed quickly. "Thomas, is that blood on your hands? What happened?"

"Nothing." Thomas rubbed his knuckles up and down the side of his jeans, smudging the obvious evidence.

"I would say it's not nothing." Principal Wiggins glanced back at me, recognizing me as one of his previous students when he had been a Biology teacher my freshman year. "What happened here, Miss Hampton? I expect the truth."

The real problem with breaking up a fight is that it always led to this. In the spirit of a twisted, Shakespeare, angsty prince, *to snitch or not to snitch, that was the question.* I stood there, with my lips slightly parted, contemplating how to settle this.

I glanced at Bellamy out of the corner of my eye, who raised a brow my way. No help there, then. I sighed. I needed to tell the truth. I didn't care if that meant I was a snitch. It meant that Thomas would get what he deserved for beating up a poor freshman.

"Thomas thought it'd be funny to use Jimmy Dawson as a punching bag. He ran off before you got here, when Harlow stepped in."

My mouth hung open and every head in the vicinity slowly twisted towards football guy.

"Is that so, Mr. Caruso?" Principal Wiggins glanced back at Thomas who glared at the floor.

"He doesn't know what he's talking about," Thomas snapped.

Football guy – Grayson, I reminded myself – shrugged. "Bet if someone tested the blood on your knuckles – now on your jeans too, by the way – they'd be able to prove it." Thomas rubbed his knuckles on his jeans again, trying to wipe the blood off as fast as he could. "Still on your jeans, genius," he said with a sigh.

"Alright, Miss Hampton, Mr. Caruso, please go to the front office and wait for me to meet with you. Thomas, you come with me." I wondered if Principal Wiggins would grab Thomas by the ear like teachers and principals did in old movies. He looked just angry enough.

I picked up my fallen backpack and followed behind Principal Wiggins who had Thomas walk in front of him. Bellamy continued to glance my way. Hot fire licked along my cheeks and I knew, without a doubt, that I was blushing.

"So, about that phone number." Football guy – Grayson or Mr. Caruso or whatever – walked backwards as we strode through the nearly empty halls of the high school, eyes watching me in their peripheral like they had the night before when his friends had catcalled to me.

I did the same thing as I had before, I ignored him. Instead, I thought of the complicated mess I had now gotten myself into. I would definitely need to call Erika and see if she or her dad could give me a lift home. My bus was likely long gone. I hoped my mom wouldn't notice my extended absence.

"Let's make a deal, you give me your phone number and I promise to wait twenty-four hours before I call," Grayson grinned.

"I don't have a freaking phone, so no, you can't have my number," I snapped.

The last few steps to the door of the front office were the longest. I reached it and threw it open, ahead of everyone else. Despite my extreme desire to slam it shut behind me, I held it open until they had all passed through.

"Hmm, that is a problem," Grayson mused, sidling up next to me again. "I guess I'll just have to take you home, so I can drop you off, and you can accept my offer to take you on a date." He nodded as if that idea somehow solved all his problems.

"Are you messing with me? Am I on a new edition of *Practical Jokers*?" I honestly could not fathom his interest. I sank down into one of the front office chairs and he sat next to me.

He shrugged, those wide shoulders of his taking up more space than what his cushioned visitor's seat offered. I slid over a little bit. Mrs. Donovan watched us from her perch, eyes curious as if we were acting out her favorite soap opera.

"I'm not messing with you," he assured me. "I like you. I think you're cute and we should go on a date." He smiled. "And you should let me drive you home today."

"Thanks, but I can get a ride myself." Maybe. Hopefully.

"Do you not like me?" If he was offended by my responses, it didn't show. He merely asked as though truly curious to know the answer.

"You didn't step in to help that kid," I replied.

"Who? Jimmy? He would have been fine. Besides, no one else was stepping in either. You don't seem angry at them."

"I am," I said. I was absolutely, blood boiling, furious. "It's not okay to just let someone get hurt and it's disgusting that they not only let him get hurt, they encouraged it. Thomas could have seriously injured him, and everyone was shouting as if it were a professional wrestling match. So, yes, I'm angry at them!"

I hadn't realized that my voice had risen until Mrs. Donovan coughed quietly in reprimand. I sighed and counted the threads of the chair covers to calm myself.

"Well, I did step up for you with the Wig."

"I don't like that name."

"Why? Everyone knows he's bald as a naked mole rat under that horrid wig of his. It's ironic that his name is Wiggins, isn't it?"

I didn't answer. Sure, Principal Wiggins had a reputation of being harsh in punishments and lazy in every-thing else, especially since he had forgone teaching for his administrative role, but I'm sure if he heard anyone call him "The Wig" his feelings would be hurt. He had been a fair teacher when I had him.

"I just don't like it."

"Okay, I won't say it." Silence stretched until Mrs. Donovan went back to her typing. Those clicking keys were the only sound aside from the low hum of jazz music in the background.

"Harlow?" Principal Wiggins stood at the door with a red-faced Thomas in tow. "If you will please follow me back." He turned to Thomas. "You," he snapped, pointing to a chair. "Sit and don't move."

I left my backpack on a chair next to Grayson. When we bypassed Principal Wiggins' office and continued on to the conference room where I had met Bellamy the first time, I wavered. Bellamy sat in the conference room, in the very same seat he had before. I chose a seat a moderate but sufficient distance away.

"Am I in trouble?" Did they think that I had anything to do with the fight? What had Thomas said?

"No, you're not in trouble, Harlow." Bellamy's strong baritone was soothing to my nerves and that knowledge only caused them to tense once more.

"Miss Hampton," Principal Wiggins began, "I actually brought you here because I was on my way to grab you before you made it out of class. I assure you, Thomas will be dealt with, but I was coming to retrieve you because I know you've had a meeting with Mr. Wood-stone here. He's very excited to accept you into a pre-college program."

"A pre-college program?" I turned to him. "I thought you weren't a recruiter?"

"Well, um..." Principal Wiggins continued to blunder, going through many more 'ums' and 'wells' before Bellamy leaned forward, stopping him.

"I never said I wasn't a recruiter," he said. "The program I have suggested for you is similar to a technical degree. You will receive training outside of a classroom. If you would like to attend a few classes, I'm sure we can arrange that as well. Unfortunately, I can't tell you much more until you agree to it first. We will then have you sign a nondisclosure agreement."

I put my hand up, stopping him. "Wait? Nondisclosure agreement? What?"

"Miss Hampton, this program is very beneficial to those who are accepted," Principal Wiggins assured me.

"I'm sure that's very true," I replied respectfully, "but I can't afford it."

"Everything will be paid for."

The words 'paid for' fluttered through my mind like free range birds, chirping and nipping at my wants and desires. I could have some sort of degree. Get a better job. Maybe a car. Better medication and doctors for my mom.

"Paid for," I repeated. Maybe I really was being pranked.

"I've already talked to you about the program, Harlow." Bellamy leaned forward, a strand of his long, dark hair escaping the band that kept most of it held together. "I'm here because you are a perfect candidate. You would start right away. We would even be able to pay you for your studies and interests in us. Much more than what you make at Alex's Diner."

"How do you know where I work?"

Stupid question. Alex probably was fairly popular and he only had so many employees. He had already admitted to me once that he bragged about me like his own daughter. On top of that, I didn't live in a large town, anyone could see me at any time walking to and from work.

"Never mind." I shook my head. "It doesn't matter." I took a deep breath. "Look, I'm sorry, Mr. Woodstone–" The look in his eyes was incendiary. "Bellamy," I corrected. "I just can't be sure what I'm getting into until I get more information. How do I know that the program you're offering won't tie me up for several years in requirements? There are scholarships that do that."

He nodded, the molten heat in his eyes gone and replaced by sweet warmth. "I've asked Principal Wiggins to give you as much information as he can. I'm going to step out of the room for a moment. When you're done talking, I'll take you home."

"You don't have to. I'm sure I can get–"

The fire returned. "I'll take you home," he repeated. I closed my mouth and nodded, mute.

"Alright then, I'll be out in the front office with Mrs. Donovan." Bellamy stood and strode to the door, opening the wooden panel, stepping through before he let it swing shut, leaving me alone with Principal Wiggins and a hell of a lot of baffled thoughts.

"Harlow." The air conditioner kicked on, cool air blowing into the room. "I think you should consider Mr. Woodstone's offer."

"I don't know." It was really hard to sit there, stare my principal in the face, and tell him no.

I listened as Principal Wiggins talked about missed opportunities and opening and closing doors, and I continued to nod my head at the appropriate intervals. Minutes ticked by.

"So, please, Harlow. Please give this a shot." Did I really have a choice?

"I don't really think his program is the best fit for me," I said.

"This is one of the biggest opportunities you might receive. I promise, Harlow. I've known Mr. Woodstone for many years now. He's a good boy – man." Principal Wiggins smiled. "He's a good man. You'll be in good hands."

"Can you tell me anything else about the program?" I asked. "I promise I'll consider it, but I need to know what *it* is."

Principal Wiggins leaned back in his chair, the wig on his head shifting. "I know that the program is very selective," he replied. "And just because you say yes, doesn't necessarily mean that they'll accept you later on. They'll have you take a test of some sort, I've been told it's different per person. Some take physical tests, some written, and some a combination. They want to make sure that everyone they accept into the program is right for it. The program is tailored to each person and there are teams. I don't know exactly what each team does, but I do know it's significant work." Principal Wiggins nodded his head in thought. "Bellamy has been in the program for a few years now. He used to be such a quiet boy. He's really come out of his shell since he joined. It's done him a world of good." He looked at me. "They won't keep you if you don't want to be there. The agreement is just to keep everything they tell you confidential."

Somehow, in the midst of his impassioned promises and the dropping temperature in the room, my brain must have frozen over. Because somewhere along the conversation, I felt my mouth opening and my voice saying, "Okay."

"I'll give it a try." Maybe it wouldn't be so bad. Maybe they had people to help my mom. Maybe I could get a better job, take public transportation, and earn enough for a car. Maybe things could be better. I wanted them to be better.

"You won't regret this," Principal Wiggins said. I hoped he was right.

CHAPTER 5

My skin was cold and clammy from sitting under the air-conditioning unit in the conference room for too long. Bellamy didn't comment as he led me back out into the office lobby with a hand on my arm.

I dragged my gaze across the floor, memorizing each thread of the carpet that hadn't been replaced in well over thirty years. Grayson lounged back in the same chair we had left him in, with his legs straight and crossed at the ankles. The moment I stepped through the doorway, he smiled and straightened.

He stood, moving towards me. "Thanks," he said. One heavy arm swung over my shoulders, dislodging Bellamy's hand. "I'll take her home."

I moved my hands to his fingers, laying precariously close to my breast – which he didn't appear aware of – and gripped the digits tightly before maneuvering out from under his grasp. I dropped his hand and frowned at him.

"No. Thank you," I snapped. "I'll walk." I stepped away from him and grabbed my bag from the chair beside us.

"No, you won't." The distraction of Grayson was overshadowed by Bellamy's deep rumble. "I will be driving you home. Though she appreciates the offer, Mr. Caruso, it won't be necessary." My eyes widened as Bellamy used Grayson's last name in much the same formal fashion as Principal Wiggins, edged with authority though Bellamy's tone was layered with disdain.

"Are you sure that won't threaten your job?" Grayson's eyes narrowed as he studied Bellamy. "I didn't know male teachers could give their female students rides. I wonder what the school board would think of that."

Bellamy grinned, but it was a decidedly unfriendly facial expression. The stretch of his mouth was a quirk that made him seem more like an unyielding feral animal.

"Lucky for me, I'm not a teacher, Mr. Caruso." The bite in Bellamy's tone as he spoke was enough to make my eyes widen. "Harlow, this way, please."

I followed, refusing to peek over my shoulder at Grayson's expression as we left the office. I chose, instead, to focus ahead. Bellamy held the door for me as we walked out into the abandoned hallway, and did the same when we reached the glass doors leading into the staff parking lot.

As we stepped outside, the temperature skyrocketed at least fifteen degrees, heating my cold skin and causing sweat to form across my shoulders and forearms before we even reached his car. The humidity swept over me, a daunting wave of heat-drenched air.

Bellamy unbuttoned his suit jacket, peeling the material off his shoulders and reaching up to loosen his tie as he unfastened the top button of his pristine, white dress-shirt. The clothes didn't fit him, in my opinion. They were too constraining, like bindings meant to cage rather than clothe. The new grin he flashed my way was much more relaxed.

"This is me," he said, as we stopped in front of a familiar BMW. I halted in front of it, the strap of my bag almost sliding off.

"This is—"

"Yup," he said before I could finish. "Marv was very upset with you when you jumped out in the road." His low rumble proclaimed his agreement with Marv's feelings.

"You were there," I said, speaking my realization aloud. "You were the one driving." I stared at him over the hood as he opened the passenger side door.

"Please get in." He gestured to the car. "It's hot out here, I'd like to get some air conditioning going before I start to stink in this monkey suit."

I slid into the seat and he closed the door behind me. The dashboard was littered with various screens and buttons – all excessively high tech. I curled my hands into my lap, trying not to touch any of it, sure I would break the first thing I came into contact with. The driver's side door opened and Bellamy's arm shot out as he tossed the jacket into the back seat. He sat and began rolling up his sleeves, revealing dark ink lines.

"You have tattoos?"

"Just the one so far," he replied, rotating his arm so that I could better see the design. A deep green stem grew out from his inner elbow that blossomed into a deep purple flower with pouting petals. "I had it done overseas. It's designed with a thicker needle. Would you like to feel it?"

"What kind of flower is it?" I heard myself ask as I tentatively reached out to touch the markings.

"It's an iris blossom," he replied. His skin was warm and rough against my palm. I followed the lines with a finger, stroking the raised impressions the needle had left in his skin. It was beautifully done.

"I like it."

He smiled, a wide smile that bled into his eyes, making them sparkle. "I'm glad." He pulled away and started the car.

"How do you know Marv?" I asked. "Does that mean you know Knix too?"

"Yes, I do," he answered as he backed out of the parking space.

I glanced at the window. "Are we going to see them?"

"Not yet."

"Where are we going?" The car slowed at a stop sign.

"I'm taking you home."

I knew I needed to get home, but still, I had to will myself not to be disappointed. I couldn't stop the question that sprang from my lips. "You're serious?"

Maybe it wasn't smart to wish he was driving me anywhere but straight back to my house, yet curiosity had me. There were suddenly so many questions I wanted to ask. I just didn't know how to phrase them. A car ride to my house was too short for me to be able to even skim the surface of all the answers I needed.

He peered at me as he made the turn.

"Of course I'm serious. Are you going to tell me where you live or should I surprise you?"

I liked a challenge. "Surprise me." His lips twitched, but his eyes smiled.

"As you wish." I grinned. *Princess Bride* references I could totally get on board with.

Bellamy leaned forward and pressed the radio button. Soft indie music drifted into the cab. I listened to the low hum of the emotional lyrics, thinking that they suited him. If I was being honest, Bellamy was already an enigma to me. He could have just as likely turned on heavy metal and I would have thought the same.

"Do you mind?" he asked, nodding towards the music.

I shook my head and he relaxed, his shoulders pushing back into the seat as he adjusted and stretched out a bit more. I tried to imagine Knix in his position, though I wasn't sure why, and I found the image amusing. He was much too big to fit in such a small car. He probably had to have his cars custom made, as well as his clothes, the doorways in his house, and more.

I drifted, watching trees, buildings, parks, and people all go by in the window like a television show without any one main character. I wondered what it would feel like in the driver's seat. In control. I had never seen this kind of show from that side of the car. I was always the passenger, just along for the ride.

Bellamy drove the car, handling the beast like it was a sweet animal under his care. When he hit the interstate, he slid into pre-five o'clock traffic. I tried to distract myself, reading the license plates that passed us. Being so close to the ocean, so close to a port city and tourist bedrock, I wasn't surprised to spot a few northern states fly by.

It wasn't until we had passed a few exit signs that I began to get antsy. How far could he be taking me? I think Bellamy sensed my apprehension because after a quick glance my way, he reached into his pocket, pulled out his phone, and passed it over to me.

"I don't need your phone," I said and at the same time he asked, "Can you send a text for me?"

Of course, I thought. He wasn't giving me his phone. That would be stupid. My cheeks tightened with embarrassment. He smiled as I slid the lock across the screen to open it.

"Um...who do you want to send a text to?"

"Alex." He clicked his blinker on and navigated the BMW's front end into the fast lane. How much farther did we need to travel? This definitely wasn't the way home. Another concern hooked my brain when I realized what he said.

"You know Alex?"

The blinker clicked off.

"We all know Alex. I'm sure Knix has told you."

"I know Knix knows Alex, and I know that you know Marv." I paused, thinking about his words before I continued. "Is there anyone else I know that you know? Do you know Erika?"

If Bellamy knew Marv well enough to drive his expensive car – at least, I assumed it was Marv's car, he seemed more likely to own a BMW – and Marv and Knix knew each other, and Knix knew Alex, odds were that they were all buddy-buddy and Alex had just neglected to tell me so. Then again, it's not like I was one of his close confidants. Still, it stung to be left out of the loop.

"Your friend, Erika?" He reached up and turned the radio off. "No, I don't know her. Although I do have a few files on her. We wanted to know how close you two were."

Was he kidnapping me? Principal Wiggins said I was

in good hands. "We're very close. She'll want to know where I am. I should text her too. Can you tell me where we're going now?"

He grimaced. "It's not a secret, Harlow, but I would prefer you didn't tell her. Don't worry, I'll have you home in time to be in bed before your shift tomorrow. You did say I could surprise you."

"I lowered the phone to my lap. How do you know about my work schedule?"

"I know Alex, Sweetheart, remember?" His smile stretched across his lips when he laughed. It was a good laugh, like he was genuinely amused. "He's your boss and I asked."

"He shouldn't give out information like that," I harrumphed, picking up his phone again as I pressed myself back in my seat.

I slid open the lock pad again and found the message icon leading to his text messages.

"You have a new text," I said looking down at the sender's name. "Who's Texas? Is that like a nickname or something?"

What parent names their kid after a state? I considered this and immediately thought of all the parents that name their children after cities and countries. Those poor Brooklyns, Londons, Chinas, Dakotas, oh my.

"Not a nickname, it's his real name. Here, give it to me, I'll take care of it."

"No!" I jerked the phone as far away from him as I could. "You're driving. I'm not letting you text. I'll send it, just tell me what you want to write."

"Fine." His smile disappeared. "What did he say?"

"It says, 'Are you bringing the package?'" I relayed the message, curious about the way his jaw tightened.

"Tell him that I'll be delivering the package within the

next hour."

I squinted at him, expecting him to crack a smile, but he didn't tell me he was joking. I had assumed he would be with me for the next hour, but maybe we would be done by then. I shrugged and typed out a quick, shortened version.

Bellamy: In another hour.

The response was almost instantaneous.

Texas: Who the hell is this and where is Bell?

I glanced at Bellamy, before typing my reply.

Bellamy: My name is Harlow, I'm riding with Bellamy. He's driving right now, asked me to text for him.

The wait was slightly longer this time, but no more than a few minutes before the phone was buzzing in my lap again.

Texas: Where are you?

I looked out the window and scrunched my eyes as we passed the next green exit sign. I caught the sign number and turned back to the phone.

Bellamy: We just passed exit 98.

Texas: You'll be here soon. Thank you.

Bellamy: What about your package?

Texas: Don't worry about it.

I dropped the phone. Who was this guy? I peered at Bellamy.

"What did he say?" he asked.

"Nothing." I grabbed the phone. "Do you still want me to text Alex?" I asked, my hand hovering over the phone. He shook his head and I placed it in the console between us.

"Awful lot of typing for nothing to say," he mused, ignoring my question. I guess he didn't need to text Alex anymore. Bellamy steered the BMW back into one of the slower lanes. "She handles beautifully, doesn't she?" He angled forward to rub one hand on the dashboard. "Marv knows I'll treat her well, so I'm the only one aside from him allowed to drive her. Although if Texas or Knix really needed this baby, he wouldn't say no."

I didn't comment on my own previous thoughts, but I was smug knowing that I was correct in my assumption that this car was Marv's.

"Bet she carries a lot of packages for you, huh?" The remark was met with a few moments of quiet.

"Not usually, no."

"Somehow, though, I don't believe you." I turned away from him, glaring out the window.

"I know you're confused, Harlow, but please remember what Charles told you."

I wrinkled my nose. "Charles?"

"Principal Wiggins," he explained. "I'm not a bad guy, Sweetheart." He peered over at me beseechingly. "Texas isn't either. You might like him. Don't worry, we're good people."

"Who is *we*, Bellamy?" The sound of his name rolling off my tongue felt comfortable and odd at the same time.

"I'll tell you when we get there." He refocused on the road, flicking his blinker again, to the right this time, and maneuvering onto a narrow stretch of road with two lanes.

"As long as I'm not going to be trussed up like a turkey when I get there and ransomed off," I grumbled.

"Sweetheart, you don't have any money." He sounded frustrated, exasperated. I could relate and it just made me want to pummel him. Not that it would do much good. He was a lot bigger than me and the one time I had hit someone, I didn't even know how to hold my fist. I stroked my thumb in apology for earlier and it throbbed in response. "It's part of the reason why we picked you. We have something to offer you." I opened my mouth again but he spoke before I could utter a word. "No, please, no more questions. Wait until we get there."

"Fine," I said.

I folded my arms over my chest, sliding even further down in my seat. I faced the window once more and stared hard, trying to fixate my attention. Trees passed. The car jerked and moved over rough pavement, the shock absorbers making me feel as though I were riding in a private, quiet, train. Every now and then, Bellamy would slow or turn. I tried to count the turns but forgot them almost as quickly as he made them. It didn't matter. Nothing mattered. Even if I were to be kidnapped, it's not like anyone would really be worried about me at home.

Bellamy's cell buzzed in the console and I ignored it, keeping my eyes trained on the sky. It buzzed again and finally, I deigned to glance at it. The screen was lit up with not one or two, but four text messages, back to back, and the name reflected back was familiar. The phone vibrated once more as another message came through and Bellamy reached for it. I snatched it before he could touch it and though his lips quirked, he didn't say anything. I unlocked the phone and clicked on the last message before scrolling up and reading from the latest unread text.

Marv: Plans changed, call me if ur not driving.

Finally, I thought, someone understands the 'no using cell phones while driving' rules.

Marv: Knix texted me. He and Tex are already there.

Marv: Yo, I might need a pick up.

Marv: Need pick up. @ Mom and Dads.

The last text had been sent only minutes before. I

wondered if we were already too far away though.

"Marv says he needs you to pick him up," I relayed.

Bellamy inclined his head, nodding. "Did he say where he was?"

"At his Mom and Dad's." I watched Bellamy for his reaction. He simply bent his head and continued watching the road. I guessed we were already on the way.

Bellamy: Hey, it's Harlow. Bellamy's driving, but we'll be there soon.

Marv: U not letting him use his phone?

I sighed, maybe I thought too soon about someone else understanding roads as non-texting zones. I simply repeated a portion of the last text.

Bellamy: He's driving.

Marv: Good girl. C u soon.

The way his praise made me smile should have bothered me, but it didn't. Oddly enough, that didn't bother me either. I was just happy to have him thinking of something other than the incident with Cleo.

There was scarcely any traffic on the road. The trees, large and beautifully kept palms swaying in the wind, towered over us. Every so often we would pass what appeared to be houses built on stilts. I knew these. They weren't really houses, more like mansions. Some were blue and brightly painted with circular driveways and fountains at the center of their yards. Some were partially obscured by short brick walls and iron gates.

About twenty minutes into the lavish community, the BMW slowed and I sat up to see which house we were stopping at. Bellamy turned into one of the larger stilt homes. It was flanked by a brick wall and an iron gate in the middle. Bellamy reached for his visor and pressed a button there. The gates parted, swinging inward.

He rolled down the driveway slowly, coasting to a full stop in front of a large yellow mansion. There was a set of slightly curved, white stairs leading down from the front door with the same iron rails. Beneath the house were sets of wide, ornately carved beams that held the structure above ground. It looked so elegant, it was difficult to imagine the kind of strength built in and the intelligence used to create such a masterpiece.

The front door opened and Marv stepped out, followed by a short, older woman with smooth blonde hair contained beneath a colorfully adorned, floppy sunhat. She kissed his cheek and waved towards the car before striding back into the house and closing the door. It wasn't until Marv made his way down the steps that I realized he would probably want the front seat. I unbuckled my seat belt.

"What are you doing?" Bellamy looked alarmed as I loosened the strap across my chest and pushed it towards the door.

"Moving," I said. "He probably wants the front seat. It's *his* car, after all." He visibly relaxed, sighing.

"Oh, no, don't worry about it. Put your seat belt back on. Don't get out of the car."

"But–" The door behind me opened, interrupting any further protests.

"Hurry, before she decides to come out here and ask us all back in," Marv said as he slid into his seat and shut the door. "I do love that woman, but she is hard to get away from sometimes."

I heard the click of his seat belt, and Bellamy stared at me until I refastened my own. I peered over my shoulder as Marv pulled out his cell phone and began typing away. He looked both young and refined in his tailored gray suit. It was cute in a childish way with his hair mussed, likely from his mom's petting. I had seen many moms ruffle their kids' hair, even though mine never had. He didn't move to fix it.

"Gonna stare at me the entire time or you gonna ask something?" I jumped at the question. Marv hadn't even lifted his eyes, but I knew his inquiry was meant for me. Bellamy wasn't staring.

"Sorry," I mumbled, twisting back and leaning against the leather seat, though I still peeked at him through the rearview mirror. Marv swiped his finger across his screen a few more times before raising the phone to his ear.

"Hey, we're on the way."

His voice rose above the silence in the car. I wished Bellamy would have turned on the radio again. I didn't feel comfortable doing it myself because it would seem rude now that Marv was on the phone, but without the radio, it felt too much like eavesdropping.

"Yes, we have Harlow." My eyebrows rose. He was talking about me, and my eyes strayed back to the rearview mirror, watching him. "He just got me. We'll be there in a few minutes. Make sure to clean up your mess. We wouldn't want to lose her in your mountain of trash."

I heard the brief ending of whoever Marv was talking to as he pulled the phone away from his ear. They were yelling.

"–not trash! It's equipment!"

"Yea, yea. I'm sure all of the ladies like your equipment. Be there soon."

Marv ended the call and set the phone down on the seat before looking up and catching my eyes. I blushed, sinking as far as I could into the seat so that he couldn't use the rearview mirror, himself, as a spy glass.

CHAPTER 6

Marv was right. We arrived in a much smaller neighborhood not too long after stopping to pick him up. The houses were not as ornate as the stilt mansions, but they were no less beautiful. Bellamy drove through the streets as I pressed my face against the glass, watching the new sights go by. Without regular transportation, I wasn't as familiar with my own town or the cities surrounding it as most people. The car turned again as Bellamy navigated the streets of the well-kept neighborhood. It felt as though we were caught in a never-ending circle until the car finally pulled into a back section near an outdoor pool with a few people sunbathing on personal foldout chairs. The smell of grilled food reminded me that I hadn't eaten anything since lunch and now that it was nearing 6 pm, I was hungry.

Bellamy parked the BMW in a spot next to an equally elegant silver Impala. Marv slid out of the backseat, opening my door before I could even reach for the handle. Unbuckling my seatbelt, I stepped out between the two vehicles and followed Marv and Bellamy towards the upscale condominium building. A large, square-faced clock pointed outward high above the front doors as they led me around the side and through a glass patio.

"Back elevator is quicker," Marv said.

I nodded as we stepped through the doors into the cool, modern interior. The building was even more beautiful from the patio. The lobby was only a few yards to our left with two silver-doored elevators behind a large countertop manned by a young woman with her hair twisted back into a severe braid. I winced a little at how it made her already bony features even more prominent. She watched us with hawk eyes, but said nothing as I followed Bellamy and Marv towards a completely different set of elevators, my shoes squeaking on the white tile. I could feel the heat of her glare on my back, and thought I probably looked like a homeless straggler compared to the guys. They seemed more than appropriately attired, in their professional suits, to be coming home to a place like this. I glanced down at my ripped jeans and t-shirt with a sigh.

A large man, wearing a pair of white, paint-splattered jeans and a dark-gray polo with an "MP Condos" logo over the left side of his chest stepped out when the elevator signaled its arrival.

"Mr. Woodstone, Mr. Carter. So good to see you." The man beamed.

"Hey, Rodney, how's your little girl?" Bellamy grinned as he clasped the man on the shoulder.

Marv put his hand out and wrapped one arm around my shoulders, squeezing me closer to him as he adjusted us into the smaller space of the elevator. Bellamy propped the doors open with his arm.

"Oh, she's good, thanks so much for asking, Mr. Woodstone! Well, I'll be letting you all go now. Good seeing you again!" The man waved as Bellamy joined us and the doors slid shut.

"Do you think he paid her any attention?" Marv asked. I glanced up between him and Bellamy.

"No, he's a good guy. He doesn't ask questions."

My head twisted in Bellamy's direction as he looked down at me with a smile. Even though I wanted answers, I kept quiet. I'd save my questions for later. Marv slapped a hand on the button for the ninth floor.

"So high," I whispered, staring at the glowing button.

I didn't realize that I had spoken out loud until Bellamy and Marv each looked down at me. In the enclosed space, they felt even larger than before. Though, in reality, Bellamy certainly was the bulkier presence.

"Scared of heights?" I saw the way Marv's lips quirked, one corner tilting up in amusement.

I frowned at him. "No."

"Uh huh," he said. He didn't press me though. Instead, the one hand he kept on my arm ran up and down, warming the exposed skin there. It was soothing.

We reached the ninth floor and stepped out into a short, L-shaped hallway. "This way," Marv announced.

His hand fell away and I trailed behind them as Bellamy pulled out a set of keys. He ended up not needing them though because as soon as we were close, the door swung inward and Knix stepped out. He was dressed impeccably in a pair of blue-jeans, tight around the thighs and a navy V-neck t-shirt. The clothes molded to his massive frame like a second skin. I tried not to drool.

"Hey, Harlow." He smiled with sharp, happy eyes.

"Glad you could make it." He gestured inside. "Welcome." I looked up at him, unable to help the smirk on my lips.

"Fancy meeting you here," I said drolly.

Though no one had said anything, I wasn't the least bit surprised to see him. I stepped through the door and into a tidy apartment that smelled like the ocean breeze. Their condo was masculine in its décor, a Foosball table to the side of the living room, an Xbox under the massive flat screen TV, and wood toned coloring. Despite the manly decorations and furniture, it was all neat and orderly. I walked towards the windows on the far side wall.

"Why don't you have a seat?" Knix offered.

I sighed and nodded before turning back to the couch.

"Alright," I started, "you brought me here, so what do you want?"

"Are you hungry?" Knix asked. He moved towards the kitchen as Marv and Bellamy disappeared down a hallway.

"For answers," I replied. "Where are they going?"

"Bellamy probably wants to change. He doesn't care for suits too much. Marv is probably on his way to torture poor Texas – he likes the suits, Marv I mean. He won't change."

"Hmm." I stared towards the hallway.

"So, food?" Knix bent and opened the refrigerator. "Or would you prefer take out?" He closed the door and pulled out his cell. "I think I have a Chinese and pizza place nearby still in my contacts."

"Whatever is fine," I said. "I don't expect to be staying long."

"Where's your bag?" Knix asked curiously. He stopped

in front of me as he moved from the kitchen back into the living room. "I thought Bell got you from school."

"He did," I replied. "I left my backpack in the car. Why is it important?"

He shrugged. "I thought you might want to do some homework while you're here. At least until we get everyone situated." He sat next to me, his big body taking up more than half of the whole couch.

I squirmed.

"Or you could just start talking and we could take it from there," I suggested.

Mysteries were not my forte. There was a reason I stuck to classics and fantasy: predictability.

"Oh, Little Bit." He shook his head. "Where would the fun in that be?"

Voices rose from the hallway, causing both of our heads to turn.

"I'm telling you, you're going to die under that mountain of shit someday." Marv walked back into the living room followed by another boy.

The newcomer was tall and slender. He wasn't quite as tall as Knix, then again, I couldn't imagine anyone else with his size. He was what some might describe as lanky, but there were subtle muscles under the skin stretched across his arms.

Two beauty marks adorned the area above the left side of his lip. His hair was dark and appeared gelled back slightly on top only to fall into a soft wave at the end. I realized there that it wasn't actually gel, but water and the ends had dried. He looked like a journalist from an old black and white movie. Low slung jeans molded to his legs, held up with a loose brown belt and a white cotton t-shirt similar to Knix's.

"You'll appreciate my 'mountain of shit' when you need it to track your cell phone or–"

"Tex, come meet Harlow," Knix interrupted.

While it was said with a light air of friendliness, I could tell that it had been timed. Whatever Tex had been about to say, Knix didn't want him to say it in front of me. I had seen the way Knix's eyes had flickered to me before narrowing slightly in irritation just before the words left his mouth.

"Texas." The new guy held out a long-fingered hand – piano fingers, I thought – as he introduced himself.

"Hi." I took the offered hand.

Texas' face was fascinating. From a distance, he could have been anywhere from sixteen to twenty-five with a youthful, languid stance. Up close, I detected more intensity. The tops of his eyes were slightly curved and his lips tended to frown unless he was speaking.

Marv readjusted the tie at his neck before sitting primly on my other side, squishing me even further into Knix. He slung one leg up and over the other, laying an ankle across his knee before leaning back into the cush-ions. Texas moved away to take a seat at the breakfast bar, watching us.

"So," I began. Marv turned towards me, a raised eyebrow, daring me. "Am I being kidnapped or what?"

Knix laughed, the sound startling me. He put one big palm over his stomach as if he couldn't contain himself. "No!" He continued to laugh, choking out between breaths. "No, you're not being kidnapped."

"How many times do I have to promise something to get you to believe me?" Bellamy's voice drew my head back in the direction of the hallway and my eyes widened.

He stood there, arms crossed, in a fitted white shirt

that was nearly see through with all of that tan, dark skin. His shoulder length hair was pulled back away from his face, highlighting his straight features, and a pair of black rimmed glasses sat on the bridge of his nose.

"She's a smart girl, Bell. She wouldn't believe anything you tell her." Marv waved his hand, the light glinting off his Rolex watch. I was drowning in confusion.

"Please," I said. All eyes fell on me. I sighed. "Just tell me what I'm doing here."

Knix patted my thigh, the fingers stretching across the fabric of my jeans like a massive, warm, bear paw. "Alright, Little Bit. Why don't we order some pizza and we'll put it all out there?"

He stood and moved back to the kitchen to retrieve his phone and dialed for the order. Bellamy took Knix's emptied space next to me, not filling it nearly as much, but still taking up a considerable amount of room. I let my head roll back against the couch.

By the time the pizza arrived, I had calmed down. I stuffed a few slices of meat lovers' delight in my mouth, chugged the can of soda Bellamy handed me, and laid back while the rest finished their meals. I watched as Marv used a fork and knife to cut up his pizza into small bites. Knix folded his in half and ate it like a taco, while Texas ate his crust first. Bellamy seemed to be the only one who ate it the normal way – just a lot slower.

"Alright." I slapped my hands on my thighs, drawing their attention. I sat up straighter. "Let's get this little intervention over with, shall we?"

Knix rubbed a napkin over his lips before he spoke. "Is this an intervention? I didn't think you had done anything so terrible – at least not yet – do you have something to tell us?"

I frowned, twisting my body so that I was facing the rest of the group and ignored his comments. "From what I can tell, you seem to be masquerading as some sort of college recruiting organization." I paused to take a breath. "That's obviously not the case."

"What makes you say that?" Bellamy shook his head, laying his paper plate to the side before sitting forward. "I thought I was quite good at that job and we *are* hoping to recruit you."

"For what, exactly?"

Knix sighed. "Alright, Harlow," he said.

I bent my head back in his direction. "You'll tell me?" I asked.

"You're right," he agreed. "We aren't recruiting you directly for college. We're recruiting you for something else."

"We need a girl with certain skills, of a specific disposition, and with the willingness to be trained," Texas interrupted.

I stared across the living room at Texas as he swiveled towards us on one of the barstools. "What kind of skills? What kind of disposition?"

Knix shot Texas a look and Texas huffed, returning to his pizza.

"You came highly recommended," Knix replied. "From the information we've gathered, we've determined–"

"Wait, hold up." I raised both of my hands, palms facing out, in front of my chest. "First of all, who recommended me? And second of all, what 'information' are you talking about?" I narrowed my eyes suspiciously.

Someone groaned, but I couldn't tell who it was. Bellamy stuffed another slice of pizza into his mouth while Marv quirked a brow at me when I looked at him. Texas sulked over his own plate.

"I don't—"

"No, hold on," Knix cut me off with a raised hand of his own. I let mine drop. "Alex was the one who suggested you. I believe he wanted to recruit you on his own, but he's a bit overworked at the moment."

"He hasn't been by the diner as much as he used to," I agreed. That still didn't explain why and what Alex would have recruited me for.

"As for the information that we've gathered..." He paused with another sigh. "We needed to make sure that we weren't getting into anything we couldn't handle."

"So, you what?" I demanded. "Stalked me? Sent Bellamy to kidnap me from school with the intention to interrogate me?" Okay, maybe that was a little dramatic. But still...

"We ran a background check. School and medical and any possible police records checked." Texas' voice drifted closer as he stood and moved back into the living room area. "Your SAT and ACT scores – which were considerably good. I do wonder why you took them if you aren't going to college."

Feeling defensive, I straightened my back. "They were free because of my mom's lack of income and I thought if anything changed, then I'd need those scores."

"You mean if you somehow found a way to go to college?" Knix asked.

I stared at my lap

"You could," Texas said, shrugging as he scooted a pizza box over on the coffee table and took a seat there. "If you wanted."

"So, you're the cyber stalker then?" I clarified. "Find everything you needed?" I added sarcastically.

"Yup." He smiled, though the expression didn't reach his eyes. "That's me, the cyber stalker."

"And yes, we did find out what we needed to." Knix moved closer, picking up one of my hands and held it between his. He leaned closer, eyes meeting mine with a seriousness that startled me.

"You need us, Harlow. You need what we can offer you. All we want to do is help you. Think of this as an internship, a job opportunity or whatever you want. All you need to do is agree to work with us and you'll see that we can change things for you. Change them for the better."

"What do you need me for?"

I was perplexed. I wasn't particularly strong or talented. I certainly didn't have the connections that Marv apparently did. I didn't have Texas' cyber stalking skills. I wasn't as large and imposing as Knix, or as sweet and intelligent as Bellamy. Why would they need me? They had said something about skills and dispositions.

"What kind of skills do you think I have?" I asked. "Why is my disposition so important?"

"Harlow, do you remember when Bell talked to you about your gymnastics?" Knix's voice was soothing as though he was trying to keep me calm.

"Yes, but how does that–"

"Every person has a set of skills that make up their talents," he continued. "Sometimes those skills may seem innocuous or even unoriginal, but they can be twisted and molded into tools used for bigger purposes. We want to do that with you if you'll agree to be a part of our program."

"Why me?" I stared back into Knix' eyes and tried to fathom why they would want to mold me. What had I done that was so great it had caught their attention?

"Do you remember when you jumped out in the

middle of the road to save a cat that wasn't even yours?" Marv asked.

Knix never took his eyes away from me even as I shifted to look away.

"She's mine now," I defended.

"I assumed you'd keep her." Marv smirked. Knix reached up and smoothed back a lock of my hair that had fallen in front of my face and I blinked, distracted, even as Marv continued. "The point I'm trying to make is that you're different. You're different because of your decisions and actions. It's not the talents and skills that people have that make them unique. It's what they do with them."

Marv folded a hand down his chest and smoothed his dress shirt. "Most people would have ignored that little kitten and kept walking. You didn't. The inherent qualities of you as a person, your character, define who you are. It's what makes you so valuable to us. It's why we chose to recruit you. We take on some pretty rough jobs as a team and we're looking for a softer piece in our box of tricks."

"Why?" I asked as Knix straightened and pulled away from me. Despite the distance, I still felt his warmth.

"Pure force is not always the best way to get a job done," Bellamy answered.

The room fell silent as I took in their expressions. They watched me with unreserved interest and hope.

"What do your instincts say?" Texas prodded. "Does your gut tell you that we're bad guys? That we're going to hurt you?"

"I don't believe most people get hurt because someone planned it," I replied quietly. "But..." They held a collective breath. "No. I don't think you want to hurt me."

"So, will you give it – give us – a chance, Little Bit?"

I closed my eyes and counted to three before I opened them again. "Okay."

All eyes were on me.

"Okay?" Marv clarified.

Texas' lips quirked.

I nodded. "I'm not saying I'm trusting you indefinitely. I'm not saying I'll do whatever you ask of me. I'm just saying I'll try whatever it is that you're offering."

"That's all we ask," Bellamy said.

"But I do find it curious," I continued. Marv arched one brow. "What would a group of guys like you need with a girl like me?"

"We–" Knix began.

I touched the wrist closest to me, stopping him. "You explained that you need someone willing to be trained, but what will I be trained for?"

I released his hand, pulling into the thoughts swirling in my head. Words began to form on my lips almost as fast as they appeared in my mind.

"Iris," I said. "That was on the black card that Bellamy gave me. It's the name of your organization, right? If Bellamy has a tattoo of the flower, he's been in it for at least a few years. Iris is the name of a Goddess, isn't it? The Greek Goddess of the Rainbow–"

I stopped when Bellamy slapped a palm on his thigh. His face was red as he held back what was quite obviously laughter. When he opened his mouth to take a breath, as it looked like he had been holding it in, he released a hoot of unbridled amusement. It wasn't long before Texas, Knix, and even Marv were chuckling along with him.

"I told you." Bellamy gasped. "I told you she was perfect."

"She's damn smart, Bell," Knix replied. "I'll give you that."

I waited for them to finish laughing. It dragged on for some time even as I frowned at them in confusion. What was so funny? Knix collapsed onto the couch next to me.

"So, what?" I snapped. "I'm right then, and this is about some Greek Goddess that you all worship as some cult or something?" I didn't actually believe that assessment, but I felt like the butt of a joke and didn't like it.

"Of course not, Little Bit." Knix shook his head. "We're part of an organization called Iris. It's more of a nod to the system that we go by. You're right, Iris is the Goddess of the Rainbow and I suppose the organization was named that in deference to how our teams are split."

"How are they split?" I asked.

Knix put a palm on the back of his neck and leaned to the side, stretching and cracking the muscles there. "We can't tell you more until we're sure you're committed. The only thing I meant by how teams are split, is that they're defined by color. No cults, I promise."

"Alright, then, tell me the rest." I crossed my arms over my chest and sat back against the cushions, waiting. "I'll agree to be committed." Knix flicked a glance at the guys.

"It's a bit more complicated than that," he replied, looking back at me.

"Uncomplicate it then."

He sighed. "I can't do that."

"Well, then what the hell am I doing here?" I stood up. "You drag me out here to talk and then you won't tell me anything. What was the point in pulling me away, huh? What was the point in even trying to recruit someone if you won't tell them what it is exactly that you're recruiting them for?"

Knix watched me with assessing eyes. "I want you to talk with Tex," he announced suddenly. "He's much better at explaining some of these things. He knows what he can and can't answer and he'll do his best to clarify what he can."

"Delegating tasks then?" I frowned.

"That's what we're about, Harlow." He rose from the couch, arching over me with this massive frame and bulging muscles. I knew I was small to begin with, but next to him I felt even tinier, and I wasn't sure if he was using an intimidation tactic or if he simply couldn't help it. "We work as a team. This is a part of Tex's job, and I won't take that from him."

The man in question stared at me from his position on the corner of the coffee table before rising to his feet. He held out one long-fingered hand, palm out, waiting.

"I don't bite," he said with a smile. I narrowed my eyes at him. I knew that he wouldn't bite me. He was an adult for goodness sake, but when I let my hand drift up and those fingers closed over mine, he leaned forward and whispered close to my ear, "Unless you ask me nicely."

I reared back, but my hand was firmly in his grasp and he simply tugged me along behind him. I felt more than a little out of control, but as I glanced back over my shoulder, I realized that I wasn't scared. I had been honest when I admitted that I didn't think these guys would hurt me. More than that, I thought that I could trust them to protect me if I really committed to being part of their team. It was an odd feeling for a girl who hadn't ever had someone else to rely on.

CHAPTER 7

Texas didn't drop my hand when we entered the bedroom. Instead, he held it and led me to the double bed pushed up against the wall under the only window the room boasted. The comforter covering it was smoothly laid over the mattress. Clean and pressed and smelling like vanilla, the dark blue was a contrast against the bare white walls of the room.

"Alright." Texas sat on the bed, tugging me along until I did the same. "Let's get to it, shall we? What do you want to know?"

I paused for a moment, glancing around the room at the plain, gray walls and lack of decor. His fingers tapped a staccato rhythm against his leg as he waited. A lingering scent of heated vanilla reached my nose as his coffee brown eyes watched me.

"I guess I'd like to start with Iris," I finally decided.

"Okay," Texas released my hand, using his own to rub at his pants' legs before standing up and striding across the room to a computer desk. "Well, to start, Iris is a not-for-profit organization that builds connections for members of the community."

"What community?" I asked as he flicked on one of the computers set across the desk and began typing.

"That's confidential," he replied as the printer hummed to life.

"That's not even a major question." I frowned, crossing my arms over my chest.

He shrugged. "I'm sorry. I can't answer that."

"Fine," I huffed. "Go on."

"If you decide to join us, you'll need to sign a non-disclosure agreement—"

"Principal Wiggins said something about that, is he a part of your organization?"

He hummed for a moment, tilting his head to one side and cracking his neck. "In a way, I suppose," he replied.

Great, I thought. *Information as clear as mud.* Instead of snapping at him, which had proved to have little to no effect, I took the opportunity to check out the rest of the room while I debated another question.

The computer desk was actually two tables pushed together in the diagonal corner of the room with wooden drawers that appeared hand-made underneath. The top of the desk was loaded with cords, wires, screens, hard drives, and a bunch of other techy-what-nots. The walls were bare, but not unclean. There were no marks, no scratches. Not even where the bed might have been moved in from.

"Harlow, are you listening?" I had taken so much time in quietly dissecting his room that I didn't notice Texas was still talking

I shook my head. "Sorry," I mumbled.

Instead of huffing in frustration or annoyance, he

merely smirked at me, the lip near his beauty marks curving slightly upwards.

"I said that we would come back to the non-disclosure agreement later. Right now, you're more of a temporary, trainee recruit. We're feeling you out. You're feeling us out. We're finding out if we click together." The way he said that had blood rushing to my face and his smirk bloomed into a full grin.

The printer began to spit out leaves of paper while he turned back to his desk and rummaged through a couple of the drawers, looking for something. When he found what he was looking for – a dark colored phone model – he popped open the back and checked something inside, then went back to searching through his drawers.

"So, I'm temporary..." I said. "Does that mean that I won't actually get any information?"

He shook his head as he opened another drawer, leaving the first open with papers and cords poking out of it. "No, you'll eventually decide whether or not you want to join Iris. When you get to that point – like we all do – we'll tell you everything."

"So, when I'm officially a member of Iris, you'll tell me what I want to know?" I clarified, my brow furrowing.

"Precisely," he said.

The printer stopped.

"Because that makes perfect sense." I huffed. "How am I supposed to know if I want to join if I don't know what it is?"

Texas shut the drawer and turned back to me. "That's why I'm telling you what Iris is."

"A nonprofit organization," I stated.

He nodded. "Yes. There are plenty of opportunities

that will become available to you if you take this job with us." His stare was intense, eyes heavy and deep.

"But that still doesn't answer what you need me for."

"I'll tell you three things," he replied. "Number one: what you stand to gain if you say yes. Number two: what will be expected of you if you say yes. And Number three: how Iris can change your life."

"Like it changed yours?" I guessed.

Curiosity ate at me. What had given him the intensity in his expression that both scared me and drew me in? He was obviously well off enough to afford the tons of tech supplies scattered around his room. I knew computers didn't come cheap even though they were required for necessities like job hunting, college applications, and even school work.

His condo was filled with various things that guys liked – the big, flat screen I had seen in the living room, the Foosball table, the refrigerator full of food. It was also relatively clean. No matter how normal Texas and Knix and Bellamy dressed – I had a feeling Marv didn't dress in t-shirts and jeans often – there was no concealing the fact that they had money. Or maybe Marv was the only one with money and he didn't mind helping his friends out. I didn't even have a phone. What I *did* have were electricity and water and rent bills waiting to be paid back home on my kitchen counter.

He shook his head. "I think that's a story for another time." The door creaked and we both looked up. Bellamy lumbered in before dropping onto the bed next to me.

"How far have you gotten?" he asked.

"I'm getting to it," Texas replied.

Bellamy blinked lazily and yawned. "Okay, I just came in to hang. Ignore me." He winked at me and I felt myself flush before I turned to face Texas once more.

"There are a lot of opportunities working for Iris, Harlow. Job opportunities if you'd like. Schooling. Connections. Safety. Friendships. Family," Texas said as Bellamy leaned back and began to play with the ends of my hair. "These are the benefits."

I nodded my understanding as he continued. "Of course, pros never come without cons. Some of the work we do, it can be a bit tricky."

"What do you–" He shook his head as Bellamy leaned forward and put his hand over my mouth to stop me and in a fit of frustration, I opened my mouth and licked his palm. Bellamy laughed as he leaned forward and looked me in the eye.

"Bellamy told me that you attacked a man much larger than yourself today," Texas commented with a frown as he watched on. "I can believe it."

"I didn't attack him," I said as Bellamy pulled his hand away. I barely punched him, for all the good it did. My thumb was still sore.

"Nevertheless." He turned back to his computers and pulled the stack of papers from the printer before rifling through them, double checking the paper tray and adding more. "Why'd you hit him?"

"He was hurting someone. No one else was willing to stop him." A fact I was still mad about.

"It could've been dangerous." Bellamy leaned back against the bed again and I felt his fingers on my hair.

"And?" I mimicked his tone. "You weren't there. I asked someone to help. He didn't. If I hadn't stepped in, who would have?"

"I'm not saying it was a bad thing, Harlow." Texas set the papers on top of one of his computers and turned towards me. "Just that it was a risk. Weren't you embarrassed?"

"Embarrassment isn't worth someone's life," I snapped. "My school isn't exactly the nicest or the safest. But life's that way. If what you need is someone to do what you tell them to, no questions asked, you might as well take me home now. That isn't me."

A moment of quiet stretched between us before Bellamy coughed to cover his laughter. I spun to face him, my mouth opening, ready to tell him off too. Texas' quiet laughter made me pause. I rotated, frowning.

"What's so funny?" I demanded.

Texas' hand covered his mouth as he chuckled. "You are," he said.

"I don't understand." Bellamy leaned forward, swiping two fingers under each eye, before putting one hand on each of my shoulders.

"You're perfect, Harlow. You are exactly what we need. We need someone willing to jump into situations that aren't exactly safe," Bellamy said. "We'll undoubtedly need to train you a bit – I've seen you rubbing your thumb. You tucked it in your fist when you hit him, didn't you?"

Baffled, I nodded absentmindedly.

"Rookie mistake. Don't worry about that, though. We'll start you on some PT and self-defense. I think we'd prefer if you could take some courses, but we don't really have the time for that. So, Knix and I will likely be the ones going over basics with you. We'll start you on that next Monday, though. You can relax this weekend." His palms squeezed my shoulders reassuringly before releasing me.

"I have to work on Saturday and I'm babysitting this Sunday and I have school Monday. How are you going to teach me self-defense?"

Bellamy was already shaking his head before I

finished, but before he could reply, Texas spoke up. "You're not going to work tomorrow – I texted Alex and asked him if he could get Joanna or someone to cover your shift. Babysitting shouldn't be too stressful. We want you to chill for a little bit before you jump in with us. As for school, we'll send someone to pick you up after you get out. You're only going for the next week anyway."

"I have a few days the next week too," I argued.

"You're not going," he said matter-of-factly.

"What do you mean I'm not going?" I felt my brows puckering, creating a slight V between them.

Texas answered. "Most of your final exams are scheduled for next week. We've bumped up your World history exam. You'll likely need to take some of your exams during your lunch period, but it's done so that all of them should be over with by Friday."

"What?!" I jerked away. "You can't do that?! The school–how did you–why–you didn't even ask me!"

I didn't have time to study for all of my exams this weekend. I still needed to finish the book for my English paper. There was so much to do. Panic flared.

"Hey, hey!" Texas redirected my flustered attention. "It's okay, calm down. I'm pretty good at the school thing. I can help you study."

"Help me study?" I slapped my forehead. "What about my paper? What about work after school next week? Work!" They had changed my work schedule too. "You can't just take away my shifts, I need those shifts!"

"Don't worry about it, we've got it covered," Bellamy replied lazily.

Don't worry about it?! I thought.

"I need the money, you jerk!" I slapped his chest. "I

need to call Alex." I held out a hand. "Let me use your phone."

"Nope." He reclined back in Texas' bed.

I calculated the chances of getting away with murder. "Knix!" I screamed.

Bellamy shot up. "Fuck, come on, Harlow." Panic bloomed over his face. "It's not a big deal, calm down."

"Don't tell me to calm down," I snapped. "Knix!"

"Why are you freaking out, Bell? Who is she going to get you in trouble with?" I wanted to punch Texas, but the heavy thud of resonating footsteps stopped me. The door swung open and Knix stood on the other side, his expression filled with concern.

"What's going on in here?"

"Nothing," Bellamy replied quickly.

"They changed my schedule, got rid of my work shifts, and won't let me call Alex to fix anything," I corrected with a glare Bellamy's way.

Texas was lucky he was on the other side of the room or else I would have included him in my irritation.

Knix visibly relaxed. "Oh, that's it?"

Bellamy relaxed.

"That's it? Is that not enough?!" When the childish urge to stomp my foot rose, I didn't ignore it. I slapped my foot on the floor of Texas' bedroom as I stood and whirled in a circle, pointing at both Texas and Bellamy. "Do something!"

Bellamy laughed, at first shaky and then with more power. "Yea, it's not a big deal. Even Knix thinks so."

"Not a big deal?!" I practically shrieked.

"Hey, hey, hey." Marv's voice sounded from behind Knix. "What's everyone yelling about?"

I pivoted as Marv slid around Knix's body and into the room. "Take me home, right now."

He held up both hands. "Whoa, okay." He glanced at Bellamy. "What did you do?"

"What did I – why does everyone blame me?" Bellamy pointed to Texas. "What if it was him?"

"Fair point," Marv replied, looking to Texas. Instead of asking again, though, he merely raised one aristocratic eyebrow.

"She's mad about missing work," Texas supplied.

"It's not about missing work," I corrected, fuming. "It's about the fact that I have bills to pay and you can't just–"

Marv pursed his lips and waved a hand to stop me. "We took care of that."

"You what?" A dull throb bloomed at the back of my head.

Knix spoke. "Your rent and utilities are paid for up until the job ends. You can make a decision then: go back home, work for Alex – you know he would never fire you – or you can work with us and maybe go to college if you like."

"You paid my bills?" I asked, shocked. He nodded. "Why?"

The look he gave me was unreadable. "Call it faith," he said. "I think you're smart enough to know a good opportunity when it's presented to you. If you don't believe me, I'd be happy to have Texas send you documents of proof."

I shook my head, but not to say no. I didn't feel like I was in a room with guys who had enough money – money that I would have worked almost forty hours a week just to break even – to pay for all of the bills my mom and I needed to pay like it was nothing, but I was.

"Can I go home please?" My voice was much quieter. It felt strange going from yelling to virtually whispering in the matter of minutes. It unnerved me how much it reminded me of my mom's mood swings. I needed to get back and check on her.

"Harlow?" Texas stood and reached out, but I shuffled away.

"I'm sorry, this is just a lot to take in. I need to think about it and I'm tired. I want to go home."

I scanned the room, looking for a clock. How late was it? One of the computer monitors on the corner tables was a black screen saver that bounced a digital clock around the surface. That and the darkness outside Texas' window told me it was past time to go.

I heard Knix sigh before he pointed to Marv. "You take her home. Make sure she has a way to contact us if she needs to." He dropped his hand and turned, studying me. "Call us if you need anything. I mean that, Harlow. Anything." I nodded. "Get some sleep and if you show up at Alex's Diner tomorrow, please know that I'll be there to take you right back home. You need to study for your exams."

I didn't have the energy to argue.

Marv asked me to give him a few minutes to get ready and I agreed, sitting back down on the bed. Everyone filed out except for Texas, who remained behind, choosing instead to go back to his monitors. He rifled through a box under the tables and pulled out various tech parts before going back in and retrieving a small, square, black box. He fiddled with the late model android phone he had pulled out of a drawer earlier. I only recognized it because it was similar to one Erika had owned.

After fiddling with it for a few more minutes, Texas pressed a button on the side and held it until the screen lit up. I waited patiently for several moments as he typed away and scrolled through the phone. He grabbed the papers he had printed earlier and began writing notes, scribbling something across the pages.

These guys were strange, a compilation of rich and elegant to earthy. Their styles were so different. Even though Marv and Texas looked similar in many aspects – their piano fingers, their dark hair, their black and white movie good looks – they were like night and day. Texas' room was clean overall, but there were clothes spilling from his closet that revealed worn jeans, khaki board shorts, and faded t-shirts. Marv appeared more put together, immaculately dressed at all times.

Bellamy looked just as handsome in a suit as Marv did, but he, too, was a contrast. They obviously had similar tastes in cars if Bellamy's care for the BMW was something to go by. Out of all of them, Knix seemed to be even more out of place. A tech nerd, a rich boy, an earthy but keen car lover, and then the leader. That's what Knix was, though no one had said so. He called the shots. I didn't miss the way they deferred to him. Who was *he*? Who were *they*?

"Okay," Texas announced, halting my inner thoughts. He pushed his chair back and came to stand in front of me, handing me the phone. "This is yours. I've already installed all of our phone numbers as your contacts as well as the number for Alex's Diner and his personal number." He paused, pointing to a few buttons on the screen. "We're all on speed dial. Knix is one, Marv is two, Bellamy is three, and I'm four. Alex is five, call him if you can't get ahold of us."

"You're giving me a phone?"

He shrugged. "Knix said to make sure you could reach us. It's got unlimited texting and minutes, but I would be careful about data. Our plan has a good amount, but the four of us already use a lot and we're trying to cut back."

"You're all on the same plan?"

Was that normal for people who no longer lived with their families? Maybe it was cheaper. I held the phone in my hand and I really wanted to hand it back. I didn't need it. I had existed and lived just fine without one, even though I felt like an outsider in my own school. I didn't know a lot about social media, just what I got from Erika. But holding the phone, warm from Texas' hand, felt safe.

"Yup and now you are, too," he said. I stared at the screen and he sighed. "Just say thank you, Harlow."

I blinked. "Thank you."

Texas gave me a brilliant smile. "You're welcome. Now, come on, Marv is probably done talking to Knix now." I followed him out into the living room where Marv was, in fact, done talking with Knix who was cleaning up the pizza mess. Bellamy was gone.

"Ready?" Marv stood by the front door, waiting.

"Uh huh." The phone was a new weight in my pocket but not a burden. I tried dissecting my confused emotions as I trailed behind Marv, into the tenant elevator and then out into the parking lot, only to give up when it became impossible.

"You okay?" Marv stood just outside of the passenger side door. He had it open and was waiting on me.

"Oh, yea, thanks."

I slid into the leather interior and he peered at me for a moment more before closing the door with a solid push. I scrutinized him as he crossed around the front end, surveying the way he moved, standing tall, comfortable in his own skin.

When he got in and started the car, backing out of

the parking spot, I continued to watch him closely, under my lashes as I pretended to pick at my nails and the fabric of my shirt. He never once extended his hand towards the radio, so it was left silent and the lack of background noise made me all the more aware of how close he was. I pushed my legs up against the backpack I had left sitting on the passenger floorboards.

"Is your mom going to ask where you've been?" It took me a moment to realize that he'd asked me a question, I was so focused on his physicality and the way he moved.

"Oh, um, maybe." I bit my lip. "It depends on if she's awake or not." It also depended on if she was coherent or not.

"I understand she has some medical issues?" His voice tilted slightly up at the end as if he were clarifying an answer he already knew by turning the statement into a question.

"How did you – never mind." I was the one stopping myself this time. It shouldn't surprise me anymore. They likely knew my entire life story. I would like to know how, but my guess was Texas. He was the tech guy. "Yes, she does."

"That must be hard." I shrugged in response. "Her records said that she has...what is it? Bipolar disorder as well? I've heard that can be difficult by itself."

"She didn't really know she had it until later in life. She wasn't diagnosed right away." I picked at a thread on the hem of my shirt.

"How is she?"

"She has good days and bad days." Really bad days. But that was likely normal with her medication. I often found that she would skip several days in a row of taking her medication. I was away so much with work and school sometimes I feared coming home and finding her lifeless body. It was a nightmare that had ruined more than a few nights of sleep.

"Do you have those too?"

"Do I have what?"

"Good days and bad days," he replied.

I twisted my body to lean against the seat and stare openly. "Doesn't everyone?"

"What do they look like?"

"My good days and bad days?" I clarified.

He nodded.

"Well, I suppose my good days look just like this except without the weird guys carting me around the city, stealing me from school and such." He smirked. "My bad days happen when bills come in and I have to sit down and count how much I made and how much I get for groceries and how I'm going to get to the store. It gives me a headache and it just stresses me out. But loads of people go through that, so it's not as bad as it could be."

I didn't consider why I was telling him this. I wasn't usually so open. The conversation died down as he concentrated on driving while I gave up my concentration of him and listened to the quiet hum of the engine instead. The rhythmic beat of the car flying over the road lulled me and I found myself gazing out the window, staring at passing trees and cars and signs.

Something occurred to me. "Do I need to tell you where to go?" I flipped back over, sitting sideways in the seat again. Marv had both hands on the wheel, conscientious.

The closer corner of his mouth lifted slightly. He was even more stunning when he smiled. "No."

I sighed and pressed the button to slide the window

down an inch or so to let in fresh air. Within the next few minutes, he flicked the blinker and pulled off on the exit closest to my house. The lights of the BMW flashed across the front entrance of my neighborhood and then again across the darkened duplexes and dirty mailboxes that lined the streets. I supposed it undoubtedly looked like a rundown community, but it was actually one of the nicest, safest places my mom and I had ever lived.

Marv parked the BMW and walked around to open my door again. It wasn't unheard of, the kind of gentlemanly behavior that he and the other guys exhibited was different, but it wasn't something I was used to.

"I'll come by tomorrow to take you to school. Bright and early, Sunshine." I took his proffered hand.

"Tomorrow's Saturday," I reminded him.

He shrugged, the dress shirt stretching over his shoulders under the pristine jacket. "Then I'll come by tomorrow morning for a study session."

"I don't know, my mom isn't used to strangers." I hesitated on the corner of the street.

Could I call the whole thing off and tell them to put my life back in order before tomorrow? Likely not. Did I want them to? Frankly, I wanted things to be different. I had always wished for it and the idea of sending them away and never seeing them again made my chest clench up and start to ache.

"–promised Knix I would," Marv was saying.

"How about meeting at the diner?" I suggested.

He tilted his head, considering me quietly. "I can do that," he said, nodding slowly. "Be there by 9 am."

I sighed, but agreed to the time. I waved him back to the car and hurried to the front of my building. He frowned, but reopened the driver's side door, watching me over the top. The lights illuminated the outside of my duplex and front hall until I closed the front door behind me and locked it. I peered from behind the curtains of the window next to the door as Marv put the BMW in reverse and backed out.

"Harlow?" My mom's croaking voice reached me and I turned, padding across the floor as a soft meow echoed behind me, followed by a light scratching of the wooden surface. Cleo came around the corner of the hallway, meowing once again and I realized she must need to go to the bathroom and was likely hungry again.

"Hey, sweet girl." I bent down and scratched behind one ear while she meowed again. "Give me a minute and I'll take care of you, okay?" I released her and moved to the open doorway of my mom's bedroom.

She laid like an exhausted queen among her pillows. The room was still relatively clean after I had cleaned up from the mess before, meaning that today had been a good day and she hadn't suffered any episodes while I had been gone. Her eyes met mine when I entered and she smiled sweetly, so different from the woman I often came home to; the one who was angry at the world, paranoid, and in pain. This woman was my real mom.

"Hey, Mom, sorry I was out so late." I sat on the edge of her bed. She lifted a frail hand towards me and I grabbed it, kissing her knuckles. "Are you hungry? Have you eaten? I can make you something?"

She shook her head. "I had some of the soup you left me in the fridge. I'm sorry about the other day." She frowned, her eyes glistening. "These episodes are getting so bad, I can't control them. Maybe something else is wrong."

"It's okay, I understand. It wasn't really you." I pressed my lips to the skin of her knuckles. Even wrinkled and spotted, I cared for them because they were the hands that had fed me as a child, tucked me in, and cared for me.

"I love you, Baby girl."

"I love you, too, Mom." I sighed and let her hand fall back to the duvet. "You have a doctor's appointment coming up. I'll be babysitting for Mrs. Grace again and she's taking you to the appointment. Have you been taking your medication?"

"I don't know, Baby. Sometimes, I do. Sometimes, I think I already have and I'm scared of taking too much on accident. It's likely what's causing these episodes. I'll talk to the doctor about it."

"Okay." I rubbed the back of neck with my hand and stood up. "I'm gonna go and clean up a bit before bed."

"Who were you with tonight?"

"Just a friend." I leaned down and kissed her forehead. "Get some rest. I love you, Mom."

"Night, Baby," she said as I reached the doorway.

"Night, Mom."

I gently eased the door closed behind me before moving down the hall to let Cleo out for some bathroom time. I didn't have the money to get her a proper litter box, so it was unsurprising that I found a few wet spots throughout the kitchen and hallway. I cleaned up as best I could and then laid out some old papers throughout the kitchen, hoping that if she had to go again in the middle of the night or tomorrow when I was gone, she'd do it there. By the time my head hit my pillow, I was more than ready to sink into oblivion.

CHAPTER 8

Alex's Diner was filled for the Saturday morning rush. Normally, I would have been among the waitresses rushing around with trays of coffee and eggs, but not this morning. I spotted Marv sitting at the counter talking to Alex. He was dressed down for the morning in a pair of slick, black slacks and a light-blue button-down rolled up to his elbows. There was a light smattering of stubble on his chin and jaw line as if he hadn't shaved in the twelve hours since I had last seen him. I liked him like this, I decided, still dressed up, but more casual. He appeared more approachable.

"Well, look who decided to show up this morning." Marv's head came up as Grayson Caruso popped up from an otherwise empty back booth. I groaned and hung my head, debating whether I should just turn around and walk out. Grayson was dressed casually, in a pair of jeans cinched at the waist with a dark brown belt, and a light-purple, cotton t-shirt with a band's logo on the front.

"I was wondering when you would show up. I asked

that girl – " He gestured to Shanavia, one of the regular Saturday morning waitresses, as she hurried by with several steaming plates of the pancake special. "But she said you weren't working this morning. Guess she lied. Where's your section?"

"I'm *not* working," I snapped, hefting the bag I had lugged with me all the way from home onto the other shoulder to relieve the stress on the one it had previously been cutting into. "She didn't lie, and I'm here to see a friend."

"Here, let me get that for you." Grayson smiled, reaching for my bag. I gripped the strap even tighter and twisted away.

"It's fine. I'm busy. I'll catch you later." I tried to glare him into backing off.

Marv caught my eye, but he wasn't looking at me. Instead, his gray eyes were narrowed on Grayson. I walked around Grayson and headed straight for Marv, my hand rising to touch his arm. Marv's pinched lips separated as he glanced down at me before they lifted in a smile.

"Hey, Sunshine."

"Ready to start?" My smile was strained as I tried to ignore the sneaking suspicion that Grayson was not going away.

"This is your friend?" Grayson asked behind me.

I could have murdered him right then and there. Marv's face hardened and he put a hand on my shoulder, sliding my bag off before placing it on the back of the stool next to him.

"Hop up," he commanded before turning his full attention to Grayson. "She's fine. You don't need to concern yourself."

I bit my lip, peering back and forth between the two

of them before flicking a pleading look at Alex. He was just as interested in watching the train wreck about to happen as Shanavia, who had paused in the doorway of the kitchen.

Grayson stared at him. "I see that." His eyes flickered over to me for a brief moment and he plastered a smile back on his face.

The smile and pleasant expression didn't reach his eyes. It was the kind of smile I had seen him give to teachers and friends alike. It was nice enough, but underneath was a thread of detachment, an apathetic guise that lingered in his blue eyes.

Even in school, he never would have noticed someone like me, while he might have been smiling and ribbing his football friends, he had always smiled an eccedentesiast's smile, the smile of someone hiding something. An actor's smile. A politician's smile. Something familiar in his expression made me think he wasn't as intimidating as he would have everyone else believe.

Grayson didn't appear offended when Marv moved so that he blocked me. Instead, he pinched his lips even as he smiled and turned towards me. "I guess I'll leave you to it, then. I'll see you in school on Monday, Harlow."

I blinked, shocked that he would give in so easily. When he moved to slip by me I was slow to adjust and his hip bumped into mine. For a second I thought his hand might have grazed my ass, but when I turned he was already distracted, having pulled out his phone. He stopped in front of the booth he had been sitting at and dropped a few bills on the table even though it was obvious he hadn't ordered anything yet, or if he had, it hadn't arrived.

When Grayson passed by us once again, he grinned – the odd remoteness I had noted before buried beneath genuine amusement. "Call me when you don't have a guard dog," he said, handing me the phone he had been typing on.

The weight in my hand was familiar, but he couldn't have – I touched the back pocket of my shorts and sure enough, my phone wasn't where I had put it. *That's why he grabbed my ass!* I realized. Grayson waved once before he disappeared out the front door.

Marv's voice was a low, fuming presence. "Give me your phone." I didn't have time to hand it over before he plucked it out of my palm and slid away the unlock screen. I watched him in stunned silence – less than a week and I had drawn more attention from boys than I had in the past four years of high school. Maybe someone dropped me in an alternate universe or I was stuck inside an extended dream.

"Damn it." Marv's curse had my attention immediately. I touched his arm again, holding onto the fabric of his expensive shirt. "That asshole texted himself from your phone so he has your number. I was hoping he just put his in your phone. I'm deleting it anyway. If he texts you, don't answer. If anyone texts you that isn't already in this phone, ignore it. I'll talk to Texas and see if we can't get you a new number."

"It's not a big deal." I shrugged. "But is it okay if I put my friend Erika's phone number in it?" I asked as he handed the phone back to me. I just wouldn't answer Grayson. He would get the idea that I didn't want to talk to him sooner or later and give up.

Marv eyes and lips tightened again. "Yea, that's fine. We'll transfer it over when we get you a new phone. I'm still telling Knix. Bellamy said something about a guy, was that him?" I nodded, assuming so. Marv cursed quietly as he retook his seat. "We didn't really think there'd be a problem." He frowned as I began pulling out my books. "We should've listened."

"He's not really a major problem. He's just someone from school," I said. "I don't know him all that well actually."

"We'll figure it out," he assured me

Alex smiled, and passed me a menu. "Looks like you've become Miss Popularity," he teased.

"Not really." My face heated, overcome with embarrassment and I hid behind the glossy pages of brightly-colored pictures of food.

"Let's get to work," Marv interrupted. "Did you bring what you need?" I nodded and pointed out the study materials I had already laid out on the counter.

For the rest of the afternoon I sat with Marv as Alex, Shanavia, and a few other part-timers worked. Every so often, Marv would allow me a brief break and I would talk to Shanavia when she wasn't too busy. She agreed to work my Sunday shift because Joanna was already working. I picked at the fries Alex had brought out and drank my water. When Shanavia's shift ended and she waved goodbye, Marv closed my History textbook and quizzed me.

"I think you've got most of it covered. We've gone over a lot."

"I still need to write my English paper, but I won't be able to get to that until Monday when I can use one of the library computers to type it up." I sighed, rotating my stiff shoulders. Hunching over the counter while writing out equations for my geometry exam had made my whole back stiff.

"Actually, I have something for you." He produced a slim, silver laptop from the messenger bag I hadn't noticed hanging from the back of his stool, and I nearly fainted. He passed it over and I gripped it, afraid it would slip from my fingers and crash to the tiled floor. I stared at it, and traced the circular logo on the case.

"I can't take this." I had never had a computer before. I wouldn't know how to use it or take care of it. Didn't laptops need cases and antivirus systems? Those would cost even more money. Libraries only had the big box computers. Sometimes they would get the newer desktop computers with flat-screens, but even those were attached to some kind of hard drive with wires and cords and..."I can't take this," I repeated.

"Yes, you can." He sipped his coffee.

Gently, so as not to scratch the surface, I set the laptop down on the counter. "No." I shook my head.

Marv tapped the top of the counter with those refined hands of his. "Don't be difficult about this, Harlow."

I pouted, looking longingly at the laptop. He only called me by my name, I realized, when he wanted me to do something. In this case, it was accepting an elaborate gift.

"I don't want the damn computer," I lied, crossing my arms.

He rolled his eyes, but before he could reply his cell vibrated. We were sitting so close on the stools, I could feel the resonance. He retrieved the phone and held up one finger.

"We're not done. You're keeping the laptop. You need it for school."

"School's almost–" I started to protest. He answered the phone and I stifled a frustrated growl.

"This is Marv," he answered. I glared. "Yea." He smirked my way before whoever was on the other side said something that immediately had his full attention.

His hands fell away from the counter, his back straightening. "Now? You're sure?" He paused as he listened to the other person. "I can be there in..." The phone switched hands as he checked his Rolex. "Twenty minutes, give or take. I've gotta take Harlow home."

I shook my head and whispered to keep from interrupting his conversation, but still loud enough for him to hear. "I can walk home. It's not a big deal." Those sparkling, gray eyes of his rolled once again and he ignored my statement.

"Yea, we're leaving now."

I began gathering our supplies.

Alex came out from the back, wiping his hands on a dish towel.

"We have to go," I said.

He nodded and waved us away. Marv threw a few twenties on the counter, much more than necessary, but I didn't comment. I followed Marv outside and scrambled to get into the seat the moment he opened my door, with his other hand still holding the phone to his ear.

"Alright, I'll be there." He said his goodbyes and hung up, slamming my door shut behind me.

I left my seat belt unbuckled since we were only five minutes or so away from my house, something that made Marv frown. When he pulled up to the curb, I reached for the door handle.

"What are you doing?" he snapped. "I got it." Before I could assure him that it was fine, I could open my own door and had for the first eighteen years of my life, he was out of his seat and striding around the front end of the BMW.

"It's fine, I can open my door," I argued when he pulled it open.

Marv scowled down at me as I stepped out. "What

would my Mother think? She raised me to always open doors for the elderly and beautiful women." My feet refused to move, and I stood on the sidewalk like an idiot, blinking up at him until he ushered me to the house. "Go on, I'll see you later." Before I could turn and follow his orders, he reached into the car and pulled the laptop out, putting it in my hands. "Take that."

"Wait!" I called, clutching my bag and the laptop as he rushed around the car back to the driver's seat.

"No more arguing!" he yelled back.

I watched him drive off, glancing down at my over-flowing arms before turning and heading inside. The front door slammed behind me and I flinched, pausing to listen for my mom. I sighed when there was no responding call. Cleo meowed from the living room, drawing my attention, and I made my way to her for a quick pet. She purred and slid her small, furry body in circles around my ankles for a few minutes until I finally managed to pry myself away from her. I slipped into the back hallway, and peeked into my mom's room to make sure she was asleep. The pills I had measured out for her that morning were still there and I huffed in frustration, but I couldn't force them down her throat. At least the sandwich I had put next to them was gone.

Cleo brushed against my feet and ankles as I managed to make it to my room without creating any more thunderous noises. I cracked the bedroom door in case my mom called for me and sat down, opening the screen of the brand-new laptop. The monitor lit up with a beautiful picture of the ocean. The white sands and the clear water resembled something I had seen in brochures to the Caribbean and not the actual beach that I had spent the night on with Erika only a week before.

"Boys are crazy, Cleo." I sighed, rubbing one hand

over her soft back as I opened the word processor and began typing an outline for my English paper.

Hours and several high-lighted Chbosky passages later, I was ready to gouge my eyes out with Cleo's little claws. I rolled over and slid my phone out of my pocket to check for messages. There were none, but I was bored. This was my first Saturday night off since I had started working at Alex's Diner. I didn't quite know what to do with myself. I was all studied out for the time being, though. So, I clicked through to Knix's number and started a new message.

Harlow: is Marv ok?

His reply was almost instantaneous.

Knix: Hey, Little Bit. Marv's fine. What are you doing?

I giggled, his texting voice was so proper, then again, so was Texas'. I wondered if they were all like that.

Harlow: nothing, bored. U?

He ignored my attempt to change the subject to something he was doing.

Knix: You should be studying.

I groaned, and rolled over onto my other side. Cleo meowed her disapproval as I unseated her from her sleeping place.

Harlow: noooooo

Knix: You better not fail your exams. Retaking them will not be fun.

Harlow: I'll pass

Knix: Go to sleep, Little Bit. I know for a fact that your mom has an early appointment tomorrow and that means you'll be up as well.

In the past, I had pulled all-nighters several nights in a row and no one noticed. My chest ached and tingled at the fact that someone was worried about me for a change. I didn't need it, I could be independent if I wanted to be, but he cared and I liked that. I liked having someone remember me and taking time to worry about me even if I didn't need it. It made me feel cared for.

Harlow: What about u?

I asked because it seemed likely enough that he and the guys were always constantly busy. I didn't know nearly as much about them as they knew about me. I recognized that if I agreed to work with them that would need to change.

Knix: I'll be going to bed shortly. Goodnight, Little Bit.

Lying awake in my bed, I decided that I liked it. I liked them. The pet names were sweet, even them trying to give me things that I didn't want or need was sweet. I looked over at the half-opened laptop. I wouldn't keep it, but for as long as I had it, the computer reminded me of Marv, of all of them. Cleo curled up behind my knees, the warmth of her little body and sleepy purrs lulling me to sleep.

CHAPTER 9

rs. Grace's house smelled like bleach and old lady perfume, specifically Chanel No. 5. It was a nice smell, but the acidic taint of bleach and Lysol to hide other smells made it unbearably sweet and nauseating. Jazzy and Devin, Mrs. Grace's five and three-year-old grandkids were already up by dawn, sitting on the living room floor, pop-tarts in hand, watching Sunday morning cartoons.

I clicked around on my new phone, finding the game Slither where I led a snake around eating dots for several minutes before that, too, became boring. Erika had been overjoyed at me finally getting a phone. She had texted me the best apps to download from the app store that the phone came preloaded with, but I was too scared to download anything. I knew those things costed money. I only had Slither because Texas had apparently downloaded it beforehand.

I set the phone down on my stomach and watched Jazzy and Devin munch on their sugary breakfast and stare, wide-eyed, as a cartoon pig danced on the screen to an upbeat song about cleaning the house. The phone vibrated to life midway through the episode, startling me so much that I dropped it over the side of the couch. I scrambled after it, picking it up with a prayer that the screen hadn't shattered upon impact. My sigh of relief drew Devin's attention as he glanced at me for a moment before returning to his show.

Texas: Tomorrow 3:15pm.

I sighed. Wonderful. I now knew something was happening tomorrow, but not what. I grinned as I typed a reply, deciding to turn up the sass and tease him.

Harlow: 3:15pm, huh? Sounds like a great time of day.

I grinned as I hit send. I'd been texting Texas a lot since I got the phone and one thing I had learned was that trying to sound sarcastic with texts was difficult for others to interpret. I still tried and even though he rarely got it, it was still funny to me.

Texas: Bell will pick you up in front of the school.

I thought for a second; how could I turn that around before typing my reply.

Harlow: I'm pretty heavy, do you think he can carry me wherever it is that we're going?

There was brief pause between texts and I could picture his face, dumbstruck and unsure. I giggled, drawing the attention of Jazzy and Devin who, with their mouths half-full, turned their heads towards me at the same time. Jazzy, the younger of the two, stood on her chubby legs and shuffled over to me. Her fat toddler fist, clutching the pastry, raised it to my face.

Her, big, brown eyes were curious and loving. I couldn't bear to disappoint her, so I leaned down and took a small bite, thanking her for sharing. She smiled, her skinny, white, baby-teeth contrasting with the darkness of her skin, before waddling over to her brother who returned his attention to the TV show once again. They were the sweetest kids. My phone buzzed.

Texas: You're not heavy and you'll never refer to yourself as such again or I'll tell Knix. Bell will be picking you up in a car.

There was only a brief second before my phone vibrated again, alerting me to another text from someone else.

Bellamy: Smartass.

I grinned, unrepentant, before I sent him a winky face and reopened my conversation with Texas.

Harlow: What's Knix gonna do?

I was taunting him, I knew it. It was too much fun, more fun than I'd had in a long time. My phone lit up again, but this time Knix's name crossed the screen and I gulped as I opened the message.

Knix: If I hear you calling yourself heavy, I'll spank you. Be good.

I wasn't even offended that Texas had tattled. I simply grinned and sent an angel Emoji before putting the phone away. Mrs. Grace came home a little after lunch while Jazzy was playing dress up and Devin sat at the kitchen table coloring his way across some computer paper I had managed to find, with a few broken crayons.

"How were they today?" she asked, setting her giant purse on the counter as I wiped away the PB&J mess they had left after lunch.

"Good, Jazzy is in the den," I said. Mrs. Grace was quiet as she went over to Devin and brushed his springy curls lightly with her hand, kissing his forehead. He grumbled and whined, pulling away from his grandmother's affection and continued to color on his paper. "How was the appointment?" I finally asked. She sighed, petting her grandson's head again as he dutifully ignored her.

She was quiet for a moment, her eyes averted and my hands started to sweat.

"It's not good, Baby." I knew it wouldn't be, but hearing it hurt. All the good that had filled me from talking to the guys bottomed out and drained away. I gripped the edge of the counter to keep my hands from shaking as I nodded my head. "You might wanna go home, now. She's gonna need you," Mrs. Grace suggested.

I let go of the counter. "Thanks for taking her."

She wouldn't look at me as I passed her, but she nodded. Her house was so full of life, Jazzy and Devin's toys in strange places, sticking out from the couch cushions, hiding under the entertainment center. They had so many years left. Sometimes, in the moments when my mom let paranoia and her mood swings take over, it felt like she was already gone. But she wasn't, not really. Because even amidst all that, there were times when she came back to me like she had the night before.

I crossed the street to my duplex and stood at the front door for several minutes, attempting to steal myself against what I might find. I took a deep breath, reached for the door, and twisted the knob, letting it swing inward. Cleo's distressed meow came from somewhere in the house. I rushed in and followed it to the kitchen where her little black and gray form was barely visible under my mom's chair. She hissed, and meowed, and cried out when I entered, but my mom didn't seem to notice that her shoe was planted firmly on Cleo's tail. I eased closer, trying not to startle my mom or Cleo. The little kitten meowed at me in desperation, begging me to save her. I slowly lifted my mom's foot, glancing up to see if she would react. Cleo meowed again, hissed at me and my mom, and sprinted out of the room.

"Mom?" I sat across from her, keeping my hands in my lap because I was afraid to reach for her.

Her dull eyes fluttered before they refocused, seeing me for the first time. "Hey, Baby." I sighed in relief and slid my palms toward hers.

"What did the doctor say?" I asked. I needed to know.

"I'm sorry, Baby." Her words were a whisper that cut me to the core. I bit the inside of my cheek, hoping the pain would keep me from floating away or being crushed by the impending wave of desolation. "I'm trying," she said. She stopped, her eyes filling with tears. I held her hand, squeezing it tight. "I forget, you know I change – he said I probably shouldn't take my normal medication anymore. He gave me a new prescription. I hope it works. I'm just so tired, Baby. The chemo makes my bones ache."

"I love you, Mom. Whatever happens, I'll make sure you're okay." I took a breath, deciding to tell her a piece of the guys' offer, hoping it would ease her a little bit. I had a choice to make and I hoped I was making the right one.

"I got a job offer," I said with a small smile. "It looks like it'll have a decent income." I had to trust that the guys would keep their promises and would help. If they wanted me, this was my price, I decided. "You can go into a nice facility if you want. You don't have to, but I'm sure they would be able to take care of you better than I can. I'm gone most of the time and I know you need someone..." I trailed off, guilt eating the rest of my words.

"It's not your fault, Baby." Her hands tightened on mine. "But I'm so proud of you. A job? I didn't know you were applying to new places." Her head hung low in shame, as if not knowing about my life was a crime. Most of the time, she didn't know her own life.

"I didn't apply," I assured her. "Alex – my boss – suggested it and recommended me."

"What is it?"

"Recruitment, I think." I realized that I truly had no clue what they wanted from me. Even if I did, I suspected they wouldn't want me to go around telling everyone. She nodded her head, eyes boring holes into the table, once again losing the light in them.

"Maybe you should call Michael. He'll help you when the time comes, he knows all of those legal documents."

"Mom–"

"I'm tired, Baby," she interrupted me. "I think I'll go lay down." I didn't know what to say, so I nodded and let go of her hands when she pulled them away to stand. As soon as she was out of the room, I put my elbows on the table and dropped my head into my palms. It hurt. Everything hurt. So much.

When I crawled into bed later that night, after a somber day of cleaning and studying – though I could hardly keep my attention on any one thing – I stayed awake. I decided to cancel our home phone after programming my brother's phone into my cell and called to tell him about Mom. He hadn't seemed happy, but there hadn't been any real sadness behind his promise to visit if anything should happen. My head ached thinking about it.

I stared at my ceiling, the fan attached to the light cast shadows against the wall. My bedroom was a dark and mild representation of me as a person; the walls bare and the mismatched furniture all pieces purchased from garage sales or thrift stores. My phone vibrated on the nightstand.

Heaviness weighed over me, spinning in my head, making me dizzy. What would happen in the next year? What would happen in five? Would she still be here? Would I? My phone buzzed again and again, the sound prolonged as someone attempted to call me. I rolled away from it, putting one hand under my head as I curled in on myself.

Even if Michael did come back, he wouldn't stay. He only called, only talked to me out of some sense of duty. He felt guilty, I knew, for leaving me alone with her. He, himself, had admitted that he couldn't handle her anymore. The phone clattered on the nightstand again, the screen lighting up against the ceiling. I wanted to turn it off, but I didn't have the energy to reach for it.

What would I do when she was gone? I wouldn't go with Michael. He would offer to take me with him, but I couldn't picture it. Would I go to college? What would I go for? I didn't even know what I wanted to do with my life.

I was so lost in my own thoughts, the scraping at my window startled me back into reality. When the glass slid open, I clambered for the lamp on my dresser, holding it up over my head, my heart pounding. The figure slinking through my window straightened and I lunged, the lamp flying. The cord stuck, but he was close enough that it descended on the stranger's head.

"Shit!" One arm shot out and knocked the lamp away before it made contact with his face. It crashed to the floor, the fabric top falling off. "Harlow! It's me!"

I gasped and sank to the floor, one hand clutched over my heart. Marv bent down, breathing heavy. "Jesus," he snapped, wiping his face. His hand came away sticky from a small cut at his hairline. "Were you trying to kill me or something?" he demanded.

"I'm sorry," I whimpered, my heart still racing. Tears burned my eyes, and relief flooded me. I tried to shove them back because now that the pressure in my mind had popped, they kept coming. I gasped for breath.

"Hey, hey, hey, none of that." Marv knelt down in front of me, fingers running over my brow, down my cheeks and my jaw line. "I didn't mean to scare you so bad. I just needed to get in to see you. Didn't you get our texts? We tried to call."

"I was in bed." My hands shook so much that he had to lift me up and deposit me on the bed before retrieving the lamp to put it back on my dresser.

"If I had known you were going to attack me when I came in, I might have rethought ringing the front doorbell." He sat next to me. "Are you okay?"

"I'm fine." My grip on the blankets hid my trembling as he sighed and leaned back, his big body taking up more than half the bed.

"No, you're not," he said. "What's wrong? Your mom had her appointment today. Is that it?"

"How do you know that?" I hiccupped and wiped my nose with a corner of the blankets clutched in my fists. "How do you, Knix, Bellamy, and Texas know everything in my life? That's not fair. If you're allowed to dig into my private affairs, yours should be free game too."

"Whoa." He sat up. "I'm an open book. You can know anything you want about me."

"What's Iris?"

"Anything but that," he amended. I growled in frustration and he grinned. "Technically, that's not specific to me, so you can't call me a liar."

My urge to hit something swelled. I stood from the bed to face him. "Why are you here?"

"You would know if you checked your phone." He

sighed when the thing in question began to buzz again, the prolonged vibration indicating another phone call. Reaching over, he plucked it from my nightstand and answered.

"Hey," Marv answered. "Yea, I've got her." Those gray eyes of his slid over me. If I looked close enough there were flecks, shinier than the rest of the clouded tones in his swirling irises. It made it look like he had burning, silver stars swimming through his eyes.

"I'm getting to that – did you – yea? I'm not surprised. She's a little defensive." I wished I had the courage to hit him. I didn't like him talking about me while I was sitting right there. "Yea, talk to you later." Silence stretched between us, thick and uncomfortable after he hung up. He lounged against my sagging mattress as though he was in a king's palace.

"So," he began, "I take it things didn't go well."

"You already know, don't you?" They already knew so much about me, I didn't have any secrets, any privacy, or any boundaries.

"We want you to come to us if you need us, Harlow." His starry eyes hinted at sympathy, making me want to choke. "But I know girls like you. We've all had our run in with the type–" His body, though not quite as massive as Knix, or quite as broad as Bellamy, overwhelmed me when he pulled me to him and hugged me to his chest. "You're incredibly selfless. You do more for anyone else than for yourself. You give and you give. You're strong willed, but you don't think so. You just think you're trying to make it."

"I am making it," I mumbled through his shirt. "And you don't really know me. You only just met me a week ago."

"Hush." One hand came up and cradled the back of

my head. "Even if we had known you for years, you wouldn't tell us. So, you might use the excuse that we're just getting to know each other, but you haven't told your friend Erika anything either, have you?"

I wasn't normally so comfortable being touched by people I didn't know, but it felt nice to lean against Marv's chest – even if I didn't want to listen to what he was saying.

"You aren't a burden, not like you *think* you would be to your brother, or your mom if she was working full time and supporting you."

I brought two hands up and pushed, creating enough distance to look up at him. "You know about Michael?" He raised an eyebrow and I gave him a sardonic look. "Of course you do."

He shrugged, running his fingers through my hair. "I know you have a brother. I know that the relationship between him and your mother is strained. It doesn't take a rocket scientist to figure out that he couldn't hack it and left you to deal with the fallout. We're not like that, Sunshine. We stick with our family. We support them, protect them–"

"Your family doesn't seem to need that."

The smile he turned my way made me feel guilty. I was jealous. He knew it and I knew it. Not of his wealth, but of his family. I had watched him and his mom and how they acted towards each other. I had seen the way she looked at him, like he was her baby – her loving miracle – no matter what. I wanted that kind of tenderness and devotion from someone else.

"No, my blood family doesn't need my help. But that doesn't mean my other family doesn't."

I knew he meant Knix, Texas, and Bellamy. The way they worked together was so odd before, but when I realized that they truly were family – in their minds, at least – it made sense. It felt like he was offering me a place there and it was tempting, even with the price tag attached.

Families could rip you open, soul and body, and you would always come back because that's what we were conditioned to do. Family is blood and blood is the strongest connection in the world. No matter the insult or injury, they were family, so they had to love you and you had to love them back. I didn't love my brother anymore. My mom was growing further and further away. Soon I would be alone.

"You're not going to be alone," Marv said. I blinked at him before realizing that I'd just said everything I was thinking aloud and my face flushed bright red.

Fingertips traced the edge of my jaw line, drawing me away from my embarrassing thoughts. He smiled down at me. His eyes shimmered with empathy and compassion. A part of me wanted to twist away from him and order him to leave, but his eyes told me that he understood what it was like to lose someone – and even though my mom wasn't gone yet, she would be eventually.

"We're each a cog in a big machine," Marv said. "None of us are burdens. Sometimes, we get a little rusty and we need someone to take us out and fix us or we get a little dirty and need to be cleaned. That's just the wear and tear of time. That stuff happens to everyone. It doesn't make what we do or who we are any less important. Your problems are not burdens. You just need to be taken care of for a little bit before you can run smoothly again."

My eyes itched, tears threatening to spill again. I cursed them. I had just stopped crying. Cheeks on fire, I held my breath to keep from breaking down. Goose-bumps trailed up my bare arms and down my back. I shivered against his chest, burrowing a bit because he was so warm. Fatigue threatened to drag me under.

"Come on, let's go to sleep, Sunshine." Marv twisted, sliding away from me as he set me back against the bed. He tucked my covers around my side, turning me over to face away from him with gentle hands before unbuttoning his dress shirt.

"What are you doing?" I asked. He picked up his phone, typed a message and sent it before I heard the telltale sound of his phone being turned off. I peeked behind me.

"I told the guys that I'm staying the night with you. They'll call your phone if they need me. I don't have my charger." He reached for the button of his slacks and I flipped back into position, staring at the wall with wide eyes.

I didn't last thirty seconds before I asked the question that weighed on my mind. "Why?"

He didn't reply as he lifted the covers and crawled beneath them, moving close, spooning up against my back. The heat was a welcome reprieve against the cool air of the room. I waited for an answer, but I didn't have any fight left in me to make him tell me if he wasn't going to offer it up.

Marv's boxers brushed against the backs of my legs as he slid one corded arm around my middle, bringing me closer to his chest. I reached down and gripped that arm, holding it tight like one might a teddy bear as another slid under my neck. He was so close, so warm. It was too much. Yet, it was also perfect.

CHAPTER 10

Sweat stuck to my skin, making me feel unbearably sticky beneath the blankets, but my feet were like frozen blocks of ice as they peeked out from beneath my comforter. Keeping my eyes closed, I jerked them back under the blankets and one ankle smacked into a hairy leg. I stiffened, eyes sliding open before turning towards the body on the other side of my bed. That's when I realized Marv's arm was still around my waist, holding me to his bare chest, which was also lightly matted in drying sweat.

Moving slowly, so as not to wake him, I scooted to the edge of the bed closest to me before sliding the blankets off to the side without uncovering his body. I lifted the arm around my waist and turned so that my butt was the first thing out from under the covers. I touched down on the cold, wood floor with the tips of my toes, shivering.

"Stop it." The arm around my middle tightened and jerked, drawing me back under the sheets and into his embrace. I blinked up at him, stunned.

"You were awake the whole time?!" I seethed, glaring up at him as his lips curved up while his eyes remained closed.

"You're cuddly and warm." His lower lip stuck out and I blinked again at the image it presented. I never would have thought Marv was a cuddle maniac.

I resisted the feeling of how good it felt to be held. Maybe I needed to get a boyfriend. I'd never really seen the need for one, but now I was in constant contact with hot guys who liked to touch. I went limp in Marv's arms, my glare dropping away though my eyes stayed fixated on him. In the early morning light, his hair revealed more sandy highlights that were naturally hidden by the rest of the dark brown strands.

"I have to get ready for school," I reminded him.

One storm colored eye lifted, the focus of the pupil blurred, and he groaned. "I forgot that was still a thing for you." He shifted, releasing me and I found myself not in too big a hurry to dart away.

"Yea, at least for the next two weeks," I replied, slowly pulling the blankets back once more. I stood up and padded across the room to dig through my dresser.

"Week," he grumbled.

Right, I had almost forgotten about getting out a week early thanks to them.

"I'm going to get dressed," I said, holding the clothes I had chosen close to my chest. "Don't leave the room." If my mom found out I had let a boy stay the night, whether she was in a good mood or not, she would lose it.

I hurried across the hall to the bathroom, flicking on the light. The bulbs illuminated the blue tiled shower and the cracked sink. Flipping the lock and setting the clothes on the counter, I took a breath and stared at my reflection. Brown clumps of hair hung down past my shoulders and over my breasts. Brown eyes in almost the same shade stared back at me. Red lines cut into the skin of my cheek where I had slept on wrinkles in my pillow-case. My hands shook.

A knock on the bathroom door had my hands flying for the knob. I yanked it open and gawked. "I think you might be late." Marv stood there fully dressed in his clothes from the night before with a cell phone in each hand, mine and his. I grabbed the collar of his dress shirt and yanked him in, eyes scanning the hallway as I slammed the door behind us.

"What are you doing?!" I hissed, panicked. "I told you to stay in the room." He continued to look down at his phone, scrolling through messages and reading.

"Knix texted me. You're not going to school today." He typed something into the phone and dropped it into his back pocket before looking up. "Why aren't you dressed yet?"

"I would be if you would give me two minutes!" I whisper-screamed as loud as I dared. "What if I had been naked when you knocked?"

He shrugged. "I thought you'd be done by now."

"It hasn't even been–" I stopped, closed my eyes, sucked in a deep breath, and released it slowly. I did this several more times before I felt calm enough to open my eyes. Marv stared back at me, patiently waiting for my meltdown to end. I wanted to strangle him with his own dress shirt. Instead, I focused on one thing. "What do you mean I'm not going to school today?"

"Our time line has moved up." He reopened the door quickly, setting my phone on the sink counter before stepping back out into the hallway. "Get dressed, we're leaving as soon as you're ready. I'll be in your room."

I changed out of my pajamas and into a pair of longer, jean cutoffs and a plaid, button-down shirt in record time. I tossed my clothes into the laundry room as I crossed to my bedroom and slipped in as fast as I could. The bed was already remade, the corners tucked in all the way around as I had seen in military TV shows. I frowned at it as Marv sat in the lone corner chair, a pair of underwear hanging from one post of the back-rest. Blood flooded my cheeks, setting them aflame. I scrambled across the room and yanked them away, hiding them behind my back as his eyes came up from his phone. Hopefully, he hadn't seen them.

"Ready?" He stood.

"I have to check on my mom first. I'll meet you at your car."

He sighed. "Bring your phone. I'll be waiting out front."

I paused as I turned back to my bedroom door. "You didn't...?" I left the question hanging in the air.

"I parked down the street," he assured me. "Now go. Hurry." I dropped the underwear next to the bed and kicked it under the mattress with my toe before dashing back across the hall to snatch my phone from the bathroom counter where Marv had left it. From the doorway to my mom's room, I couldn't hear him lifting the window screen.

"Mom?" I whispered into the darkened bedroom. A lump under the covers stirred. "Mom?"

"Go away!" she yelled back.

I sighed. Bad morning. I hoped Marv wouldn't be too upset with waiting.

"I'm off to school," I lied. "Do you need anything?" A wrinkled fist shot out from under the covers, lifting the blanket enough for her to glare at me.

"I said, go away!"

I exhaled slowly before creaking the door open just a bit more. She slammed her blankets back down over her head.

"I might be gone later than usual today. There's some crackers and snacks in the cabinets if you get hungry."

"Get out!"

I waited a second, then two before finally nodding, though she couldn't see, and backed out, closing the door behind me.

Back in my bedroom, I pulled out my phone and checked the messages. What was I supposed to bring? What did Marv mean that the timeline had moved up? There were no less than two text messages from Marv already telling me he was in the car and parked in front of the house across the street from my duplex. A single text from Knix sent an hour or so ago and another from Texas, less than ten minutes before.

Knix: Tell Marv to check his phone.
Texas: Bring alternate clothing.

What? Why did I need extra clothes? What kind? I typed a reply to Texas and asked, but Marv texted me once more a minute or so later asking where I was. I decided to just grab something extra and if they didn't like it, we could always come back. At least I had something to bring. It would have felt odd leaving the house without a book bag on a school day. I ran back to my room and dumped the contents of my school bag onto my now pristine bed. I tucked in another shirt and pair of shorts as well as a light jacket just to be on the safe side. As the summer heated, everyone's AC would be running at full blast.

I reached under the bed, scrambling for the laptop that Marv had lent me – no time like the present to return it – as well as my Chbosky novel. They went into the bag and I zipped it up, sliding both straps over my shoulders. Keys in hand, I paused at the front door, mentally ticking off a checklist. A low meow had me cursing and rushing for the kitchen as my phone pinged. Another text from Marv.

I poured fresh water into a bowl and put a can of tuna out in Cleo's usual spot. Big, round cat eyes watched me as I flitted from one counter to another, preparing the items and putting things away. I scrambled faster every time my phone vibrated, but still it didn't feel fast enough. I rinsed my hands, wiped the wetness from my fingers on the back of my shorts, and I rushed for the front door. Cleo followed, completely uninterested in the food and water I had just set out for her and I shooed her away. I opened the front door and nearly jumped a mile when I heard a voice from behind.

"Where are you going?"

Spinning, my hand clutched over my chest, I gasped. "Mom!" She stood in her bedroom doorway, her gray, frizzy hair pulled at the top of her head in a small, barely there, bun – the strands thin enough that I could see through to her scalp. "You scared me." I panted. "I told you, I'm going to school."

"What is that thing doing here?" She pointed one thin finger at the kitten at my feet that looked up at the both of us like a young child between two arguing parents.

"It's a kitten, she's staying here until I can find her a better home. Her name's Cleo."

"I don't want it here. It could have rabies." She

grimaced, letting her hands fall to her sides before rising to clasp the front of her robe closed. "I'm already sick enough as it is. If you're going to live under my roof, you respect my rules, or I'll have to toss you out, just like your brother." I didn't bother mentioning that after so many threats and even a few actual tosses, he had decided to leave on his own.

"I'll find her a home as soon as possible, Mom, but right now, I have to get to school."

"No!" she yelled. "You will get rid of that thing right now, young lady!" She stomped past me, through the living room, and into the kitchen. Cleo meowed up at me from my feet. I listened to the sounds of my mom rifling through the kitchen before the shattering of glass had me hurrying in behind her. She was standing above Cleo's food with the tuna can dumped over and the glass water bowl smashed at her feet. "I want that thing out now!"

"Okay Mom, I'll find her a new home," I said hurriedly, hoping that if I appeased her she wouldn't get any worse. "Let me clean that up." I rushed forward and bent down to start gathering the broken bits of the glass bowl before she could step on any. My cell phone pinged again in my back pocket and my back stiffened.

"What was that?" I closed my eyes at the question, but there was no doubt that she knew exactly what it was.

"It was my cell phone," I replied, standing. I glanced at her over my shoulder and shook at the way her eyes narrowed on me.

"I haven't given you a cell phone. Where did you get it?"

"The landline was turned off and I decided to get one in case Michael ever–" I started.

"I said, where did you get it?!" she shrieked.

I trembled, the broken bits of glass clenched in my grasp, cutting into my skin. I loosened my hold.

"Erika gave me an old phone of hers and I–" It sounded like a lie even to my own ears, but maybe that's just because it was.

"Give it to me." She held out one hand, while the other remained on the lapels of her robe. The phone buzzed again. I mentally cursed the guys for their continued texts and myself for not having put the phone on silent.

I dropped the glass in the trash and reached into my back pocket, retrieving the brand new looking device. I placed the phone in her palm and she began to click through it, reading the screen.

"Who are these boys?" she demanded.

"Friends from school and work," I said slowly. It wasn't exactly another lie. I *had* met them at school and work.

"Why are they texting you so early and so much?" She read through some of the messages, her eyes squinting as if she found them difficult to read.

"I-I..." I didn't know what to say, how to respond without another lie, because even I didn't know what they were texting about. I hadn't read the last few.

"Respect," she said suddenly, pulling her face away from the glowing screen. "I never said you were allowed a cell phone." She moved to the sink and I stepped forward, one of my feet almost tripping over Cleo as she rubbed against the inside of my ankle with her hackles raised towards my mom. "No more of this," she said. "You need to learn to respect my rules."

I watched in shock as she stuck the phone down the sink drain and leaned over, flipping the garbage disposal switch up. Loud cracking noises shattered my stunned silence as the blades inside began to whir, destroying the phone. I lunged for the switch on the wall, but my mom stood before it as if daring me to shove her aside. Air clogged my throat as I stood there and listened to the sounds of the phone screen fracturing, the metal and glass pieces sticking to the insides of the disposal, which was just one more thing I would have to pay to fix.

After several moments of the raucous volume, she finally reached back and flipped the switch down, cutting off the horrendous noise. Her feet shuffled across the vinyl kitchen floor as she paused and glanced back down at the cat.

"Remember what I said," she snarled. "Get rid of it."

I stared at the sink long after she was gone, scared to reach in for the remains of the phone. I would have to explain to Marv and the guys what had happened. I would also have to take Cleo with me today. I was half-terrified that if I left her here, even for another day, that I might come home to find her as the next thing pushed down the garbage disposal. It didn't matter that the thing was now beyond any real repair and likely wouldn't work. If she wanted to, my mom could very well do something equally horrible and I couldn't let that happen to Cleo.

Spotting a dish towel on the counter, I used it to pull as many of the cracked and broken pieces of the cell phone from the sink drain as I could. I kept the pieces bundled tightly in the towel, holding it close to my side with one hand while I bent down and scooped Cleo up with the other. I was sure Marv was still texting me, but considering the condition of the phone, I knew I wouldn't hear any more pings or vibrations, nor would I be able to respond.

Cleo meowed at my face as I opened the front door

and juggled her and the towel while trying to lock it behind myself. My book bag bumped against my back as I strode across the street. Marv's dark, shiny BMW was parked across the street just as he said it would be in his last text – the last one I had been able to read.

The bright, yellow school bus that I would have normally ridden to school at this time of the morning stopped several houses down and kids began to board. I glanced at it once before continuing across the street to the BMW. Marv opened the driver's door, but I opened the passenger door and slid in before he could make it around the back fender. He frowned, but returned to his side, and slipped back into the leather interior.

"What happened? I've been texting you like crazy. What took so long? Why are you bringing that?" He motioned to my cat as she curled up in my lap.

Cleo meowed back as though she recognized him, and purred under my soft strokes. I inhaled deeply, rubbing the underside of her chin. Somehow just being near the animal calmed me. "My mom caught me trying to leave," I said. I held out the kitchen towel. "I'm sorry, but the phone didn't make it."

His brow puckered, but he took the towel from me, opening the flaps I had folded it into to reveal the damaged pieces of the cell phone Texas had given me. He stared down quietly before picking up one battered chunk of screen and turning it over and over in his hand.

"I'm sorry," I repeated, quietly. My eyes burned with embarrassment. "I'll try to pay you back," I offered. Cleo bumped her head against my hand when my petting paused.

"She did this?" he finally asked. I nodded, keeping my eyes trained on the black and gray cat in my lap. "What did she freaking use, a blender?"

My head jerked up. The tone of his voice was the furthest thing from angry. It was shocked, yes, but also curious and slightly amused. "It was the garbage disposal," I admitted. "She heard it and demanded I hand it over. She was yelling at me about Cleo when–"

"Cleo?" Gray eyes peered at me from beneath his dark brows.

I gestured to the cat in my lap. "Cleo," I repeated. "She was yelling at me about having a cat in the house, saying she probably has rabies. I told her I was just keeping her until I could find her a good home, but she told me to get rid of her today, and I was afraid that if I left her there..." Everything spilled out from between my lips before I could stop it; the words coming like a flood bursting from a dam.

"It's okay, I understand." He refolded the flaps and turned, placing them behind us on the floor of the back-seat. "We'll take Cleo back to the condo. Texas rarely leaves. He'll take care of her until you can find someone else to keep her."

"Thank you. I'll try to find someone else to take her as soon as I can." He reached forward, his eyes softening, the stars coming out to sparkle. With one thumb, he drew a line across my cheek and then traced it for several seconds.

"You don't have to thank me, Sunshine." He smiled. "I don't mind helping you – so long as you stay out of the roads."

I chuffed at the reminder as he drew back and started the car. The school bus roared by as we headed in the opposite direction and I was thankful for the tinted windows of the car.

"Here." Marv passed me his cell phone as we stopped at a stop sign before turning out of my neighborhood.

"Text the guys for me. Let them know your phone is out of commission and that we're on our way."

I nodded and pulled up their names one by one before typing a text to send to all of them. I copied and pasted the same message to each of their numbers.

MARV: THIS IS HARLOW. MY PHONE IS BROKEN. MARV told me to tell u that we're on the way

SLOWLY, BUT SURELY, I WAS GETTING THE HANG OF texting, though I found it difficult to keep up with their speed and precision. It was just faster all around to shorten things. The replies were almost instantaneous.

KNIX: WHERE ARE YOU?
    Texas: What happened to your phone?
    Bellamy: K

I RUBBED A HAND DOWN MY FACE AS I READ THEIR TEXTS. I decided to start with who had replied first and work my way down. At least Bellamy didn't need a response. I sent Knix a reply first and then Texas.

MARV: WE'RE JUST NOW LEAVING MY HOUSE.
    Marv: My mom found out about the phone and broke it.

. . .

I paused, looking over at Marv. "Can you do me a favor?" I asked.

His tornado gray eyes flicked to me once before refocusing on the road. "What's the favor?"

"I don't want the guys to know how my mom broke the phone," I said quietly.

No one else needed to know. It would be embarrassing enough letting them see the shattered remains. Marv's phone vibrated in my hands as I waited for his reply.

Texas: I'll have a new phone for you by tonight.
    Marv: I don't really need one

"If they ask, I won't lie to them," Marv finally said, drawing my attention back. "But I won't tell them what you told me if it makes you feel any better."

"Thank you," I replied. A few seconds later, the phone vibrated once more, Knix's name popping up.

Knix: You're getting a new phone.

I bit my lip and narrowed my eyes at the screen before clicking back to Texas' name. I sighed in frustration as I typed.

Marv: Tattletale
    Texas: He's the boss. You have to listen to him.

· · ·

I GLANCED OUT OF THE CORNER OF MY EYE AS MARV leaned forward and began flicking buttons. The radio came on along with a blast of cool air. I typed a quick reply.

Marv: I LISTEN TO MARV.
 Texas: You should.

I SET THE PHONE ASIDE, DONE WITH TEXTING, AND TURNED back to Marv as he drove. "Why can't I go to school today?" Cleo butted her head into my hand again, urging me to scratch her ears. I complied.

"Knix and Bellamy won't be able to work with you tonight. They're busy now. We're supposed to train you on communications before we take you out to work with us."

"What are they doing?" Soft classical music drifted between us, quiet enough for talking, loud enough for the notes to be heard. Marv grimaced, but remained silent. "Can't tell me?" I guessed. He nodded. "What kind of communications training am I getting?"

Sharp eyes caught mine and held for a moment that seemed to stretch on forever. It would have been dangerous if he had held my gaze for too long since he was driving, but when he broke off to glance at the road, I felt unexpectedly disappointed.

"You surprise me," he muttered, shaking his head. "It's not really communications, but that's what Iris calls it. It's normal stuff like etiquette and body language and you're going to be doing self-defense training as well, though that's less communication and more general," he said. "Bell's already informed Principal Wiggins. We'll just push the tests you had today further along in the week. He's working something out with a few of your teachers. You might be able to do a few of them from home with your computer."

"How do I surprise you?" I focused in on that little bit, perhaps because it had been said so quietly under his breath, while the rest of it had been in a normal, polite, tone.

"It's nothing," he replied, slowing as we came to a red light. I squinted at him, pursed my lips, and waited. Marv heaved an exaggerated sigh as he looked over at me. I smiled as he began talking. "It wasn't an insult," he explained. "Most people would be less understanding than you've been. You're putting a lot of trust in me – us – and we can't tell you everything, yet. But you're extremely collected about it all. I wasn't like that when I first started."

"Am I supposed to demand answers?" I asked. "I didn't think I would get them either way."

He chuckled. "You're already demanding answers," he said. "But you've been a lot easier to deal with than other people we've recruited. You'll get your answers, eventually." The BMW slid into a small space onto the highway between a semi and a green minivan. "We like those who ask questions. We don't want you to just follow us blindly or not question orders–"

"Orders?" I bit the inside of my lip. I wanted to ask about the other people they had recruited, but it didn't seem like the time. "I didn't realize you were giving me orders."

He smirked, flashing me an amused grin. "Not yet, Sunshine."

"I don't know if I like the sound of that."

He shrugged. "It's a lot like work. You take orders from your tables, don't you?"

"That's different. I can always refuse service." I held that right and I knew Alex would back me up because I wouldn't just do it without reason.

"It's the same thing with us. You can always say no, and we'll respect that. I've told Knix no many times."

"You have?" That didn't sound all that bad.

"Orders aren't really orders, they are more like requests, but we call them orders. And yes, I have. There are some things I can't do, some things I'm uncomfortable doing – not many, albeit – but still..."

"So, I can say no? Just like that?" Cleo purred into my fingers.

Marv pursed his lips, silence lingering as I supposed he thought about his response. "You can always say no," he started. "But we – Iris and especially our teams – ask that you consider each and every option before you refuse something. If you say no without truly contemplating your abilities to do a task, or what it could do or who it could help, then the likelihood of people coming back to you for help or for requests goes down. Our whole organization runs on people who have agreed to help others."

"But you're not all 'yes' men?" It was less of a question and more of a statement, yet I heard my tone go up at the end as if I wanted to make sure I understood what he was saying.

"No, we're not all 'yes' men." He glanced over with that smirk of his back in place. "Or 'yes' women."

I stroked Cleo's fur and concentrated on where we were heading for the rest of the drive. Marv drove down I-77 for another fifteen miles before pulling off onto a different road than Bellamy had taken before. Weaving in and out of morning traffic, he avoided potholes and rough patches along the pavement. Cleo whined when my hand stilled and I jumped. Big, kitten eyes stared up at me, upset and hungry for attention. I kissed one little kitty ear – the undamaged one – and continued to scratch down her back.

The song on the radio changed, the melody slowing considerably as one of Yiruma's more recognizable pieces, *River Flows in You*, began to play. The song was so familiar and sweet that I smiled, tilting my head to the rhythm.

"You know this song?" Marv's tone suggested surprise.

"Sure," I replied. "It's one of my favorites."

"What other kind of artists do you like?"

"Classical or otherwise?" I asked.

He turned down a narrow street. Trees arched over the road, Spanish moss darkening the way.

"Either, I suppose."

"Well, I really like Julian Lloyd Webber for classical music. His take on *The Moon* with the English Chamber Orchestra was beautiful. I obviously like Yiruma. I think he's a very talented pianist."

"What got you into classical music?" I blushed, not wanting to say. "What?" he demanded. I tried to think of an excuse while I covered one cheek with my free hand, keeping the other on Cleo. "You're red, is it really that bad?"

I groaned. No hiding it, I guessed. "Watching cartoons growing up, Bugs Bunny had a few episodes where there was classical music playing in the background and it made the show funnier and I realized that classical music wasn't as boring as everyone thought it was. It had a lot of emotion, not just sad or lovey dovey–"

"Lovey dovey?" He laughed.

"Hush," I commanded. "You asked." Cleo butted my hand again when it stilled. "Anyway," I drew out the word. "Hearing it on those old cartoons, I decided to look up more and learn a little bit about the artists and their instruments, I guess."

"You like Webber, so you must like cellists, huh?"

I shrugged. "Sure."

"What else do you listen to?"

"Pop, soft rock, classic rock." I listed them off. "Breaking Benjamin is one of my favorite bands." He nodded and we fell back in comfortable silence.

CHAPTER 11

The BMW left the smooth concrete of the road and bumped along the gravel driveway of a barn style building with faded, white trim along the roof and a wraparound porch. Twin shadows moved across the roof and the sound of high-powered drills and nail-guns shattered the serene quiet of the surrounding area. Trees lined three sides of the property while an extended lawn reached out towards the road. The last house we had driven past was half the size of the monstrosity before us and a good two or three miles back up the road. I wondered who lived here.

"I thought we were going to drop Cleo off with Texas," I said.

"I will," Marv replied. "Don't worry."

"Then why are we here?" I asked. Marv shook his head and started walking.

Shouts could be heard from the backside of the house and I trailed behind Marv as he strode toward the porch. He waved to a few guys who passed by, their eyes lighting up with recognition and camaraderie. A few paused when they spotted me, their eyes curious and zeroing in on Cleo as she surveyed them from my arms.

"Aww." One man slowly approached and cooed at her. A friend followed close behind them, their eyes big and wondrous as Cleo preened under their attention. Marv shook his head at them, took me by the arm, and steered me through the front door. I had never seen such big men coo over a small kitten.

The more men we passed, the more attention Cleo got. Some got all big-eyed, staring with wonder and adoration while others put whatever tool they were wielding down and reached out to pet her on the head or scratch behind an ear. Cleo merely yawned and meowed every so often, allowing them to worship her. Marv finally released me when he realized I would still follow him without coercion. I wasn't about to be left alone with these strangers if I could follow him.

I ducked my head after another bulky man stopped to pet Cleo. When he patted me on the head as well before heading back to his work, I barely resisted the urge to reach for the back of Marv's shirt. We managed to make it past most of the workers without too many stops and I noted they all seemed relatively fit, even the older men. Assuming it was because of the type of work they were doing, I focused on where Marv was heading and followed.

The living room was an open space with an elaborate chandelier. The place smelled like pine and I breathed deeply, inhaling the scent. To the left was an equally spacious kitchen with a rectangular island. The counter tops had yet to be installed, but it was still beautiful. To the right were wooden stairs leading up into a balcony hallway that overlooked the living room and kitchen.

Four doors lined the downstairs wall, and the second to last opened before Knix stepped out.

"Finally." The sound of his boots on the hardwood floor ricocheted in the open space.

Marv raised his brow. "Was there a time limit? I came over as soon as I got her in the car." He gestured to me and Knix's eyes followed.

"Hey, Little Bit." Strong, masculine lips curved up in greeting. Gooey liquid squished in my stomach, warming me. Butterflies fluttered.

"Hey." I halfheartedly raised my hand in reply. Knix smiled again, then turned his attention back to Marv.

"It's just about lunchtime for the guys. They'll take off for an hour or so, and we can get her into some training while they're gone."

Marv put a hand to his unshaved chin and scratched. "Isn't it a bit early for lunch?"

"They call it second breakfast, I call it first lunch," Knix's low-toned chuckle washed over my skin, making me shiver, and I leaned into Marv's side involuntarily. Marv glanced down at me before leaning back, pushing his lightly muscled arm back into me, causing yet another bout of shivers. Knix continued, "They're working so fast, I let 'em have more than a little leeway when it comes to their breaks."

"You're a good boss." Marv waved his hand dismissively. "Anyway, here she is. I've gotta go pick up some stuff."

"Just get everything ready for tomorrow, that's all I ask," Knix said.

"Bellamy can pick her up after the guys get back," Marv replied. "Should I run out and grab you something?"

"Nah." A wide palm slid between the golden strands

of Knix's hair as he rubbed at his scalp. "I've got a few snacks packed away in the cupboards for emergencies. The guys usually don't find them in there since they're already finished with them." That same wide palm dropped and reached for me, pulling me away from Marv and under his very large shadow. "I'll take care of her."

Marv caught my eyes. "Will she bite me?" he asked, gesturing to Cleo. I looked down at the bundle in my arms, purring away, and shook my head. He sighed. "If you'll give her to me, I'll drop her off with Texas. We were gonna take her there anyway."

"You adopted a cat?" Knix's eyes widened with surprise. "Come on, seriously?"

My head jerked back and I glared up at him. "You don't like cats?" I demanded.

He chuckled, a thick finger chucking me under my tilted chin. "I like cats just fine, Little Bit. I'm just teasing." I relaxed, passing Cleo over to Marv. She whined when our arms brushed and she was unseated from her comfy place, but curled up nicely enough when Marv soothed her, a palm to her back, rubbing lightly as he strode away.

"This way now." Knix led me out into the backyard, which was even more enormous compared to the front. Glancing around, I noted several different places he could fit another house and another and another – the entire back yard could be filled with half a neighborhood. "What I'm gonna teach you today are some basic self-defense steps – Harlow, are you listening?"

I jerked back to face him. With everyone gone, I didn't exactly know how to act around him. He was in charge. He commanded attention just with his size, though usually his demeanor didn't make him seem intimidating. This wasn't the friendly, easy going Knix I had come to know. The agreeable man with too much muscle mass was gone. In his place was a serious, commanding Knix that finally made me understand some of the guys' reactions. Tattling to Knix became a threat that I suddenly understood.

"This is important, Harlow."

"Why?" The moment I asked, I wanted to reach out, wrap my hand around the word, and shove it back inside my mouth.

"Because dangerous situations happen, whether we want them to or not. Unfortunately, it's simply a fact of statistics that as a woman, you'll likely end up in those dangerous situations more often than any of us would like you to. We want you to be prepared."

"What about my communications training?"

"This will help you in that area too. We'll get into that later." His palm came back down over my head, rubbing lightly. "Right now, it's work time – stand here." He gestured for me to take up position directly to his front. I was glad I had left my bag in Marv's car. At least I didn't have to worry about where to put it.

"Here?" I stood my ground, shaking as I planted my feet, feeling like an idiot.

He nodded. "Alright," he began. "In a dangerous situation, what is your first instinct?"

"Run?" I asked.

"Very good," he replied. "And I want you to do that if you can. If you have a choice between fight or flight, always choose flight but in the instance that you *have* to fight, I want to prepare you the best I can. I know that you don't know how to punch."

I flushed, my eyes sliding to the ground. Firm fingers tilted my head back up.

"No, it's nothing to be ashamed of," he said. "You just haven't been taught properly. That's what I'm going to do today."

"You're going to teach me how to punch someone?" That didn't sound so bad. I could get behind that.

"Not just how, but where." He dropped his hand away. "Look at my body." I did as he asked, glancing over the t-shirt he wore, the way it outlined the dips and hollows of his abdomen, the way his jeans clung to his powerful thighs. I gulped. "Where would you hit me first?" Knix asked.

"Uh..." My eyes remained fixated on the bulging muscles of his body. He was immense, like a stone statue brought to life. "Your um...pelvis?" I peered up at his face, catching the way his eyes glinted in approval.

"Yes, you're gonna want to go straight for the groin. Another good place to hit is my throat." He grabbed my hand and raised it so that my fingers grazed his neck, over the strong lines. I gulped. "–the throat controls a person's breathing. If you hit the groin or the throat, then your attacker is incapacitated – even if only momentarily, it will give you the opportunity you need to get away."

"I thought that I was supposed to fight." I ran a hand over the side of my face, pulling my hair back and tucking it behind one ear.

"In this exercise, I don't want you to fight me if you see a way out." As I thought about it, looking up at Knix, I knew he wouldn't run if he didn't have to.

"Why can't I just fight the attacker off?" I asked.

"No," he barked. I blinked at his intensity. "The point is to get away. Not to fight. I don't want you fighting at all if I can help it."

"Then what's the point of this exercise?" I huffed in frustration.

"There may be circumstances in which you cannot avoid a fight. I don't want to give you the skills to start a fight, only to end one." Knix took a deep breath and as he released, the tension ebbed out of his muscles. "There may be occurrences where it happens." He took a deep, calming breath. "Now, what I'm going to have you do is ball up your fist for me." I stared at him for a moment, waiting; for what, I didn't know. When he didn't do or say anything more, I followed his instructions and balled up my fist and presented it to him.

"That's right," he continued. "Now when you're making a fist, don't put your thumb inside. I'm sure you learned this the other day, but when you end up throwing the punch, the fingers on the outside will automatically be pushed inward with the force. If you hit hard enough, you could break your own thumb."

That explained the soreness of my thumb following the fight at school. I nodded my way through his next instructions as he had me do a few punches into the air with both hands balled into fists. Knix maneuvered himself behind me, hands on my hips and I wavered as the heat of his palms reached me through my clothes.

I wouldn't admit it to him or anyone else, but his intensity was damn near impossible to resist. He was this giant god, an educator, friend, and protector. It was attractive. I shook my head at the outrageous thoughts spilling through my mind and focused on the task at hand as he rounded back to my front.

"Alright, now hit me."

I paused. "What?" He couldn't be serious.

"Did you think I was just going to have you punch air all day?" He raised his eyebrow at me. "You need to move your body like I showed you. Follow through with your punch. It's difficult to understand just how important it is to master this unless you have practice hitting someone."

"Can't I just hit a punching bag or something?" The idea of hitting him was preposterous. I might actually be able to do some damage to an inanimate object, but Knix? No way. The very idea was laughable.

"No." He huffed. "Now, hit me." My fist waved, unsure and I reached out, landing a light punch to his chest. He groaned, and I jerked back. Had I hurt him? I stared down at my fist. No, I couldn't have. Knix was monumental and I had thrown the wimpiest punch in the history of wimpy punches.

"What," he stared at me, "was that?"

Hesitation made my voice tremble. "Um...a punch?"

"Do it again," he commanded. "But this time, put some force into your punch instead of just touching me."

I was shocked. Knix had never talked to me – or to anyone else that I knew of – like that before. I frowned in irritation. I didn't like the idea of hitting someone, and I would have rather been doing, or learning, something else. There was a point to this, though, I knew. I pulled back, aiming for just the right place. His throat was too high for me to reach and no matter how angry I was at him, I couldn't stand to think of going after his balls. Tightening up my fist, thumb just under my knuckles like he taught me, I swung. I turned with the movement until my punch smacked him right in the stomach, I followed through all the way.

He chuffed, the sound offensive, but bent slightly, a hand raising to rub the area. Mirth twinkled in those oceanic eyes of his. "Not bad, Little Bit. That's the way you do it." His eyes sparkled as though he knew just what his tone had done. Maybe I needed to be mad to hit someone. For the rest of the hour, Knix went over several different defensive positions. He stressed that the goal of each situation was to get away, not stay and fight. His instructions were only to help me escape not start or cause fights. Even as he stressed that, I couldn't imagine myself doing so. His focus allowed me to settle into a similar mindset, soaking in every lesson he taught me. After every successful attempt at mastering a new position, a new defense skill, he would praise me. I found myself not wanting to let him down, not wanting to disappoint him.

When construction guys began to trickle back in from their lunch break, they picked their work back up and the noise level rose. Sweating under the intense southern heat, Knix led me back into the house. A dark shadow emerged from one of the upstairs rooms and I started in surprise.

"Bell," Knix said. "I thought you were–" He cut himself off, glancing at me. Whatever it was he had been about to say, I was apparently not privy to it. "I thought you weren't going to be here 'til later," he corrected. I picked at the hem of my shirt in irritation. It wasn't like I would scream their secrets to the world. If I had to trust them, they could trust me too, couldn't they?

Bellamy's dark hair was loose around his face, hanging to his shoulders. "I got done early. Thought I might come and check out the place." He stopped in front of us. "Maybe pick up Harlow while I was here." He grinned at me. "Hey there."

I shifted from one foot to the other. "Hey," I replied. His bronze skin was a stark contrast to the loose fitting white t-shirt and whitewashed jeans he wore. Several braided bracelets lined one wrist opposite his tattoo.

"Yea, we just finished up. You can take her. Did Marv tell you about her exams? Did you get in contact with Wiggins?"

"Yea, I did." Bellamy ran one palm through his hair, pulling it back away from his face. "She can take her history exam online. I already got the teacher to send it to me. She can do it at the apartment and she can work on her paper today." His eyes flashed as he glanced at me.

"Good, take her and get that done." Knix pushed me towards Bellamy, his hand warm in the center of my back. "I'll see you later, Little Bit. Be good."

"No promises," I shot back.

Bellamy laughed and ushered me outside, and into a new car, a newer model SUV. The ride back to their condo was much shorter this time. I rolled down the window and let the speed of the car whip wind at my face and through my hair. When we pulled into the parking lot, I hopped out and followed Bellamy to the front doors.

We used the regular elevators this time. I scanned the area for the bitchy looking front desk attendant, but she wasn't there so I guessed it was her day off. As the elevator doors closed behind us and Bellamy slapped one of the buttons, I was curious enough to ask about why we had used the service ones before.

"Marv's paranoid," was his response.

The moment we stepped through the doorway, I was startled by an attractive male butt encased in sweatpants swaying as Texas crawled along the floor next to the couch.

"Come on, little one," he cooed. "I'm not going to hurt you, I swear."

Cleo's hiss of uncertainty had me laughing. He was

on the floor, crawling, trying to appease my cat. She recognized my laughter and shot out from beneath the couch, near Texas' feet. Before he could react and grab her, Cleo's little, fuzzy body was wrapped around one of my ankles. I bent down to retrieve her while Texas sat up, pressing his back against the coffee table.

"We were doing so well," he said. "I don't know what happened."

I shrugged. "Cats are fickle, I guess." I petted her back and she purred in my arms

Bellamy chuckled as Texas stood and glanced between us. "What's up? I thought you were at the construction site."

Bellamy looked down at me before addressing Texas. "She's gotta do homework," he said. "Take a test, work on her paper, that sort of thing."

"Ahh." Texas hummed as he moved back towards his room.

Bellamy shuffled in the opposite direction. "I'll make us some lunch," he announced. "I'll let you know when it's ready."

With Bellamy heading one way and Texas heading another, I wasn't quite sure where to go until Texas turned around and gestured for me to follow him. I clutched Cleo to my chest and let him lead me back to his bedroom.

"Okay, Marv dropped your bag off a while ago with–" He motioned to Cleo. "Bell probably already forwarded you the test. It should be in your email. You get to work on that. Let me know when you finish. We'll be out in the living room or in the kitchen if you need us. You can get changed in here if you want to shower in the bathroom. We won't bother you."

I guessed I was using his room then because the

moment he was done informing me, he turned and left the room. I sighed, placed Cleo on the pillow at the head of the bed, and shifted to sit down. Cleo curled up, scratching her paws along the surface a few times before falling asleep.

Opening the laptop that I retrieved from my bag, I scrolled through my emails and found one forwarded from an unfamiliar address. Sure enough, my history teacher had sent me an online version of the final exam with instructions on how to go about completing it. I could already feel the pressure of the test throbbing in the back of my brain, but I got down to work and opened the document. The sooner I started, the sooner I could finish and it would all be over.

CHAPTER 12

I finished my test rather quickly and moved on to my paper which took up the bulk of my time. After an hour spent on an analyzation of the character developments within Chbosky's *Perks of Being a Wallflower*, I decided I had depressed myself enough. I shut the laptop after saving the pages and cracked the sore muscles in my neck. I was thankful that my teacher had allowed the class to choose books that we were all interested in rather than force us to write something about Shakespeare or Edgar Allen Poe. They were great writers, yes, but so overdone. If I read one more obnoxiously complex play or horror-stricken poem, I would vomit.

Stretching, I rose from Texas' bed and headed for the hallway. Cleo continued to sleep on Texas' pillow. I tiptoed down the hallway, intending to sneak up on Bellamy and Texas. I imagined their faces when I jumped and screamed. Carl, from work, had caught me doing my side work enough, zoned out, and scared the crap out of me multiple times. I tried not to think about how comfortable I had become with the guys that I was doing this.

I reached the corner of the hallway, and just beyond were the living room and the kitchen. I peeked around and saw the back of Bellamy's jeans. They were in the kitchen. Before I could jump out, though, I heard one of them say my name. I couldn't tell who spoke, it was whispered so low, but the hushed voice had me thinking that they were trying to stay quiet, to keep me from hearing. Without intending to, my tiptoeing had a new purpose. I sidled back, my spine pressed to the wall.

"–should've asked Marv's cousin or his sister, maybe another girl from Iris," Texas was saying. "She's going to need to go in with him tomorrow night and I'm not sure she should. It's dangerous."

Bellamy's low rumble replied. "His sister isn't old enough to attend one of these parties and I've only met Quinn once or twice, but even I know she'd rather cut off her own ear than be forced into another socialite gathering. From what Marv says, she gets forced into it enough. Another Iris girl would have been preferable." I frowned. It sounded like they were referring to a party. Was I going to one? I looked down at my old clothes. "But we were looking to add to the team anyway. She works with us. Marv likes her. I like her."

"I don't know if she works with us, yet." My head turned at the bite in Texas' words. Did he not want me around? He seemed nice enough. He was even willing to give me information and phones. Had he changed his mind? "I haven't gotten to spend any time with her."

"Neither have I," Bellamy said.

"You at least got to have contact with her at the school. You were her first contact on behalf of Iris."

"Do you want me to head out?" Bellamy didn't sound

like he wanted to. The offer was given gruffly. "I can head over to the construction site or call Marv and ask if he or his parents need help."

There was a pause where silence reigned. It could have been Texas considering his offer. In truth, however, I pictured his face pinched with guilt. These guys cared about each other. I knew he would never intentionally push Bellamy out of his own home. At least, I hoped not.

"No," he finally said. "No, don't do that. I'll be fine. She'll have to work with me at some point. It doesn't matter."

A thousand thoughts swept through my mind. Were they fighting over working with me? What was this about a party?

I crept back, sliding along the floor until I got to Texas' bedroom door. I opened it and closed it to alert them that I would be coming in. Almost guiltily, they jumped at attention, scrambling to get into the living room before I got there. Standing in the doorway with my hands clasped behind me, I rocked back on my heels as though I was unsure of entering, as though I hadn't just been eavesdropping on them.

"Hey," Bellamy spoke first. "You done?"

I nodded. "Just finished."

"Cool, lunch is ready. I was just about to come get you."

Sure, I thought, but I didn't comment.

We sat in the living room, and each ate a bowl of chili with a side of cornbread. I had never tasted anything so delicious. I wolfed down the food and was done before either of them had finished half. They stared as I got up, rinsed my dishes in their sink, and placed them in their dishwasher.

"Do you think she even breathed between bites?" Texas asked.

"I don't know about breathing, but she sure inhaled that food," Bellamy replied.

I ignored their teasing. "What else are we doing today?" Would they tell me about the party? The slightly angry, betrayed part of me dared them to lie to me.

Bellamy popped up from his seat on the couch. "Shopping," he said.

My eyes widened, and my mouth dropped open in surprise. It was the furthest thing from what I had expected him to say.

"Shopping?" I clarified.

Texas was the one who replied. "Yes, shopping. Marv wants to take you. We're all going."

"Why shopping?" I looked down at my clothes. I didn't need more.

Texas winked. "It's a surprise."

I stiffened. A party kind of surprise? I didn't ask, though. Within the next twenty minutes Texas had finished his food while Bellamy rinsed his dishes and went about the same routine that I had. I waited in the front hall, leaning against the wall, while they rushed around the apartment, grabbing shoes, turning out the lights, and all of the various other things people usually did before going out.

"Ready?" Bellamy asked as Texas came skidding around the corner, this time dressed in a tight pair of jeans cinched at the waist with a brown belt, and a dark t-shirt with a pair of converse completing the look.

"Let's go."

When we reached the parking lot, Bellamy claimed the driver's seat of the SUV. Texas reached the front passenger seat and held the door open for me. I was going to insist that he ride there, but with one look, he silenced me. I politely thanked him in a quiet voice as I reached for the suicide handle and heaved myself up into the car. He beamed.

"So, where are we going?" I inquired as Bellamy pulled out of the parking lot. "The mall?"

"One of the outlets should have something," Texas said from the back.

"Yea, okay. Text Marv. Tell him we'll meet him there."

"Oh, that reminds me!" Texas reached into his back pocket. "I knew I would forget. I grabbed it just before we left." He reached between the two front seats and handed me a new iPhone. "This is your new, permanent phone. It's under warranty, figured we would need that in case anything else happened."

I flinched. "I really don't need a phone." I pushed it back at him, but he refused to take it. "I don't want my mom to find it."

"So, you'll hide it." Texas waved away my concern. "Keep it. You might need it for emergencies. Check it out, I installed a few new apps for you." He leaned forward, the seat belt stretching across his chest.

"Isn't it just for emergencies?" I said. "I don't need any apps."

"Hush. Click that button." He pointed to a blue square with a red outline. I opened it and a small creature popped up on the screen. "It's a video game. Have you ever played Pokémon GO?"

"Uh...considering that I didn't have a phone before this, no. I can't imagine how I would have been able to."

"Oh, right. Well," he stretched even farther until his hand hovered over the phone. "It's a really cool game where you can walk around and find different creatures. Hey, look! There's a Charmander. Quick! Catch it!"

"How do I–" I slammed my fingers down on a few buttons until Texas flicked the ball at the bottom of my screen and it slapped the small, orange dinosaur looking creature, jerking back only to absorb it into the ball. "Holy cow! That's cool. How did I do that?"

Bellamy rolled his eyes. Texas grinned and proceeded to school me on the awesomeness of Pokémon hunting. I became so absorbed in finding the little, strange looking creatures that by the time the SUV pulled into the outlet mall I barely realized that much time had passed. I grudgingly closed the app when Bellamy informed me that I wouldn't need my phone with me.

"What if she gets lost?" Texas argued.

"She'll be with one of us the whole time," Bellamy reasoned. "There's no need and you're the one who told her it was for emergencies. Who would she need to contact? The only one not here is Knix and he'll likely contact us first. It's fine. Leave it."

"Maybe we should leave our phones then, too," Texas said, though I could tell he didn't mean it. He kept his phone in his back pocket, not even feigning to reach for it. He just wanted to bait his friend.

"Oh, for the love of – you and I need to keep our phones in case someone needs us. How are we going to find Marv without our phones?"

Texas wasn't listening. He had already found Marv, who stood at the closest entrance, waving his arms. As we approached, I noticed that he had also changed clothes. He wore a pair of expensive looking black slacks, a bright-pink dress shirt tucked into his waist, and a blue and white bowtie. Texas hooted with laughter.

"Dear god, who dressed you?" He was laughing so hard that his eyes began to water.

Marv arched a perfectly sculpted brow. "My sister did."

"She's got horrid taste, Man," Texas chuckled. "Never let a fourteen-year-old pick out your clothes."

"I think he looks nice." I didn't know why I felt the urge to defend him, but I thought it was sweet that he was willing to let his little sister pick out his clothes. I could remember wanting to do the same for Michael, though he had never let me.

Marv smirked. "She thinks I look dashing, Tex. Maybe you should try to leave the house in something other than nightwear." With that, he turned on his heel and headed inside, Bellamy trailing behind.

"I'm wearing jeans, you snob!" Texas yelled, following after the both of them. From there, I fell to the back of the group.

The outlet mall was similar to the regular mall, except the shops were all much more extravagant, set outside, reminding me of a place in Myrtle Beach, South Carolina that I had once gone to as a child. A vinyl canopy covered the path that separated the stores, giving the illusion that they were indoors. Instead of high blast air conditioning though, the sweltering heat poured through, only minimized by the shade the canopy provided.

Marv strode with purpose, Bellamy on his right, Texas on the other side of Bellamy. Together they were a trio of beauty. Every so often, I would catch girls and women of all ages, as they turned their heads to watch the boys. With the three of them standing side by side and me trailing behind them, I finally got a good look at some of their differences.

Bellamy was obviously the broadest, his shoulders were massive. It truly made no sense for him to be between Texas and Marv because he would frequently have to angle his body to allow one of the others closer as shoppers milled around them. He and Texas were about the same height, and though Marv didn't tower over them, he stood just a few inches over six feet.

Marv was similar to Texas in certain ways too. Both were slender, their waists tapered, though Texas' more so. Each of their shirts stretched across easily visible muscle, though Marv's clothes looked personally fitted. As my eyes traveled down, spotting the grooves and quirks of their bodies, they came to rest on each of their behinds. I blushed when I realized where I was staring and jerked my gaze back up just in time to slam my face into Bellamy's back as they all came to a stop.

"Sorry," I mumbled, pulling back and rubbing at my nose.

Bellamy turned with a grin, seemingly unaware of why I had collided with him. "No worries."

"This one should do," Marv announced.

My eyes widened at the displays. Sleek black dresses and sparkling silver numbers were caged in the glass windows at the front of the store. As they led me inside, I felt even more out of place. A woman in simple black glided over to greet us.

"How can I help you gentlemen today?" she practically purred. "Looking for something for a girlfriend perhaps?"

"Actually," Marv said as Bellamy pushed me forward. "We're looking for something for her. It's for a party–" My eyes widened. Marv had come right out and said it. It made me wonder if Bellamy and Texas had been trying to keep it a secret at all and if, maybe, they had just been trying not to disturb me. "We were wondering if you had anything you think might suit her."

"Hmmm." Tapping one long, manicured nail against her cheek, the woman – whose nametag read Lindsey – circled me. I shrunk inward on myself, feeling caged by a strange, weirdly floral smelling, animal. "We might. What kind of gown were you thinking?"

She directed her question at Marv as Bellamy and Texas wandered off to finger through the racks. "Cocktail dress. Something loose fitted maybe. She's small, but I don't want to make her uncomfortable in one of those skin-tight dresses. I also don't want it to look like she's trying too hard."

"Not used to dressing up, is she?" The woman – Lindsey – smirked.

I bristled. I was standing right in front of them! I opened my mouth to say so, but Marv interrupted me.

"She doesn't need to," he said. "She's beautiful enough without the window dressing." My heart almost stopped right then and there.

I looked back at him and he smiled my way, letting me know that everything would be okay. No matter what Lindsey said, no matter what I wore, I would always be beautiful to him. It was something I had never been told before. I had never worried, and never cared before what someone else thought about my appearance. But here, in this moment, I wanted him to like whatever I wore because he was just the kind of person who deserved to have an elegant lady on his arm. It wasn't me, but I would do my damned hardest to try.

"Alright, follow me back, young lady," Lindsey said. "Let's see what we can find." I didn't take my eyes off of Marv even as I followed behind the woman. He grinned, letting me know with his eyes that everything would be okay, that I would be okay.

Lindsey went straight to a rack at the back of the store. She spread a few dresses apart and began pulling ones in different colors. Red. Blue. White. Her arms were filled by the time she decided she had chosen enough, and she led me back to the dressing room. I thought it was odd that she hadn't asked my size, not that I knew. It had been years since I wore a dress for anything and I hadn't had the money since to spend on anything so frivolous.

"Try this one on first." She handed me the red dress before hanging the rest on the back of the dressing room door, and stepped out, closing me in. I stared at the gown she had chosen. I didn't particularly care for it, but I slipped out of my old clothes and into the red sheath, staring at myself in the mirror. It really was a lovely dress; bright red, and tighter than I would have liked. It hugged my thighs and butt, molding to my curves, but at the top it sagged open and I had to hold it closed. There was no way I was walking out in this. I stripped and started looking through the remaining dresses. "Are you almost done?" Her high pitched and slightly whiny voice grated on my nerves.

"Almost," I replied.

I selected a white and blue dress with a mesh upper bodice that crawled up my shoulders. The skirt was flared, with blue and black petals spread across the fabric. More mesh poked out from the bottom of the backside, making the dress seem longer than it really was. It was more fun than elegant, but when I looked in the mirror, I decided that this dress fit much better. I felt pretty, even confidant. I opened the door.

"What happened to the red dress I gave you?" she asked immediately.

I shrugged. "It didn't fit." I didn't wait for her to say

anything else. The only opinions that mattered were the guys' opinions.

I walked out into the store. Marv stood to the side beside Texas, both scrolling through their phones. Bellamy leaned up against the nearest wall, a bored expression on his face. They straightened and stared when they saw me. Bellamy's jaw hung open slightly. Texas raised his eyebrows, scanning me up and down. Marv pursed his lips, but didn't look too displeased. Lindsey came behind me, her brow furrowed and a frown firmly on her face. Before she could say anything though, Marv spoke.

"Not bad. It's actually quite lovely," he commented. "I like the skirt and the mesh. Modest, elegant, but still fun, still her."

Lindsey sputtered. "Yes...well...uh, I do try to choose the dresses to match the clients."

I rolled my eyes but decided to remain quiet. I didn't want to be mean.

"I'd like to see more, in a few different colors, if you don't mind?" Marv said.

"No problem!" Lindsey beamed.

"Ah, yes, I was actually talking to Harlow. What's your opinion?" Marv's tornado eyes zeroed in on me, refusing to budge, demanding he know.

"It's nicer than the first one I tried on. I like the color combination." I fingered the mesh and the blue flowers. "I don't dress up, though, so I'm not an expert."

"No, it's beautiful. Would you like to try on more?"

I hesitated. I would have been perfectly fine just buying this one if I absolutely needed a dress. I flinched at how much it would cost, but I wanted to please the guys. I tried to find the tag, peering behind me and to my side, when Marv caught my shoulder and turned me back to look at him.

"What are you doing?"

"I want to know how much it is," I said, trying again. Texas laughed and shook his head.

"Why?" Marv's brows were drawn over his sparkling, silver eyes. Confusion clouded his handsome face.

I sighed. "Marv, I need to know how much it is to know if I can afford it." It was embarrassing to admit, but I wasn't sure if I could afford even a headband in this place. I didn't particularly like Lindsey, but neither did I want to waste her time.

"It doesn't matter," Marv huffed. "I'm paying for it. So, tell me, do you want to try on more?"

"Marvin," I said, enunciating his full name. "You can't buy me a dress." His eyes scanned up, just over my head, I imagined at Lindsey.

"Can you give us a moment?" he asked. I heard the clicking of her heels as she walked away. He waited a few more moments with his hand firmly gripping my arm before his eyes turned back to mine. "Sunshine," he began quietly, and I thought I heard something else I couldn't name in his voice. "I'm going to buy you this dress."

"I–" Marv pressed two fingers to my lips to silence my protest.

"Not only is this something you're going to need very soon, but you forget, I've been in your room. I know you don't have anything like this." I flicked a panicked glance over at Texas and Bellamy; both watched on. Texas wasn't laughing now. "You take such good care of your mom, you have such a big heart, Sweetie. Let us take care of you for just a little bit. Can you trust us to do that?" He leaned closer as though he didn't want the others to hear his next words. "Can you let me do that?"

"What about Iris?" I asked. "I mean, if I'm working for them, then you don't have to spend your money."

He scratched his chin. "If it will make you feel better to think of it as Iris, then do that."

"Marv," I warned.

He shook his head. "Don't worry about it. I *am* a part of Iris and therefore, technically Iris *is* buying you this dress."

I swallowed around the lump in my throat. I didn't want them to take care of me. I didn't know how I was supposed to let them. I hadn't had anyone to help me or take care of me in a long time. My mom was too sick. Michael was gone. Who would have? A part of me was scared, truly terrified that the moment they got what they wanted – my cooperation and assistance – they would pat me on the shoulder and usher me back to my life with a farewell smile. I didn't want to get so involved in them, only to be used and rejected in the end. Marv's tone of voice, especially around his last plea, felt more like he was asking something else, something more intimate. But could I really tell him no?

"What do you say?" his inquiry drew me back to him. I shook under his stare.

"O-okay." I nodded. I would let him buy me a dress. It wasn't a commitment. It was for the party. Whatever they needed me for, they would need me dressed up.

In the end, I was pushed back into the dressing room with Lindsey who took the red dress away and presented me with a new selection. Most of the dresses were similar to the style of the one I had originally chosen. Some were more outrageous that others. Some were simpler. I glanced through several, tossing them out of the pile before I even set one foot in their skirts.

It came down to four options: the original and Marv's personal favorite, an empire-waist, teal dress that Lindsey had actually admitted looked good, a red, sheath dress with an over skirt that opened in the front and flared out, or the very last dress I had tried on: a jewel encrusted bodice with a sweetheart neckline and loose fabric that fell longer in the back than the front – it was gorgeous. I hadn't yet shown the guys. Marv had already chosen a favorite and so had Bellamy – the red dress – and anything that made Lindsey admit that someone might just be pretty was something to be considered. But this dress...it made me feel stunning.

I stood for a few more moments in front of the mirror, twirling back and forth. It was Texas who came to the dressing room door asking for me. I took a deep breath and told him to go wait with the guys; I would be out in a moment. He grumbled good naturedly about 'girls taking forever to get ready', but proceeded to do as I asked.

I slipped on a pair of thick heeled, silver pumps that Lindsey had given to me, "to get the full effect," she had said. I wanted that to convince the guys that this was right. I liked the other dresses, but I loved this one and wanted them to love it too.

Feeling more confident than I had in a long time, I strode to the front of the hallway of dressing rooms where the guys had congregated to sit in a collection of lavish settees. I closed my eyes, inhaled, and stepped out, opening them again. My eyes immediately went to Marv. His lips parted and his own eyes widened. A hand reached up to the knot of his bowtie. I glanced over to Bellamy, whose expression was blank, as though shock had wiped away all cohesive thought. Was that a good thing? Last was Texas, who had stood when I exited.

"That's the one." His voice was practically a whisper, like he didn't want to destroy the magic. I nodded, smiling wide enough that my cheeks began to hurt. I spun in a circle, staring down to watch how the dress flowed.

"I love it," I beamed.

Marv cleared his throat. "Yes...well, um...it's certainly..." He turned to Lindsey, who stood silently off to the side. "We'll take it."

Thirty minutes and two hundred dollars later – I almost choked over how much the dress cost – and I was back in the front seat of the SUV with all three guys. "Where's *your* car?" I peered back at Marv.

"I caught a ride here," he said.

"Oh." I sat back in my seat as Bellamy drove. "So, what now?"

"Hmmm?" Marv answered.

"I mean, what do we do now?" I repeated. "Are you going to teach me more self-defense? Do I need to know anything for this party?"

"No."

I huffed in irritation, flipping back to glare at him. "No, you're not going to teach me more self-defense or no, I don't need to know anything for this party?"

Marv scrolled through something on his phone. "Both."

"Why not?"

"Hmmm? Why not, what?" he replied.

I groaned, pausing to watch him fiddle with his phone. Texas did the same, but he was likely playing his game. Marv wasn't even paying attention!

"Why don't I just dye my hair pink and become a flamingo?" I said blandly.

"You would be a beautiful flamingo, Sunshine," he stated. "But we quite need you in human form right now."

Bellamy chuckled. I shot him a seething glare which only led to more laughter.

"This is stupid," I snapped.

Marv looked up, dropping his phone in his lap. "What's stupid?"

"Just tell me what this party is! I need to know. How am I supposed to help you if you won't even tell me what it is that I'm supposed to be doing?"

"You're not supposed to be doing anything yet, Harlow." Marv leaned forward. Texas glanced up from his screen. "This is just a preliminary meet and greet. We just want to show you off. If we show up with you in tow at the last moment, it will be suspicious."

"Who are you showing me off to?"

Marv grunted. "Talk to Knix," he said, then returned to his phone.

I decided that the first chance I got, I would do just that.

KNIX WAS SITTING ON THE COUCH WATCHING AN OLD rerun of a 90s TV show when we returned. I made a beeline for him, intent on getting some answers. He looked up, lines of happiness forming at the edges of each eye, his lips twitching.

"How'd it go?" he asked.

I opened my mouth to ward off his question and start my own interrogation when Bellamy cut me off. "She's beautiful." I sputtered, rounding back on him. He moved past me, grinning with the garment bag clutched in his hands. "You wouldn't believe someone could look this gorgeous."

Texas headed out of the living room, head down on his phone, and I had to wonder if he was playing his game at all or doing something else.

"Knix," I said, standing in the middle of the living room.

His head jerked up. "Yea?"

"What is this party about?" I asked. "Who is going to be there? What do you need me for?"

He arched a brow, sliding a look to both Bellamy and Marv, who stood a little behind me, holding the shoebox containing the silver heels that had bewitched them. Marv shrugged as Texas returned to the living room, sans phone, taking up position against the wall next to the kitchen's entrance. The flat screen television cut off and Knix motioned for me to move closer. I did so hesitantly. He gestured for me to sit on the coffee table directly in front of him.

"You want to know?" It seemed a silly question considering how long I had been asking, but I nodded anyway. "Okay."

"Okay?" I said. "You're just going to tell me?"

"We've received some intel that there might be a scam going on in the area. It's on the wealthier side of town – near where Marv's parents live. Apparently, someone sends out free couples' retreat invitations to specific people. When the couple arrives, they spend two days at a small private resort on an island just off the coast. The couples that have gone complain about things being stolen – family heirlooms, expensive jewelry, money from wallets, etcetera."

"Officers haven't been able to catch anyone in the act. No one is allowed to leave the island the entire time that the couples remain there, and the staff changes every time. There's no way to know how the items are being stolen or how they are getting off the island."

Marv coughed to get Knix's attention and I turned towards him. "My parents received an invitation about a month ago to go to this couples' retreat. The company that owns the retreat and island are very good at keeping what has happened on the down low, so they didn't know. Fortunately, they won't be able to make it. Since the invitation is not specifically addressed to them as a couple but to the Carters, we decided it would be beneficial if I were to take their place."

It clicked. "You need me to act as your cover."

He nodded. "The invitation is not for singles and this company is owned by very traditional, old, southern businessmen. Therefore, I can't go in with say Texas or Bellamy as a gay couple."

"Why me though?"

He blinked. "What do you mean?"

"I mean, why pick me? Don't you – doesn't Iris have girls to help you out? I'm not very good with sleuthing."

"You never know until you try," he replied, "and we were considering recruiting a few females anyway." I didn't like how he made it sound like I wouldn't be the only one. "Alex is close to Knix. We're all friends, but they've worked together, and when Knix mentioned wanting to recruit a girl, he recommended you."

That had me thinking. "Would you have considered me if he hadn't?" I had to know. Was I just a convenience?

"Little Bit." Knix captured my chin, angling it towards his and holding me to face his piercing gaze.

"We can't know the answer to that. It's like Schrödinger's cat. We would never know unless it hadn't happened that way. But it has. You're with us now." Those blue eyes flickered. "Unless...you don't want to be?"

"I..." Did I? I stared hard at him, trying to find something in his blue eyes that would tell me the answer.

"If you don't want to do this, Harlow," Bellamy said. I could barely make out his form in my peripheral vision. "We can find other ways. This job is not solely dependent on you. There's no pressure."

That wasn't quite right, though, because there was pressure. I felt it; the pressure to be good enough for them, to succeed, the pressure to take care of my mom, to finish high school. I shut my eyes, warding off Knix's penetrating gaze. The fingers on my face tightened, but not enough to hurt. He seemed to realize that I couldn't answer.

"Do you want to know the rest of the plan?" he asked.

I sighed, relieved, and nodded. He released me, and I relaxed back.

"We had to bump up our timeline because there's a meet and greet with heads of the company and their families. It's something they have never done before, and we assume it's because they want to assure people that everything will be alright, and there will be no more thefts."

"It's free?" I squinted in confusion.

"The meet and greet?" Knix scrubbed a hand down his jaw line. "Yea, so is the actual retreat."

"Then how do they make money?" It made no sense. A company wouldn't want to be caught stealing from clients. Literally stealing, and not just money fraud, though they wouldn't want that either. It sounded like the boys considered the company the prime suspect. I said as much.

Knix's face bloomed into a stunning smile that lit up the room. "That's why you are perfect for our team," he said, causing a blush to rise to my cheeks. "The retreat isn't the company's source of income. They work with a variety of collaborated businesses and wealthy benefactors in the area. This is their way of saying thank you, a perk if you will. It makes them money by keeping their benefactors and business associates happy."

"Having their things stolen wouldn't make them happy," I replied.

He continued to grin. "I was hoping you would pick up on where I was trying to lead you. You didn't let the opinionated version color your own thinking. That's an important quality to keep. But you're right. They wouldn't. We don't believe the company itself is actually responsible. We were informed of this via several different channels: Marv's and the company itself."

"What's the name of the company?" I asked.

"It's Sweratt Incorporated," Marv said. I tilted my head. "The company itself does a lot. They run the gambit for legal assistance to website development. There are so many branches to this company, it's difficult to tell where the head is. For this branch, though, it's mostly a contractor for local businesses on security systems."

"Has anything been stolen from the actual businesses they work with?"

I jumped when Bellamy hooted. "Look at her, and she questions if she's cut out for this!" I frowned at him. If this was as crucial as Knix made it seem then he needed to take it seriously.

"Forgive him," Knix said, shaking his head.

"No, as of right now, there hasn't been any reported breaking or entering. There hasn't been anything reported missing." Texas finally came around to stand next to the couch. "But that's not to say there won't be."

I nodded, and quiet fell over the room.

After a few moments, Knix stood up. "I think it's time to get you something to eat and take you home," he announced.

"I should probably go now," I agreed. "I haven't checked on my mom."

"Nope." Knix leaned down and plucked me up from the coffee table, throwing me over one wide shoulder. His broad arm wrapped around my waist, holding me up there like a box to be carried and I was so stunned, I didn't fight it. My stomach pressed down into him. His body was so warm. I could feel it through his shirt and mine.

"No?" I huffed.

"I checked on your mom just after you left this morning. Marv did it before he met you at the mall."

"We actually went to the outlet," Marv said, ever so helpfully.

Knix turned towards the front door. "We'll go out and grab dinner for us and the guys, and then we'll drop you off," he continued.

I was still focused on 'the checking on my mom' bit. "I locked the door," I grunted, pressing my palms to Knix's back, and arced up, hitting my head on the ceiling. I dropped back down with a whimper. "I have the keys." I reached back, feeling for my butt pocket where the keys were ...not. "Where are my keys?!"

I heard a jingle and Texas rushed ahead to open the front door for Knix. He held my house keys up for me to see. "Marv grabbed them from you on the way to Knix's this morning. He passed them off to me, and I made copies." He handed them to me and I noticed a few new additions. "You now have a key to our apartment and Knix's house."

"Knix's house?" I asked.

"It's the house you saw this morning," Knix said. He shut the door and carried me down the hall, into the elevator, and out into the parking lot, before setting me down next to the SUV. "Hop in."

They were going to drive me crazy, but I got in the car anyway. Maybe I liked crazy.

CHAPTER 13

After a small argument about stealing my keys, the boys got their way, and I reluctantly agreed that they could have spares for emergencies only. We picked up pizza and ate dinner before Knix dropped me off in front of my house with a new phone and a worried look.

"If she finds it, don't worry about it," he reassured me. "I don't want you getting into any trouble, but we need to get ahold of you if we need to."

I was half-tempted to tell him that he could just do what Marv did before, but I couldn't picture it being as easy for him to crawl through my bedroom window as Marv had made it seem.

Walking up to the duplex after being with the guys all day felt strange. Like I didn't quite belong here anymore, yet nothing had physically changed. I grabbed the mail peeking out from the stained mailbox at the end of our empty driveway, and jogged to our front stoop.

"I'm home," I called, quietly entering the foyer. There were a few low mumbles in the first bedroom and I followed the sleepy noises. Mom lay on her side, a fresh glass of water on her nightstand, and a plate with a few crumbs left. My phone lit up and I turned away from her bedroom before locking myself away in my room to pull it out and check the incoming text.

Texas: You will have the same number. Marv said he would prefer I change it. I can get you another number tomorrow.

Harlow: No need. This is fine.

I set the phone down, but almost immediately it buzzed to life again.

Texas: I'm exchanging the phone number tomorrow. You will keep your contacts.

I grunted and slammed the phone down once again, this time without answering. The phone buzzed and buzzed again. I ignored it until it began vibrating with an incoming phone call. Without glancing at the screen, I flicked the green answer button and began to hiss through the phone.

"Don't call me when I'm home, my mom could hear!" It was embarrassing enough to tell them about the first incident. If it happened again, I would refuse any phone they might try to give me.

"Strict parents, huh?" The voice on the other end was not Texas. I pulled the phone away from my ear, but the caller ID read as an unknown number.

"W-who is this?"

"Forgotten me already?" he replied. "That's a shame. I was wondering if you were sick or avoiding me since you didn't show up to school today."

"Grayson?"

"I guess you haven't forgotten me then." I could hear the smugness in his tone. "So, where were you today?"

"I was…nowhere, out…um…just doing errands. How did you get my number?"

"Your friend at the diner didn't tell you?"

A light went off in my head. "It's not nice to steal phones," I said.

"Ah, well. You're not wrong. But who said I was a nice guy? Besides, being nice is overrated. I'm only nice to people who deserve it."

"Yea? Then why are you talking to me?"

He paused. "I find you…interesting. I feel like we would make a good team and I'm a quarterback. I'm good at teamwork."

"Well, I don't find you interesting and maybe I already have a team. Don't call me again."

I clicked 'end call' and threw the phone at my bed, standing over it, seething. I couldn't leave it there for long, though. I needed to tell someone that he had called. Instead, I found myself picking the phone back up when it began vibrating again.

"It's not nice to hang up on someone. Seems like we have being 'not nice' in common, don't you think?" Grayson asked with a dignified huff when I answered again.

"What do you want, Grayson?" I demanded.

"Come out with me."

"What? No!" I glanced around my room.

He was a football player. He was used to cheerleaders

in fancy uniforms, who did their nails every week, and didn't have to scrounge for grocery money.

"You sure? It'll be a fun night. If you're not going to school tomorrow, then I think you'll enjoy it."

"Who says I'm not going to school tomorrow?" I didn't know if I was or not, but I assumed that I would be unless the boys said otherwise.

"Well, then let me pick you up. I'm sure you'd rather catch a ride to school than take the bus. I had to ride that thing for a whole year before I got a car."

"Oh, wow." I feigned amazement. "That must have been so hard for you."

He laughed, deep, and full, and slightly smoky. I hated that I wanted to see what he actually looked like when he laughed like that, without reserve. From what I had noticed, usually when he laughed, it was subdued. A chuckle here. A smirk with a rumble there. Nothing so filling as this laugh. It made my insides warm. Why, though, I couldn't say.

"I like you, Harlow. I'll pick you up tomorrow at 7:30 am. Be ready."

"You don't know where I live, and I never said yes!"

"Goodnight, Harlow."

I slapped the phone on the nightstand and crawled under the covers after setting my alarm. The guys were right. I needed to change my phone number. My insides rebelled at the thought that I wouldn't talk to Grayson again. Even though we still had school, who knew how many more days I would actually see him in person before he went his way and I went mine.

How much longer would Erika be my friend for that matter? I hadn't spoken to her in a few days, which wasn't unusual due to my work schedule and previous lack of phone. Still, I felt like we were growing further and further apart. She had been my constant for so long. Who would I be without her as a friend? Who was I now?

~

I ALMOST HAD A HEART ATTACK AS I OPENED MY FRONT door the next morning and found myself staring at a tall, surprisingly chipper, Grayson. He grinned, with one arm slung over his head on the door frame as he leaned against it.

"Man, girls take forever. You finally ready to go?"

"How did you–" I stepped back into my house and grabbed the doorknob, preparing to slam it shut and turn the deadbolt. "How did you know where I lived?"

"I asked that friend of yours."

"Marv?" I shook my head, inching the door forward a bit. "He wouldn't tell you." Grayson grabbed the edge and held it, shaking his head.

"The girl...Erika?"

"You don't even know her name?" I accused. "No. Just no. Get out of my way." I brushed past him, shutting the door and locking it behind me. I headed straight for the curiously empty bus stop a few houses down, glancing around for the usual one or two other bus riders that lived in the neighborhood.

"Scared to be in a car alone with me?" Grayson's footsteps echoed around the empty street as he followed behind me. "Don't worry. I won't let you jump me no matter how much you might want to."

I rounded on him. "You!" Jabbing my finger at him, I sputtered, "You're just...you're horrible!"

"Nah, just trying to give a friend a lift." He shrugged.

"We're not friends." My hands itched to go after my

phone. I had received neither a phone call nor a text from any of the guys this morning.

"So, you don't want a ride?"

I huffed, frustrated. "I have a ride. The bus has just as much ability as your..." I glanced behind him at his car, my eyes widening, "mustang does."

He shrugged again. "Well, I wouldn't be so sure since you missed it."

"What?" I froze, turning away from him, and scanned the area. It was odd that the other students weren't on the curb like usual. "No, that's not possible."

This time I did fish out my phone, wondering how I had lived without it before, to check the time. I stared down at the fat numbers on my screen. How had I missed the bus? I had never missed the bus before, not unless I had been sick or yesterday... I had missed the bus yesterday because of the guys.

Grayson's arm slung over my shoulders. "I promise to keep my hands to myself. Let me just give you a lift to school."

"You did this on purpose," I hissed through clenched teeth, shaking his arm off.

"Who? Me?" He raised his brows mockingly. "I distracted you so much that you didn't even notice you were running too late to catch your bus just so I could give you a ride to school? I wouldn't do that."

"I can just call one of the guys," I snapped. "They can give me a ride. You can go."

"And you'll go to school late?" he asked. "That won't look good on your record."

"Graduation is a few weeks away. It's not going to matter much longer anyway."

"Come on, Harlow. Just let me give you a ride." He sighed. "I wanted to talk to you anyway."

"Why?" I demanded, clutching my phone in my palm. "Why do *you* want to talk to *me*? You barely know me. We've gone to school for how long and you're just now trying to talk to me?"

"You don't trust me," he stated.

I shook my head in shock. "Wow," I deadpanned, "did you figure that out all by yourself?"

He lowered his head and grinned sheepishly. When my expression remained placid, he sighed again. "I'm really not that bad," he said, gesturing to the car. "It's just a ride to school. Please?"

I stomped over to his shiny silver mustang, stood next to the passenger side door, waiting, my bag in hand. He chuckled as he pulled out his keys and hit the button on his key fob that unlocked the doors. The interior smelled like leather and pine, likely a mixture of the seats and the scented cardboard tree hanging on his rearview mirror.

I stewed in silence as he crossed around the car. Before he reached the driver's side door, I shot a quick text to Bellamy to tell him what had happened and then put my phone away. He seemed the least likely to be upset. Even though I hadn't known the guys that long, it felt right to let someone know. I would just find out what Grayson wanted and then be done with him.

"So, what kind of music do you like?" Once inside the car, Grayson turned the ignition and cranked the AC. I turned with my back against the door, staring.

"What do you want?"

"To give a girl a lift to school. I am a gentleman, after all." That was bull-crap. I raised an eyebrow, crossing my arms over my chest. "To be fair, no girl I've ever offered to help has been as resistant as you."

"Maybe I'm just immune to your charms." I smirked.

Around him I felt like I acted different too. With Knix, Marv, Bellamy, and Texas, I felt smaller – not difficult around Knix. Maybe smaller was the wrong word. I felt intimidated, maybe? They were so strong, had so much – Marv's money, Texas' smarts – I felt almost insignificant or unnecessary, despite their reassurances. Around Grayson, it felt okay to argue back, to snap at him. He took it so well, with a smirk or a grin. Though his eyes sometimes flickered with something much deeper, even heartbreaking, for the most part, he was cheerful and teasing. I questioned his morals though. And that is what had me repeating my question. "What do you want? You said you wanted to talk to me, why?"

He stared ahead. "That guy you were with the other day – the one after the fight. I was wondering why a girl like you would know him and I realized…"

"Realized what?" I pressed when he paused.

I watched his facial expression harden as he navigated the mustang. He was quiet for several moments. "I realized you're probably more special than you think you are," he deflected, shooting me a shark-toothed smile. Somehow, even though I knew to others it might have looked dangerous, to me, it looked like a mask.

"If you were trying to impress me, Mr. Gentleman," I replied, "maybe you should have jumped into the fight."

"What would be the good in that?" The mustang slowed to a stop sign and turned out of the neighborhood. "For a chance at you possibly liking me? You don't seem like the kind of girl who changes her mind easily."

He wasn't wrong. I pursed my lips. "Why did you show up to my work?"

"To talk to you."

"Why?"

He tilted his head. "Because I like you."

"Why?"

Grayson glanced at me when he stopped at a red light. "Are you two? What's with the twenty questions? How about I ask you some? What are you doing hanging around with those guys? Also, put on your seat belt."

I twisted, placing my back against the leather seat, and pulled the belt across me. "I don't know what you mean," I said. "And you're the one who picked me up, intending to talk to me. It makes sense for me to ask you questions since you're not being forthcoming with why the hell you showed up at my house this morning."

"You really like playing hard to get, huh?" he asked.

"I'm not playing," I shot back. "I *am* hard to get." I shivered, unfolding my arms and rubbed my palms down my legs.

He laughed the same deep, rumbling laugh he had the night before. "Okay, okay." Grayson slammed on the breaks as a crazy girl in a yellow bug pulled out in front of us and slowed down. The streets began backing up and even in the coolness of the car, I felt trapped with him. "If you don't want to talk about your boyfriends, who am I to push you?"

"The pushiest person I've ever met?" I said. "And they aren't my boyfriends."

"So, you're single?" He twisted his head to wiggle his eyebrows at me suggestively.

I groaned. "Oh my god." I slapped the back of my head on the headrest of the seat. "You are impossible."

"I'm trying to be very possible for you." He swerved into a new lane, bypassing the yellow bug and shooting through a yellow light. "But seriously, what are they to you? Friends? They can't be related to you. They don't live with you, I know that." So, that's why he wanted to know where I lived. I squinted at him out of the corner of my eyes.

"Are you spying on me?"

He smirked. "Just looking out for a girl," he replied.

"Some people call that stalking." Was he just looking out for me? "Especially if you don't know the girl that well." He slowed and stopped at a stop sign, his chest curving as he looked directly at me.

"I want to."

Not knowing what to say, I didn't answer. We sat in silence as he pulled into the school parking lot and stopped the car between an old Toyota and an empty handicap space.

"Thanks for the ride." I reached for the door handle.

"I'll give you a lift back home too, if you want?"

"No," I said. "I won't be taking the bus home. I have some extracurricular activities." It wasn't exactly a lie, but I didn't want him to know that I would be with the guys.

"Wait! Harlow!" He met me around the front of his mustang.

"What?" I held onto my bag by the top handle before slinging it onto my shoulders.

"I don't want you to start avoiding me."

"I haven't been avoiding you," I said.

He stared hard at me, trying to keep me from looking away, but I did so anyway, focusing on the brick building waiting for our arrival.

"Please?" His tone was pleading. I had to glance back. The deep, damaged look in his eyes had returned, shining out at me. "Just be careful around that guy."

"I'll see you in class," I said.

I felt his eyes on every step I took away from him,

and I wondered if I would see him in class or if the guys would pull me out before the day was over.

~

I MADE IT TO MY LAST AND ONLY REAL CLASS OF THE DAY, having spent the majority of it in the library taking my final exams. All I had left now was to turn in my final English paper.

Principal Wiggins had called me into his office later in the day to tell me that, 'considering the special circumstances' – circumstances I wasn't quite sure I understood fully – I wouldn't have to finish the last week and a half of school. There was no knowing what else the guys might need me for in the coming days.

A text message dinged my phone as I walked out of front office. It was Bellamy telling me that he would be by to pick me up after school. My phone dinged again and I sighed as I read the latest message.

BELLAMY:IF THAT GUY TRIES TO TALK TO YOU AGAIN, avoid him.

IT WASN'T LIKE AVOIDING GRAYSON WAS AN EASY TASK.

I walked to class, relieved to finally have something more to pay attention to than questions on paper. Tests really did nothing to assess intelligence, just memoriza- tion. It was nice that the school would be turning over the teaching method in the next year to project based learning, where the only tests taken were the state and nationally required ones, and everything students learned would have actual real-world applications.

As I predicted, it was absolutely impossible for me to avoid Grayson because as I walked through the doorway, he was already in the seat next to mine.

"Didn't see you at lunch," he said as I approached.

"You were looking for me?" I put my bag down and slid into the hard, plastic seat. "I was taking exams in the library."

"What are you doing after school today?" He leaned closer, those bright, blue eyes of his reminding me of Knix's, but he wasn't nearly as bulky or tall. He had the football player's build, but Knix was still several inches taller than him.

"I'm busy." Getting dressed up and going to a party to lie about who I was. Not that I was nervous. I dropped my pen as I scrambled to pull out doodling materials. No need to take any real notes since I had already taken the test for this class.

"Well, what about tomorrow after school?" he asked as I leaned over and picked up my pen.

"Um…" How did I tell him I wouldn't be at school?

The teacher saved me from saying anything though, as she came in and shut the door behind her. She flipped off the lights and turned on the PowerPoint she had ready for the class. We spent the remainder of the period glossing over materials. To save myself from going insane, or rehashing that awful test and stressing over which answers I had gotten wrong, I scribbled across my notebook.

My phone buzzed in my bag and I slid a glance down at it, wondering if I could manage to get to it without alerting the teacher. I decided not to risk it and instead raised my hand to request a bathroom break. She stopped me when I passed her with my bag packed, but I had the perfect excuse. Ignoring Grayson's hard stare, I whispered an excuse about periods and not wanting to pull my tampons out in front of everyone. She nodded and gestured for me to hurry along.

Once in the girl's restroom, I closed and locked a stall door behind me before pulling out the phone.

BELLAMY: Time to go
    Harlow: Still in school
    Bellamy: Not anymore. Where are you right now?
    Harlow: 2nd floor. Girls bathroom.

I SIGHED, THANKFUL THAT I HAD AT LEAST PACKED everything away before leaving the classroom. I unlocked the stall and went to the sink to wash my hands. I always felt dirty in public bathrooms. The door to the bathroom opened and I moved to the paper towel dispenser as I assumed another girl had entered for her own afternoon bathroom break away from class.

"Almost ready to go?"

I whirled around, hands reaching out to grip the sink, so I wouldn't fall. Bellamy's coffee-brown eyes watched me from a much sterner face than I had seen on him before.

"What happened?" I asked, concerned.

He simply shook his head. "If you're done, we need to go. We have things to prepare for tonight."

"Why do you look like that? And what are you doing in here? This is the girl's bathroom, what if someone walked in?" Bellamy stepped forward and yanked my bag up and slung it over one of his broad shoulders before tugging me along behind him. "Bellamy?"

He grunted as he towed me out into the parking lot

towards the familiar BMW. I looked for Marv, maybe in the passenger side, but he wasn't there.

"Where are the others? Where are we going?" He opened the car door for me and pushed me in, shutting it without a single word. He got in and started the engine, and backed up. I glanced at him out of the corner of my eyes. "Why are you acting like this?" Why was he so mad?

He lifted the console of the BMW and pulled out a cell phone carrier box. "This is for you." He tossed the box in my lap. "New number. Don't use the old phone anymore."

"I would hardly call it old," I said, opening the box and peeking inside. "In fact, I think this is the same phone. New number?"

"Yes."

I threw the box on the floor of the car and turned to him. "What is your problem?"

He flicked a hard look at me before slowing to a stop along a back road before the interstate and pulled over on the shoulder. He turned the ignition off and jerked the emergency break up.

"Why did that boy pick you up this morning? Did you ask him to? You could have asked any one of us to come get you. You could have asked me!" he roared.

I huffed. "I missed the bus. I didn't know he would be there!" I yelled back. "He was already there, and I figured you guys would be asleep. I texted you!"

"After you were already in his car!"

"I knew you would be upset if I didn't tell you, though," I snapped. "Give me some credit."

He stared at me, his eyes sliding all over my face, his cheeks flushed. I'm sure mine were too. I didn't break his gaze. Then something happened. His eyes narrowed on mine before dropping to my lips. I bit them nervously, especially when he leaned a bit closer.

"You shouldn't have gone with him." His voice lowered, growing dark and gruff.

"He just gave me a ride to school," I argued.

"You won't need to go anymore," he said.

"I don't have a car. I might need a ride somewhere, but I promise not to call him to ask for a ride." If he called me to talk…well…I might not hang up on him. Not now that he had me a little curious about him. If he even could, with this new number I knew they would insist on.

"Goddammit!" He slammed both palms down on the steering wheel.

I jumped. "Why are you yelling?"

"I'm just irritated," he growled, twisting back. His eyes zeroed in on my lips again, his lids lowering. "You drive me insane."

"How do I–"

My words were cut off when his hands grabbed my arms, jerked me forward, and he kissed me. I was so stunned at first that I just let it happen. Then his lips moved over mine, soft and sweet. He traced my lower lip with his tongue, and I jerked away when I felt something hard touch me. He had a bar through his tongue that I had never noticed before. He pulled me back in and this time I let myself kiss him back.

His hand grazed my side, sliding to my back as I pressed into him, opening my mouth. When did my seatbelt come undone? Had it been him or me? It didn't matter because I followed his lead, shivering as my shirt slid up slightly and his warm palm touched my bare skin. Everywhere he touched, goosebumps jumped to meet him.

I had never been kissed before. Had never even been on a real date. He was my first in this way. I closed my eyes and reached up, my fingers tugging on the loose ponytail of his hair, pulling out the band that held it all back. I grabbed hold and held on as he crushed his lips harder against mine, like he couldn't get enough, like he wanted to breathe me in, consume me. I trembled under his heat.

Bellamy's hands squeezed me harder, hauling me closer, until I was almost straddling the console. It should have been uncomfortable with my head tilted to meet his, but I hardly noticed as I ran my hands through his hair and licked at his lips too. He groaned before he pulled away and rested his forehead against mine. We were both breathing hard. I couldn't believe he had kissed me. I couldn't believe I had kissed him back. It was startling and my mind reeled, my eyes glued to the lips that had – moments before – been attached to mine. He had kissed me like he needed to breathe. It felt like he had stolen the oxygen straight from my lungs.

"If you need a ride, you call me," he rasped. "If you can't reach me, you call one of the guys." I shook, trying to hold myself over him. "Promise me."

I swallowed and nodded. "I promise."

"Okay." He blinked and kissed me once more, hard, and close-mouthed, before urging me back into my seat. "Now, put your seatbelt on." I did as he said, my hands shaking as I pulled the seatbelt over my chest and buckled in. Bellamy lowered the emergency brake and turned the ignition, pulling back onto the road.

Touching my lips with the tips of my fingers, I stared out the windshield and asked myself, 'what just happened?'

CHAPTER 14

I stood in the guys' bathroom dressed in the gown Marv had bought and put the finishing touches on my makeup with light brush strokes. Texas sat on the closed toilet fiddling with his phone, trying to catch some sort of purple blob that kept escaping. He told me the name of the app, but I had already forgotten. Tucking my hair behind my ears, I leaned further over the sink counter, dabbing a shiny nude powder over my eyelids before adding eyeliner and mascara. I wasn't used to using so much makeup, especially the high-quality brand Marv had shown up with. As I glanced in the mirror, closing the palettes and makeup cases, I thought I looked pretty freaking good.

"Damn it," Texas cursed, tapping at his phone.

"What do you think?" I asked.

I needed a second opinion. Just because I thought I didn't look too bad, didn't mean that everyone else would think the same. The makeup felt heavy on my face and I wasn't sure if I hadn't used too much. I needed to look like I knew what I was doing.

Texas' dark eyes slid up from his phone and he paused. "You look…" He stared hard, his eyes analyzing the dress, the makeup, my bare shoulders. "You look amazing."

I blushed, and turned away. "Th-thanks."

He followed as I headed into the living room where Knix was quietly giving both Bellamy and Marv directions. Marv was dressed in a charcoal suit, tailored to his tall body. It tapered down over his chest to his waist. Bellamy wore a simpler uniform of a black t-shirt and jeans. He glanced at me as I entered, his eyes gliding over my skin, the dress, and my bare legs before trailing back up. My blush deepened.

"Wow." Marv's gasp drew my attention to him. He wore a thin tie that matched my dress and the charcoal of the suit accentuated his eyes. He also looked me up and down. "Now, that is a dress." He stopped at my eyes, smiling. "Ready to head out, Sunshine?"

I nodded the same time that Knix shook his head. "Not just yet. Texas needs to go over a few things with you before you go." He glanced at me, a quirk at the corner of his mouth the only approval I would receive from him. It was approval enough, and made me feel like a real princess with four attractive men admiring me.

Texas jumped to the center of the room. "Okay, yea." He pulled two small, curved, nude lumps from his pocket. They looked like hearing aids. He handed one to me and one to Marv. "Each of these will put you in contact with either Bellamy or Knix. I'm going to be in the security room with Knix. Bellamy will be serving at the function which is hosted at the DeLuca Charleston Hotel downtown."

I watched as Marv wiggled the little device into his

ear and I mimicked him. It felt foreign in my ear, like a strange headphone. "Here, push this button," he ordered.

Marv grabbed my chin and tilted my head to the side as he fidgeted with the device. A quiet shrieking noise startled me, and he began tapping something else until the volume rose slightly before cutting off completely.

Texas continued, "The party starts at 10 pm. Your objective for tonight is to be seen and identify possible targets."

"The potential victims or the bad guys?" I clarified, pushing Marv's hand away to adjust the ear device myself.

"As of right now, you're just looking for the possible thieves," Knix replied. "Under no circumstances are you or Marv to approach them. This party is all about information gathering."

"I thought this entire job was information gathering," I questioned.

"It is," he confirmed, nodding.

Texas showed us the devices that he and Knix would be using, basically headphones with mouth pieces. They would be in security, so they wouldn't look out of place sitting in front of cameras all night. I wondered how they were able to get such a convenient position. Bellamy's piece resembled Marv's and mine, I noticed as I watched him adjust it in his ear.

Knix, Bellamy, and Texas left first in the SUV; Bellamy had to help set up, and Knix and Texas needed to be in the security room before people started arriving. Marv and I were left standing in the patio on the bottom floor of the complex they lived in. As I shifted in the heels I wore, my stomach rumbled and Marv looked down.

"Hungry?" He smirked. I rubbed both hands over my

stomach, and shrugged. "They should have food there, but come on." Marv reached for my hand, tugging me to the BMW on the other side of the lot. "We can at least grab a cup of coffee and a snack before we do some spying."

"I thought spies were supposed to be quiet about being spies?"

"We're not spies," he corrected. "We're just acting like them for the night."

"For the entire job," I reminded him. He harrumphed and opened the car door for me. southern gentlemen were something else.

Marv drove us towards downtown, but detoured to a small café several blocks away from our intended destination. He parallel parked between a flashy convertible and a light-blue truck before striding around the front of the car to help me out. I held his hand as we walked down the cobblestone street towards Kat's Café. My heels were tall enough and the road uneven enough that I almost tripped more than a few times. He grinned the entire time, wrapping one arm around my waist to help steady me while I held onto the other.

"I promise, I'll be more coordinated than this when we get to the hotel," I said when we finally made it to the Café's front door. He chuckled, opened the door, and ushered me in.

The café smelled like coffee: hazelnut and vanilla bean. At the diner, Joanna burned the coffee more than she didn't and the smell never really went away. The barista at the counter was a young girl with pink streaks through her hair. She smiled brightly as we entered and welcomed us. I stood behind Marv while he ordered a dark roast coffee for himself and some sort of frappé for me. I looked up at him as the barista told him the price and then asked for our names to put on the cups. Once she stepped away to make them, he ushered me towards a nearby table.

"I figured you might like frappés. They're usually sweeter than what I like though." Marv slid a seat out for me.

"I'm not much of a coffee drinker. I've only ever had it at Alex's Diner," I admitted.

His eyes widened in horror. "Don't get me wrong," he began. "Alex is an awesome guy, but the coffee at the diner is only decent with pie or something sweet."

"But you just got a dark roast. Aren't those bitter? How can you like bitter and sweet together?"

He shook his head. "The dark roasts are dry and lighter roasts have more caffeine. If I drink that right now, I'll be up all night." He grinned. "As for bitterness and sweetness, well, I say they are the perfect combination. They complement each other, balance each other out."

His mention of staying up late reminded me of my mom. I usually had to leave her home alone when I was working and going to school, but now that I was out with Marv and, for the most part, just hanging out with the guys, I felt guilty. My eyes slid to the tabletop and I fidgeted with the edge.

"What's wrong?"

I shook my head, and pressed my hands together, clasping and unclasping them on the wood. "Nothing, just nervous about tonight, I guess."

"There's nothing to be worried about." Marv reached across the table to still my hands. "We're just two people going to a party. Sure, it's a fancy-shmancy party and those aren't nearly as fun as regular parties, but this one is special."

"Because we're trying to find out who's stealing people's stuff?" I asked.

"Nope." Marv grinned down at me. "Because it's a date with you."

My mouth dropped open. Did he think this was a real date? Before I could ask, the barista called our names, and presented our drinks at the counter. Marv stood to retrieve them. No, he couldn't mean that this was a date-date. He was a nice guy, he was sweet to me. Protective. From what I knew of him so far though, that was just his personality. The guys had said something about him having a little sister. A lot of big brothers were very protective. *Not Michael*, a piece of me jabbed. I dug my nails into my palm and smiled brightly when Marv returned, taking my cup and chugging half its contents before I felt comfortable enough to look at him again.

Marv took his time drinking his coffee, and I plucked at the small cookie he bought me, trying to buy time until we had to be at the hotel. When it was five minutes after ten – Marv assured me that arriving early to such a function wasn't the norm – we picked up our mess and deposited it in the trash on our way out.

The BMW sped through the streets of downtown until we arrived at the front doors of the DeLuca Charleston Hotel. A valet, dressed in a red vest with a gold embellished "DeLuca" on the left side of his chest, hurried up to meet us. He opened my door first and reached in to help me out as Marv came around the front of the car straightening his suit jacket.

He tossed the keys at the valet, who fumbled before catching them. "Don't have too much fun." He laughed, taking my hand.

Inside the double entry paneled doorway that led into the lobby, bright glittering chandeliers hung from the arched ceiling. Red chairs were aesthetic accents to the hotel's color scheme and intentionally placed for guests to rest at will. Columns sprouted from the glassy floor to the ceiling, making me feel like we were entering a throne room. A smiling, elderly woman dressed in a deep burgundy pant suit, matching the chairs and the valet's vest, greeted us and gave us directions to the ballroom. I practically leeched myself to Marv's arm as he smiled at the woman and thanked her before leading me down the long hallway. At least it was much easier to walk indoors.

"You okay?" Marv's quiet question was accompanied by a squeeze of my hand. I nodded.

Another set of double doors opened into a grand ballroom alive with people in similar dress: men in suits, and women in cocktail dresses of various colors. I relaxed a bit when I spotted kids here and there, running across the room from one parent to another, or towards a long, elegantly draped table stacked with snacks and a tower of champagne beverages. Waiters milled around with round trays in their hands, offering more drinks or caviar, watching and waiting to be needed.

"Marvin!" A booming voice startled me. An oversized man in a straining black suit, with an equally straining plaid bowtie, waddled across the ballroom floor past several couples dancing to a quartet in the corner. "Good to see you, my boy!"

"Good evening, Mr. Daschund," Marv said. I couldn't restrain my reaction, and my eyes bulged from their sockets. Daschund? I thought. Like the dog?

"Will you be going to our retreat with your lady friend here?" Mr. Daschund smiled brightly up at me. I wasn't tall, but he was much shorter than the average man. Marv's hand came around my waist, pulling me into his side. My hand fell across his chest to stay upright.

"This is my girlfriend, Harley." Marv's eyes flashed as he turned his head towards me. The lie slipped from his lips easily, and I understood. If anyone knew who I really was, they might assume I was one of those women that hung on the arm of the rich for handouts. I gave him a slight nod before turning to Mr. Daschund.

"It's a pleasure to meet you, Mr. Daschund." I held out my hand and the man took it, kissing the back in a surprisingly grand gesture. I didn't know men did that anymore. I had just expected him to shake it.

"Lovely to make your acquaintance, and please, call me Stephen." He turned back to Marv. "Will you be stepping in for your parents then?"

"Yes." Marv's jaw tightened as he glanced over Mr. Daschund's head, but as I peered over in the same direction, his hip butted me, and he frowned before continuing to speak. "They send their regards. Unfortunately, they are both quite busy this time of year."

Mr. Daschund nodded enthusiastically. "Yes, yes. I quite understand. Well, we're happy to have you here. Why don't you and your young lady have a dance?"

"I think that's a splendid idea, Mr. Daschund," Marv said. "If you'll excuse us."

As we walked, Marv leaned down to my ear. "You're doing good."

"You could have told me about the name change in advance," I whispered back.

"You need to know how to handle unexpected changes under pressure," he replied. "I kept it somewhat close."

Suddenly, his head jerked up and his eyes narrowed. I didn't have a moment to look towards where he was staring because with my hand in his, Marv marched to the middle of the dance floor and spun me on my heels to face him. He clasped my palm and his other hand moved to the small of my back. I didn't know how to dance; my eyes lingered on the tips of my high-heels, making sure that I didn't step on his toes as he hauled me around the dance floor with the other couples. Every once in a while I peeked up at him, and his jaw remained hardened as if he were angry.

"What's wrong?" I asked.

"Your friend is here." The bite in his tone confused me. I twisted my head. "Don't look," he hissed. "Don't make it obvious."

"Who?"

"Caruso," he said through gritted teeth.

"Grayson is here?" No, he couldn't be. It was even more difficult, knowing that's who he had spotted, to not glance around to try and find him.

"Yes."

"Are you sure it's him?" I demanded. "Maybe it's someone else."

He looked down at me. "Did you tell him where you would be tonight?"

I blinked, shocked. "How could I?" I snapped. "I didn't even know yet."

Marv glared down at me, his gray eyes flashing with confusion and anger. I raised my chin and hoped that I didn't trip in the midst of this stare-off. Finally, he sighed and broke my gaze.

"Sorry, I didn't mean to accuse you."

Something squawked in my ear and I jumped, almost head-butting Marv in the chin. Texas' smooth voice came through the ear device that I had almost forgotten about.

"What's going on?"

I looked across the grand ballroom as though I could see him through the walls. Before I could open my mouth though, Marv nudged my face back to his.

"If you're going to talk to them, look at me," he advised. "Make it look like you're talking to me and not to some creeper in the basement listening in." He smiled.

"I'm in the fucking security room, asshole!" Texas snapped. "Oh, wait. He can't hear me. Tell him he's an asshole, Harlow." His voice grew slightly muffled as he spoke to someone else – likely Knix. "No. I will not stop being childish. Marv called me a creeper. If I'm a creeper, you're a creeper."

I grinned. "Texas wants me to tell you–" Marv pressed a finger to my lips, his eyes squinting in amusement.

"–fine!" Texas' tone cleared. "You still there, Harlow?"

"Yup."

"Okay, so we've got a list of guests here. We need you and Marv to check out and talk to a few of the couples who have been to this resort and haven't been targeted. Then you can check out the family members of the board members of Sweratt Inc."

"Is Caruso on the list?" Marv asked. I looked up at him, biting my lip. Would they be angry too?

"What the fuck?!" Texas' curse made me flinch. He was completely different on the job than he had been on his own, or maybe he was coming out of his shell now that he felt I was more a part of their team rather than someone they just hung out with. "Who is this kid? Hold on, Harlow, Knix wants you."

I listened to the sound of a speaker of some sort on the other end being moved. I heard the intake of breath as a new person took over my direct line. Before Knix could speak though, I gritted my teeth and snapped back.

"I did not invite him or tell him where I would be."

There was a pause, a brief moment of breathing. "Good to know. Look to your left and you'll see Bellamy. Do so very slowly as though you're just checking out the room around you. Actually–" His voice quieted, becoming slightly farther away as he spoke to someone else. "Tell Marv to spin her."

Seconds later, Marv twirled me and I scanned the room while still trying to keep my footing. Broad shoulders in a black dress shirt and pair of slacks matching the rest of the waiters caught my eye.

"In a few minutes, Marv is going to take you over to greet a few people closer to the windows on the far-left side of the ballroom. When he does, Bellamy is going to stop you and offer you a drink. Take it. The glass he offers you has a small bug in the stem. I want you to place it on the table next to the group as close as you can without being conspicuous. Can you do that?"

I started to nod before I stopped myself. I guessed he had cameras watching, otherwise he wouldn't know where to send me. "Yes," I answered.

"Good." My heart pounded. "And Caruso would have been here whether or not you had agreed," he said. "His father is one of the Sweratt's executive directors."

Marv led me off the dance floor as the song ended and we made our way across the ballroom towards a group of three people, all older than forty. A shadow crossed the corner of my eye and I turned as Bellamy pulled up next to us.

"Can I offer you a drink, Ma'am?" He held his tray out with one hand and I grinned. His balancing skill was astronomical. He turned the tray with his opposite hand, nodding toward the glass on the edge.

"Thank you." I picked it up. He nodded once to me before sharing a look with Marv that would have taken me much longer than it lasted to unpack.

"Olivia!" Marv called out as we neared the group. A tall, thin, blonde woman turned towards us.

"Marvin?" The tone of her voice was tight and nasally. "How lovely to see you!" Her lips stretched across her face. She took one look at me and the smile dipped into a grimace. "Who do we have here?"

"This is my girlfriend, Harley." Marv introduced me with a wave of his hand before asking about the woman's business and her sons. She shot irritated glances at me throughout the entire conversation for reasons I could not understand. After several minutes of monotonous dialogue where Marv introduced me to Olivia's associates, and they tipped their noses at me, only nodding my way in acknowledgement, I was ready to go.

"Alright, well, we've taken up too much of your time, Olivia. It really was good to see you. I think Harley and I will make the rounds before heading out."

As we turned, my heels caught on the floor and I stumbled. Marv's hands grasped me around the shoulders and my free hand went out to catch the table nearby. I set the glass down a bit harder than I meant to. But Olivia was so focused on my misstep, smirking and whispering to her friends that she wasn't paying attention to the glass that I left behind. I almost hoped the boys caught her doing or saying something she shouldn't. I had the feeling she wasn't a very nice lady.

"Are you okay?" Marv asked.

"Perfectly fine." I smiled, feeling accomplished. "Let's go make those rounds. I'm ready to get out of here."

No matter how ready I was to go home and crawl into bed, Knix had us drop two more glasses around the room where certain groups were congregating. I pushed back more than a few yawns as it grew closer and closer to midnight. We were standing near one of the windows arching over the left side of the ballroom, Marv rubbing the middle of my back, and I was attempting not to fall asleep right there in his arms – rich people parties were quite boring – when a familiar sounding voice barked out a laugh to our right.

"I would have never guessed it!" Golden locks brushed the back of his neck and his smile was the sincerest one of his little posse. He looked so familiar. Blue eyes. Tan skin. Where had I seen him before?

My eyes settled on Grayson, standing just to his side and I realized that I had never met this boy before. Grayson looked strangely odd dressed up, but not in a way that detracted from his handsome features. The top button of his dress shirt was undone and he wore no tie. The boy at his side was obviously related to him, probably closely – *a brother?* I thought. Standing side by side, they could have been twins. The other boy, however, was just a smidge shorter, with hips more slender and narrow than Grayson's. His face was rounder as well, his chin dimpled. Grayson watched him with a hint of boredom.

"Josh," Grayson muttered, pulling the other boy closer. "I think you've had enough. It's time to leave."

"Nonsense!" Josh said, slinging Grayson's arm away. "We're just getting started." Josh moved away from Grayson and slung an arm around a younger girl with plump, rosy cheeks. "I think we should head to one of the clubs after this. Go have us a real party, get some fun in before the night's over!"

"That's his older brother," Marv whispered, confirming my suspicions. "Joshua Caruso. Twenty-five, lives off of his father's money. The parents split two years ago. Grayson lives with the mother." It seemed likely that Knix had ordered Texas to look up all sorts of information about Grayson and while a part of me felt a little bad that they all thought Grayson was not to be trusted, I was actually grateful for the information. I wanted to know more. Like why was Grayson babysitting his older brother at his father's company function?

Marv tilted his head in the other direction and I suspected either Knix or Texas was telling him something. He slowly straightened and moved around me as though to block me from view, nudging me towards the doorway.

"Time to go," he said.

"What's going on?" Did Grayson spot us? Did someone start checking out the glasses we had been placing all over the ballroom? Were we in trouble? My mind raced with all of the horrible things that could have gone wrong. I was sure I had messed up somewhere. I thought I had been so clever, but maybe I was just foolish. My ego took a dive and my heart beat an impatient rhythm to know what I had done.

"Nothing," Marv said. "We're just done. I'm tired. You're tired. Let's go get some sleep and regroup tomorrow."

I could have pummeled him. That was it? He had put on that serious face and I let my thoughts jump to all sorts of confusion because of it. I imagined that Knix had told him we had done enough, and the moment he had been given the go ahead, he was rushing me out. I huffed in irritation as he led me out into the hallway and back towards the lobby. The same valet waited just outside in the hot summer air, a bead of sweat trickling down the side of his neck.

"Give me just a few moments, sir." He smiled, revealing a row of slightly crooked teeth. It made him appear younger and rather charming. "I'll be right back with your vehicle." Marv nodded, and the young man strode away.

Cars drove past the front of the hotel and couples walked by, hand in hand. The lights from the buildings blocked out the stars and no matter how hard I squinted at the sky, I couldn't see them. Marv bumped my elbow with his.

"What did you think?"

"About what?" My hand dropped to sift through the layers of fabric around my thighs.

"The party?"

"It was..." How did I put it nicely? "Intense," I finally decided on. "Not really what I expected."

"What did you expect?" Marv leaned against the side of the building, crossing his arms over his chest with an interested smile.

"I don't really know," I admitted. "But it's not really my scene. I felt..."

"Different?" he supplied as I trailed off. I blushed, looking at the ground. He wasn't wrong. "Yea, I get that. I'm not really a fan of the parties myself. You did a good job tonight, though, with the job."

I lurched, my head rising, my eyes glancing around. "Are we supposed to talk about that out here?"

He shrugged. "No one's around."

Lights flashed and Marv's dark BMW stopped in front of us. The young man stepped out of the vehicle and made his way around to open the door for me. I smiled and thanked him as Marv handed him a bill that made his eyes widen.

I was so tired that by the time we got back on the interstate to head home, I found myself fading. Marv left the radio off and the soft thrum of the car over pavement lulled me. The car glided so soft and smoothly, it felt as though we were floating. My eyes slipped closed, only bits of light from other cars and highway lamps filtering through.

What felt like only moments later, a car door was quietly shut as Marv got out. I groaned and stretched, curling my toes into the soft floor mats of the BMW – my heels had fallen off sometime while I slept. The passenger side door opened and I blinked up as Marv reached across me and unbuckled my seat belt.

"I can do it," I slurred.

"I know, Sunshine." As he leaned back, Marv's cheek brushed mine and his lips pressed to the corner of my mouth. "Let's get you inside." Marv helped me out of the car and I realized that we weren't at the guys' place. We were in my neighborhood, with the darkened windows and the smell of the trash rolling to the end of the driveways, up and down the streets, lingering in the air. Disappointment crawled up my throat, quickly followed by guilt. I looked down at my dress and realized Marv's suit jacket had slid to the ground. I bent to retrieve it. He must have put it on me after I fell asleep. Marv leaned over again, purposefully kissing my cheek this time. "I'll see you in a bit," he said. "Get inside."

I nodded and reluctantly climbed the front steps to my side of the duplex. I opened the door and slipped inside. I didn't bother to peek out the window and watch him drive away. I didn't want to see it.

The house was dark and smelled musty, as though no

one had been home for a while. I started to wonder if it had always smelled that way. I snuck to my mom's bedroom door, hearing her light snores. I peeked in through the crack and noticed that fresh water sat on her bedside and a new snack had been placed there as well. I felt thankful and ashamed. I hadn't even thought of her for hours. I didn't worry when I was with the boys, and not worrying felt wrong somehow.

When I stepped inside my room, wind whistled in through the opened bedroom window and I stopped in startled confusion when Marv stood there, slowly pulling his tie from around his neck and unbuttoning his expensive dress shirt.

"What…"

"Shh." He pressed a finger to his lips before winking. "I'm pretty tired myself and we've established that your bed can hold two. Mind if I stay the night again?" His shirt was already halfway unbuttoned. I nodded and watched as he pulled the shirt out of his pants and laid it across my rickety, old chair. When he began to undo his belt, I whirled in panic, remembering that I hadn't closed my door and quickly closed it. I heard sheets shift behind me, and I took a deep breath before crossing the room to grab a ratty t-shirt and a pair of boy shorts. I peered out into the hall before escaping my room to change in the bathroom, and finally, I took out my hearing device before ducking back into the bedroom minutes later. I hung my dress on the back of my closet door as Marv fiddled with his phone, texting. I lifted the covers, and crawled in next to him.

"Here's yours," he said absentmindedly, handing me my phone. "I kept it while we were at the party."

"Thanks." I took the phone, staring at the blank screen. After getting dressed at the guys' apartment, I'd left it lying on the bathroom counter, and had forgotten about it completely. I was glad he hadn't. I checked the messages.

Knix: Tomorrow we continue training.

Bellamy:I'm sorry I yelled at you earlier. You did great tonight.

Texas: Impressive. See you tomorrow.

I was torn between wanting to sigh, grimace, or grin. Knix's text left me feeling tired all over again. Bellamy's reminded me of that kiss, and I didn't know how to take it. Texas', at least, made me feel like smiling. It wasn't serious for a change.

I handed the phone back to Marv, asking him to put it on the charger. We settled into bed, his front to my back, the heat from his skin seeping into me through my clothes. Somehow even with the hot, southern, summer air filtering in through the window, and Marv the furnace smelling like dark coffee, I was comfortable.

CHAPTER 15

The air in the room was heavy with heat, sunlight pouring in, filling every crevice in the space with its blistering temperature. The sheets were thrown from my body and I lay, awkwardly, half on the bed, half off, with my left hand and foot grazing the floor. I groaned, rolling over to face the ceiling, the muscles in my legs and back cracking with every movement. It was then that I realized that I was alone in bed.

Sitting up, I scanned the room. His clothes were gone, except for his jacket that was slung over the back of the chair stationed in the corner of my bedroom. The window was shut, though the blinds were still pulled up. If he left the way he came, it would have been difficult for him to lower them on the other side, but at least he had closed the window. During the night, I hadn't minded the warm air so much. Now, I could practically feel myself baking.

I leapt from the bed and hurried over to lower the blinds. Though the room dimmed, it did so only marginally. To me, the room looked used. Not lived-in-used, but tired, chipped chair in the corner, sagging mattress – I didn't know how Marv had stood to sleep on it when I was sure he had a much nicer bed at home – and even the old leaning dresser, with more scars than any functional dresser should have. There was still a small heart in the lower portion of the front left leg that I had carved when I was twelve.

I sighed, reaching up to pull my hair away from my neck and twist it up into a bun to let my skin breathe. As was becoming habit, I went through my phone and let my thoughts consume me. Time: 9:43 am. When had Marv left? It felt weird not being in school. I hadn't replied to any of the messages from last night, but there was a new one from Knix.

KNIX: PICK YOU UP AT 11.

I SIGHED AND PUT THE PHONE DOWN BEFORE STRETCHING again, popping even more tired muscles. The house hadn't been thoroughly cleaned since before I got the job at Alex's Diner and it was in sore neglect. I began by picking up my room, throwing dirty clothes into the washer, and then the dryer. Hunting through the house, I listened to the soft movements of our neighbors on the other side of the wall. They were loudest in the hallway right outside of my mom's bedroom door and I hoped they wouldn't wake her. She was finally sleeping peacefully.

It was odd not being around the guys. As I swept and mopped, there was a sense of disconnect inside of me, like I was back in my life before I met the boys. Every time I worried that they might have just been a really sweet dream, I rushed back to my bedroom to hold my phone before sliding it between my mattress and box spring along with its charger. I was determined to keep it hidden in case my mom got up and came snooping around.

I checked the old, mini-cereal box for the extra cash I had stored, noting that it was still almost full. I would have to ask one of the guys if they could take me to set up a bank account. A couple hundred dollars wasn't much, but now that rent was a relieved burden – at least temporarily, thanks to a very generous Marv – I could start saving. For what, I didn't know. It was strange having extra. I'd never had that before. If I hadn't gone to the party with Marv the night before, it would have felt too much like charity, but as it was, I felt closer to them, a part of their team, like I was really working for something bigger than money to live.

"Harlow?" My mom's voice came from behind me as I straightened the living room and I turned to greet her.

Her nightgown was pale and thin in many places. There were splotches of purple on the back of her right hand as she held it to her throat, overshadowing the age spots beneath. Her thin gray hair was left loose around her face, falling over one side as her dazed eyes bounced around the room before landing on me.

"Hey, Mom, how are you feeling?" I finished throwing some old newspapers from the coffee table into the trash as I faced her. "Can I get you something to eat?"

"Yes… I think that would be nice…" she said. She trailed after me as I strode to the kitchen and flicked on the florescent bulbs overhead. They heated and buzzed as I searched the fridge for something suitable. Spotting a few old, leftover containers from the week before, I decided to pour them out and see if there was soup in the cabinet. I sifted old chunks of meat and vegetables into the garbage disposal. One flick to turn it on and I realized my mistake. I quickly turned it off when the grinding sound hit my ears – still broken from the destruction of my last phone. "What's wrong with the disposal?"

I turned my head, my eyes wide. Did she not remember? "Um…" I finished throwing the leftovers away by hand before washing up. "It's broken," I hedged.

"Hmm," she replied, sitting at the dilapidated kitchen table. "Well, this house is old. Most things are bound to break every now and then." I didn't say anything as I opened a can of chicken noodle soup and heated it in the microwave. When I retrieved it the time flashed, 10:35. Knix would be here soon. I wasn't even dressed yet. I placed the bowl in front of my mom, and kissed her head before rushing to my room to clean up and dress. I returned in another pair of jean shorts and a t-shirt that covered my butt pockets where I had placed my phone.

"Why aren't you in school?" She ladled soup into her mouth, watching me with curiosity.

"Um…it's a half day for seniors," I lied, wiping down the counter. "A friend's coming by to take me around 11 am." The idea came to me when I realized that she would be curious as to why I was going to school so late in the day and why the bus wouldn't be picking me up. She didn't seem to care, and just continued to sip her soup.

The seconds crawled by in awkward silence. We were two people who lived together, but we so rarely saw each other that it was difficult to make small talk. She left the house only for doctor's appointments and emergencies. What was there for us to talk about aside from her illness? She seemed to be doing so well now that I didn't want to remind her.

"I've been thinking," Mom started, drawing my attention. "This house is getting a bit older and things are breaking down." She slid a glance at the disposal. "Maybe it's time to move on."

"Move on?"

"Yes…I've got some savings and with my disability check maybe I can get into a nursing home or just resign myself to staying in a hospital." She finished the rest of her soup and pushed it away. I retrieved it and rinsed it in the sink, thinking.

"Mom, I don't know if we could afford that, even with your savings." Her feet on the linoleum of the kitchen floor were quiet as she stood from the table behind me.

"Baby." She sniffled and I slowly turned to face her. Her eyes glistened. "I know, and you know, I'm not going to get any better. This will be the best thing for you."

It became clear. "You've already started something," I said. I was surprised.

She nodded. "When I went to the doctor last, I talked to him and he agreed. I should probably have 24/7 care, he says."

I knew she was right. I had known for a while, but I wanted to be that 24/7 care for her. I didn't want some nurse who didn't know her, didn't care about her. I couldn't stomach the image of her lying in hospital beds for the rest of her life. My throat rebelled. I was incapable of a response. I couldn't be here for her. Even if I stopped going with the guys, I would have to pick back up at work, perhaps a second job to compensate for all I had missed in the last week or so. My hands shook and I sank into the chair across from her vacated one.

"I know you worry, Sweetheart." Her cold fingers brushed the side of my face, trailing from my temple to my chin as she flipped her hand over and rubbed the back of it against my cheek. She was so thin her fingers were nothing but skin and bone. "But you'll be able to move out of here. Maybe go to college."

I was shaking so hard, my whole body panicked at the idea of losing her. If she went into a hospital, that was it, I thought. She wouldn't come out alive. My throat expanded until words weren't the only thing that couldn't pass through. I couldn't breathe. I held myself still, trying to inhale through my nose, but it wasn't working. She was still talking, her mouth moving. It was the first time in a long time that I had seen her so animated, and I couldn't hear a damn word. The phone in my back pocket vibrated; probably Knix telling me he was here. Mom's hand touched mine and I stared at the purple splotch of color against her paleness. It was another bruise. They had been the first sign of her illness.

"It'll be okay, Baby. It's gonna work out, you'll see." She kissed my forehead. "I'm tired, so I'll go lay down for a nap." She shuffled forward, heading towards the living room. "I'll see you when you get home, Baby. I love you."

"I love you too..." I heard myself say as she disappeared around the corner. The phone buzzed again, but I was too numb to feel it. My arms tingled and I could feel my face turning cold. I still wasn't breathing. How many seconds had gone by since I had stopped? It felt like hours.

I opened my mouth and a squeak escaped as I tried to force my lungs to take in air. Cool oxygen rushed in and my vision blurred. The table was hard and cool on my skin as I leaned down and pressed my forehead to the rough surface. Hospital rooms. Nursing homes. *Inhale.* IVs. Hospital gowns. Medical bills. *Exhale.* The smell of disinfectant. Phone calls from nurses. Funeral homes. *Don't throw up.*

Even when my phone vibrated with impatience a third time, I didn't retrieve it. I didn't look at the messages. I just stood up and put one foot in front of the other until I was in the front hall. I stepped out onto the hot sidewalk, seeing the big, black SUV waiting just a little down the road when I realized I wasn't wearing shoes. I went back inside and stared at the laces of my sneakers for several moments before slipping into flip flops.

Knix met me at the front of the SUV, walking around to open my door. I got in the car and blinked at the windshield. He said something and I nodded in acknowledgement, though I didn't actually hear a word. He closed the door and quickly got in on the driver's side.

"Little Bit?" I frowned. Knix sounded farther away than I expected. I swiveled my head. No, he was right next to me. Was I still breathing? Yes. Why did it feel like the SUV was caving in on me? Like my chest was squeezing in enough oxygen to keep me upright and conscious, but every other piece of me, body and soul, was sucked dry of life. My heart beat slow, sluggish, almost nonexistent. I drifted. "–low? Harlow?!"

I blinked when Knix's hands gripped my shoulders. He had pulled over to the side of the road, his face covered in concern. He shook me slightly, staring at me with wide, panicked eyes. "Harlow, what's wrong?"

My shoulders shook. My heart rate picked up. Every bird, every car that passed, every slight wind was too much, too loud. My hands trembled as I grabbed onto his arms, holding on as though I might tumble away. I opened my mouth to tell him, but a sob poured from my chest and then another and another. My cheeks were soaked in my horrible realizations and everything that made life so unbearably cruel.

"Little Bit." Knix hauled me across the seat into his lap. His massive hand stroked my hair as I sobbed against his chest, the sounds shaking me so hard, and he just held me close.

"It isn't fair!" I screamed. "It's not fair!" The stain of tears on his shirt grew bigger and bigger the longer he held me, but he didn't flinch. Knix crushed me to his chest, his cheek on my head, his breath stirring through my hair. It hurt less that way. I didn't feel so alone.

"COME ON, LIE HERE." KNIX LED ME INTO A ROOM THAT smelled like sandalwood. The floor shined beneath the dark-burgundy throw carpet. There was a double bed shoved against the wall between a table littered with tools and a nightstand. I sat on the bed instead of lying down. If I laid down, it would be too hard to get back up.

Knix pulled a folding chair from his closet, placed it a foot or so from the bed and sat directly in front of me, his hands reaching for mine. His fingers engulfed mine, his thumbs rubbing along my knuckles to soothe me. My eyes found the floor and stayed there. I was embarrassed by how hard I had cried in the car. It was only when I had finally gotten over the worst of it that he had set me in my seat, buckled me in, and drove to the complex.

"Little Bit..." I shivered under his gaze, flicking up across his face only to search out the details of his room instead. The walls were bare other than a few architectural designs tacked in different places, blueprints as well. His closet had a sliding mirror and I skipped over the horror of how I looked. Puffy splotches of red marks on my cheeks and eyes swollen from the tears. I sniffed hard and took my hands from Knix to press them to my face.

I covered my eyes. "I'm sorry," I said through my fingers.

"For what, Little Bit?" Knix's warm hands came to my cheeks, drawing my hands away. The scent of sandalwood was on him too, all over him.

"For…you know." I kept my eyes closed.

His breath fanned across my face. "There's nothing to be sorry about." Warm lips pressed to my forehead, surprising me. My eyes popped open. His chin lingered in front of my eyes as he kept his lips pressed to my skin for a few moments more. "Tell me what happened."

The command in his tone was gentle, but no less authoritative. Powerful. I found my lips opening and words spilling forth. "My mom's dying," I said, pausing for his reaction. He drew away from me, his blue eyes finding mine and holding. I continued. "She wants to move out of the duplex and go stay in a nursing home or at the hospital. Apparently, her last visit to the doctors didn't go well. She thinks it will be pointless to stay when she thinks she's going to end up there anyway." I looked at him, begging him to help me, to guide me. I needed someone to tell me what to do, how to handle this. Would we be able to afford it? Would I be able to cope?

Knix took a breath. His fingers brushed aside a lock of hair that had fallen across my face. "What worries you?"

"I-I," I stammered. "She's really sick. A tumor, and she

has um…some other problems." Bipolar disorder wasn't life threatening. I stumbled through an explanation of her trips to the doctor's, and the medications, and her mood swings. When I had nothing more to offer, he sighed and stood, scooting me over on the bed to sit next to me rather than in front of me. He leaned against the wall and pulled me to sit between his legs, my back to his front.

"You're scared," he said. "She's the only family you have and she's all you know."

"I have Michael," I reminded him. "My brother."

"Ah, but you never really see him. When was the last time you two talked?"

"Just before I met you."

He nodded, expectant. "And when was the last time you saw him in person?"

"Not since he moved out," I admitted. "We've been alone since then."

"You are not alone, Little Bit." His lips pressed to my temple. "If she needs to be taken care of, we will see to it."

I broke his hold and turned. "What do you mean?"

His blue eyes glittered. "If doctors can't help her, then we will make sure that she is comfortable."

"But…" They didn't know her, had never even met her. "Why?"

"Because she's your family." His fingers touched my neck, trailing down to settle on my shoulder. "And you are family to us – or we hope you will be."

I closed my eyes, my face tilting up, and my body angled to the side to rest against him. "I-I'm scared." I didn't want to admit it, but it felt safe there, in his arms. "I'm scared that once she goes to the hospital, she won't come back. Not alive."

Knix's nose nudged mine, urging me to open my eyes. I did. "Not everyone can get better, but we'll make sure that she has the best care, comfort, whatever she needs. I know how you feel, Little Bit." The rasp in his voice, the broken way some of his words ended, sliced me right to my core.

"Who did you lose?" I asked.

"My father was a strong man," he said. "He built a lot of houses from the ground up. He drew some of these…" He gestured to the walls, leaning back and cuddling me closer as though needing his own blanket of protection against the memories. "He passed away a few years ago. Heart attack. Left me everything he had, but I would give it all up just for one more day with him."

Tears slid down my face. "Your mom?"

"She and I don't speak. They split when I was in high school and she used to hold me over his head. I never wanted to be his guillotine. I tried to please her, make her happy so he wouldn't be miserable." He smiled, but it was filled with bitterness. "You can't make everyone happy. It wasn't until I was eighteen that I realized I could have chosen to live with him the entire time and we both could have cut her out of our lives."

"You would have wanted that?" I asked.

"Some women are born maternal," he replied. "Some grow into it, but she never did. She was angry, bitter, jealous, and paranoid. She was the woman who gave birth to me, nothing more. If it made my father happy, I would have cut her out of my life and pretended she never existed."

The more he spoke, the more his eyes shined. His face was stark, cold against the thoughts of the woman who must have hurt him much deeper than any other because she was his mother – his blood. I cried for him. I cried for my mom.

"I'm sorry," I whispered. The hard edges of his expression softened as he looked back down at me.

"I told you, Little Bit." His eyes grazed along my cheek. "There is nothing to be sorry for."

Those blue endless pools stopped, frozen in time, and he leaned forward. I backed up, confused, worried. What was wrong? His hand landed softly on the back of my head, halting my retreat. He paused for a moment, but when I didn't protest – I didn't even think to – then his lips were on mine. Brushing over them. His kiss was soft, gentle. So unlike how he appeared in stasis – an unrelenting mountain. Now, he moved with me, trailing his fingers through my hair, turning me to face him completely, and bringing me closer until my breasts were crushed against his chest. My hands crept up to his shoulders, his mouth opened and mine followed. My heart raced in my chest, beating rhythmically, speeding up my breath. My eyes slid closed when his kiss became all consuming.

"Harlow," he whispered, drawing back for an instant. "Harlow." He pressed his lips to mine once more. I breathed in the scent of sandalwood and gasped when his teeth tugged at my lower lip. How was this happening? It took what seemed an eternity for my mind to catch up with my body, but by then Knix was distracting me with something new. His hands lowered to the middle of my back, and he groaned. His tongue slid into my mouth. I reciprocated.

It was like a game of tug of war. When I retreated, he advanced, but then he would pull back and I would follow, clinging to the sensations that he created as they washed over my skin. I needed him to keep going. I needed him like I needed to breathe. His shoulders were hard, encased in muscle and when he lifted me up to straddle his lap, I sat back on his knees, feeling something poke my stomach. The sensation was immediately lost when he kissed me again.

Heat speared through me and I tugged on his shirt, sliding my hands beneath the fabric to feel his hard chest underneath. When he flicked his tongue across mine, my nails sank into his skin and he groaned. My head was a whirlwind, a fog of lust. Not wanting to stop kissing him long enough to yank his shirt up, I let go and my hands traveled up, my fingers sliding through his hair. The sandy blond strands stuck to my palms and I smoothed it back to look at his face when I finally pulled away. Our chests rose and fell, each of us breathing hard. I gulped as I gazed at him. His eyes were wide, stunned. I had never seen him so dazed. He always appeared in total control. Now, with his cheeks flushed and his skin warm to the touch, his lips full, he seemed wilder. Unabashed. Beautiful.

Just as beautiful as Bellamy.

I staggered away, nearly throwing myself off the bed with that thought. My butt landed awkwardly on the carpeted rug. He sucked in a breath and stood up, reaching down to help me. I just kissed Knix. I had kissed Bellamy. What was I doing?

"It's going to be okay, Little Bit." Knix reassured me, taking my flustered panic for fear. He leaned down to kiss my forehead again. Perhaps he thought that I was just confused or that I thought he had moved too fast, but he pulled away, giving me space. "I'm going to go make us something to eat. Why don't you sit on the bed and I'll bring it to you."

I watched him go, his hips drawing my attention. I

could have slapped myself. What was I thinking? How did I let that happen? Did this mean he liked me? Did this mean we were dating? No, at the reminder of Bellamy I calmed down a little more. Bellamy hadn't said anything about dating me. One kiss did not a boyfriend make. Otherwise, I would have two boyfriends in the course of less than a week. I sat back down on the bed and sighed. Guys were hard to understand, but I was sure if they really liked me they would have told me. Sometimes guys got heated and when they got heated, they got turned on. It was just a reaction. Bellamy had been angry, Knix had been thinking about his mom, which also made him angry. It didn't mean anything. Right?

CHAPTER 16

When the guys came home – it was odd how much I was beginning to consider their little apartment home – I was sitting on the couch reading the *Perks of Being a Wallflower*, with Cleo purring in my lap. I had been excused from training for the day. Knix had set himself up to draw another set of blueprints for a separate property and was working at the small kitchenette's table. He immediately got up and pulled Marv aside, as the guys piled in through the front door.

Texas and Bellamy's eyes lit up when they saw me, turning my insides to mush. While Bellamy hung back, Texas bulldozed right over and crash landed on the couch over my lap and Cleo. She hissed and batted at his face. He just leaned down and kissed her furry little head. I was glad that Texas seemed to have gotten over his shyness with me. Before, he had held himself apart as though I were a coworker. Now that the rest of the guys had decided I was alright and in it long term, he was just as friendly. Or maybe he just really liked Cleo.

"Guess what I did today," he urged, tilting his face up to look at me with his soft, brown eyes. A lock of dark hair fell over his forehead and I brushed it back grinning.

"What did you do?" I asked.

He shook his head. "Nuh uh. You have to guess."

"Hmmm," I hummed, glancing over him for any potential clues. His usual jeans were replaced with khakis and instead of a t-shirt, he wore a much nicer green polo tucked halfway into his pants with a brown belt to top it off. His feet were bare, but I caught the pair of brown suede loafers sitting by the front door. "A job?" I asked.

He blinked in surprise before turning his head to Bellamy. "Did you tattle?"

Bellamy shook his head back and forth quickly, grinning. "Nope. Not a word."

Texas rounded back to me, sitting up on his knees. "Did Knix tell you? Marv?"

"Full guesswork." I smirked.

He huffed, indignant. "Well, that blows. I was looking forward to making you sweat for that."

"Next time don't give it away with your reaction," Bellamy advised as he ambled over to the table, looking over Knix's work.

Texas laid back down in my lap, and sighed. "Well, yea, I got a job," he said. "You're looking at the on call, IT guy for Sw`eratt Inc. Resort and Retreat for the next week. I'm on loan," he paused, raising his hands to put air quotes around the word 'loan'. I giggled. "–from another company that they associate with."

"What company?" I asked, curious.

He grinned, poking my nose. I batted his hand away, but still, I liked how playful he was today. "Goode Construction."

"Huh?" The name wasn't familiar.

"It's Knix's company," Bellamy explained.

"Knix has a company?" Why hadn't I known that? Thinking back, it made sense though; the blueprints, the information about his dad, the guys at the worksite that had followed his directions.

"Yea, he sort of took over his dad's company and then made it his own," Bellamy explained.

"Yup," Texas agreed, "and it's useful in situations such as these. So, I'll be on the island with you and Marv. Knix and Bellamy will likely not be able to make it on. At least not for the first twenty-four hours."

"Why?"

"It's lockdown time. Sort of." Texas scratched Cleo under her chin, earning a rewarding purr and lick. "See, all of these people are business men and women. Their entire lives revolve around work and the first twenty-four hours require them to give up cell phones, laptops, and anything else that can link them to the work world. Their security is actually pretty good, so you and Marv won't have any either."

My eyes widened. What if something bad happened? How would we get in touch with them? Texas caught my eyes and sat up, hugging me to his side reassuringly.

"Don't worry. I'll be right there and unlike the guests, I am there to work. Cell phones are required for me and I'll be giving Marv one when we meet up on the island. You two shouldn't be separated and you won't be without one for more than the time it takes you to get through security to the first dinner."

I relaxed, knowing that my panic was unwarranted. I hadn't relied on a phone until I met these guys. It really wouldn't be so hard to go without one for a few hours. Then again, we were going into a potentially dangerous situation. Suddenly, I was more appreciative of the training Knix had put me through, and I wished we had practiced more again today. I must have still looked concerned because Texas took the arm he slung around my neck and pitched me forward, locking my head into his side. I squirmed and pushed, but the more I did, the harder he chuckled until he was enveloped in a full-blown laugh. His chest vibrated and I could hear his lungs squeezing in air as he held me like that, and I struggled playfully to get away. I poked him in his side and he finally released me, rolling to the floor to escape my flying fist of revenge.

He gripped my wrist and twisted me until I landed on the floor with him hovering over me. He pressed down, his eyes sparkling, lighting a fire within. I gasped, staring up at him. His smile was wide and friendly, filled with amusement. I relaxed, slumping back on the floor, and grinned back at him. A pair of feet, covered in smooth black dress socks stopped just above my head and both Texas and I tilted our necks to look up. Marv stood, feet spread apart, hands on his hips, squinting down at us.

"What are you two doing? Don't we have work to do?"

The groan that rumbled from my chest was echoed by Texas' and we glanced at each other before we broke into another peal of laughter, causing Marv and Bellamy to shake their heads and smile.

Hours later, I was back at the outlets where Marv had bought my first dress, this time with only Texas as my escort. We had been instructed to purchase two daytime outfits and another cocktail dress for the retreat. Marv had to do an errand for Knix, while Bellamy had remained behind to prepare for the coming weekend on Sweratt Island, or so that's what I was calling it. Apparently, the island didn't actually have a name. It was barely a mile long and about two miles wide. It was only large enough for a resort and spa owned by Sweratt Incorporated, a few VIP guest houses, lodging for employees, and not much else.

"So, where are we going first?" Texas flipped a glance up from his phone.

I stopped mid stride. "Um…I thought you knew where we were going?"

"I'm just the ride. I figured you would have a few stores you wanted to try first," he replied, tucking his phone away in his front pocket. "Which stores do you like?"

"I don't know. I don't go shopping all that much, but if you're just my ride, why couldn't I drive myself."

"You can drive?" he raised a brow.

"Sure." I shrugged. "I took Driver's Ed in school." We stood there a moment, glancing around at the different stores until I found one with a name I recognized. "How about that one?" Texas followed my finger and nodded, trudging towards the red and white display windows.

My phone buzzed when we got into the car not long after the store had closed with everything we needed. I was feeling proud of our accomplishment, and more than a little tired as the day had wound down. I slid the phone out of my pocket and answered on the third ring. Texas took the bags from me and stored them in the backseat of the SUV.

"Hello?"

"Harlow?"

"Erika? Hi! How'd you get this number?" I was surprised. This was a new number rather than the first one I gave her. I hadn't had a chance to message her from this one. I also hadn't heard her voice in so long. She sounded different.

"Oh, we gave it to her," Texas whispered. "Just in case." I smiled to let him know I wasn't angry.

"I got it – it doesn't matter," she interrupted herself. "You have to get home now."

"What's wrong?" She sniffled and I realized why she sounded so different, she was crying.

"I just came by to find you. I knocked on the door, but when you didn't answer…" She sniffled again, hard, as if she was holding herself together. Someone started talking to her in the background. "No…I'm on the phone with her now – hold on."

"Erika?" I was growing increasingly nervous. Texas pulled out of the parking lot, throwing glances my way, concern etched into his features.

"Harlow, your mom's hurt. I-I went in. I haven't seen you in a while and I was worried. They're taking her to the hospital now."

"What? How? What happened?" I demanded. Before she could answer though, I ripped the phone away and turned to Texas. "Can you drive me to the hospital?"

His eyes widened. "Which one?"

"Which one?" I barked into the phone.

"Triton Hospital." The tone of Erika's voice shook and I didn't want to think of what had happened. I didn't want her to tell me. I needed to see for myself.

"Okay, I'm on my way. Can you meet me there?"

"She–"

"–don't!" I snapped. I swallowed. "I'm sorry, just… don't tell me. I'll…I'll see you at the hospital." I ended the phone call and turned to stare out the window. All of the calm I had cocooned myself in was gone. Everything

Knix had done to convince me that all would be right with the world, if I let them help me, had dissolved.

"Harlow?" Texas' voice permeated by dazed thoughts. "What did she say?"

"She said that she went to my house because she hadn't seen me in a while and…my mom's hurt."

Texas didn't ask any more questions, but I noted that the speed of the SUV increased, and we flew through the interstate towards Trident Hospital. I closed my eyes and tried counting down from a hundred as slowly as I could manage in order to keep myself from going insane. When I reached -150, I opened my eyes to Texas pulling off the interstate and into the parking lot for the emergency room of the hospital. Erika waited by the entrance. I struggled to command my limbs to move.

"Stay there for a minute," he said, jumping out of the cab and running in Erika's direction. She backed away when he approached, quite obviously startled and confused. I watched as he spoke to her, his hands making small gestures as he explained something and motioned back to the SUV. Erika's eyes followed his hands, but she couldn't see me through the tinted glass of the vehicle. I pulled the lever on the car door and slid out. She visibly relaxed when she realized that I was there with him.

"Harlow!" Erika rushed to me, and threw her arms around my neck. She didn't say anything else. Her arms squeezed me tighter, and she burrowed her face into my hair. It was meant to comfort me, a hug that told me things were bad, very bad. Erika pulled away after a few moments, her eyes glittering with tears she continued to hold at bay.

"Where…" I tried to speak, to ask where my mom was, but my voice failed me.

"I'll show you to her room."

She had a room. She was staying. My insides shriveled and collapsed as Erika held my hand to lead me inside. Texas pulled out his phone. The stoic expression on his face was the last thing I saw before the emergency room doors closed us into the smell of antiseptic, bleach, and illness.

MY MOM'S ROOM WAS ENCLOSED, THE BLINDS DRAWN across the long window stretched across one wall, with the lights turned down in deference to her sleep. Erika stayed with me for a while, both of us taking a seat on the couch against the window as she explained what happened.

My mom had been found passed out in the hallway. My eyes strayed to the gash on her forehead she had incurred on her way down. While her external condition appeared minimal, and she didn't have more than a mild concussion, the doctors had decided to keep her overnight.

The ER doctor, who had been the first to see my mom when she arrived, stopped by to let me know that a new doctor would be in soon to discuss further diagnosis and treatments. Erika had informed them of my mom's medical history – she knew it as well as I did. Nurses came and went, some talking quietly, asking if either of us needed anything, some slipping into and out of the room like ghosts. After a while, as the sun began to set, Erika had to leave to return her father's truck. I told her I wouldn't be returning to school, but I would still see her at the graduation, and I let her know that I would be able to make it there on my own – I assumed one of the guys would be able to drive me.

Texas entered as she exited, his brown eyes trailing from my mom's beeping heart monitor to me. When he sat, I latched onto him, startling him momentarily when I buried my face into his chest. I let out a ragged breath and tears leaked onto my cheeks. I inhaled the scent of vanilla that always seemed to soak into his clothes and skin, allowing it to calm me. His hand rested on my hair, pushing the strands back as he tilted his chin to sit on top of my head.

"They're on their way," he whispered.

I nodded, grateful. I closed my eyes and sunk into Texas. I touched the fabric of his shirt, and breathed in his vanilla scent, trying to ground myself in the present, rather than the future as an orphan. I was old enough that I could take care of myself. I was eighteen. That wasn't the problem. What I was really terrified of was being alone. Mom hadn't been the best companion to live with in her more recent years. She hadn't always been herself, or particularly kind in certain instances when her hormones had taken over – but she was a constant, she was my mom.

It wasn't until the door opened and light spilled in from the hall, and the scent of peppermint floated to me that I cracked open my eyelids to look up. Marv stood behind Knix, who stood next to Bellamy. They entered, and closed the door quietly behind them. Knix knelt at the end of the couch in front of me.

"Are you okay?" he asked.

I couldn't answer because I didn't want to lie to him and the truth was just too painful. I kept hoping that if I didn't admit it then it wasn't true. He stared at me, his blue eyes searching, hunting for anything to make me better. I wanted to crawl into his arms and cry. I wanted to stay with Texas. Marv was standing right there.

Bellamy too. I wanted them all. They understood. They knew.

We stayed at the hospital that night, all of us taking turns sleeping on the couch and a cot the nurses had brought in. Knix and Marv disappeared regularly throughout the night. Bellamy and Texas stayed with me, ever vigilant. I appreciated the support they gave me, though I probably didn't act like it. I didn't even want to imagine how I might have reacted had I not had anyone else. Erika had to go home, but she promised that she would text me for updates. I tried calling my brother, but he didn't answer. If she died, I would have to tell him. I dreaded that conversation.

She woke late afternoon the next day. The guys vacated the room when she cracked open her eyes and her heart rate monitor sped up. She was dizzy, nauseated, something the new doctor, Dr. Mason, informed me might be likely. She would have to stay in the hospital longer. This terrified me. I didn't know why I only associated death with the hospital. I knew, even if we left, she could deteriorate even faster. Logically, I knew my fears weren't grounded. I just wanted her out of the hospital. I felt like if they released her, then she wouldn't die.

I sat with her, talking about anything I could think of, and after several hours I was relegated to the weather and whatever I had managed to glean through the hospital magazines. I was horribly inept at talking when all I felt like doing was crying. She slept a lot more than usual. Even though I hadn't been at the house as much, I would notice small things moved around that told me she had been up and about. At the hospital, she would wake for several minutes, eat with me – always something small and light – while I talked, before drifting back to sleep. The guys always seemed to know she was out because they would trickle back in, gathering around me. Bellamy forced me to go with him to the cafeteria more than once just to get out the room.

I would find Marv talking to nurses outside of the room and even the receptionist down the hall. I suspected he was paying for the room. I knew she should have been somewhere less private, cheaper. He was there though, and I knew him well enough to know that he wouldn't accept that. I dreaded having to pay back every penny, but I knew I would. I just couldn't do this by myself right now. I needed them.

The weekend drew nearer and Knix pulled all of us out of the room, promising me that he had a nurse watching over my mom. She would call if anything changed. He drove us in their SUV back to the apartment to prepare for the retreat. I wasn't feeling up to a job, but we had promised to dedicate our time to help these people and, if I was being honest, I would rather do something to get my mind off my fear. Sitting around and waiting for my mom's health to finally fail, and waiting for the impending pain of losing a parent to destroy me wasn't doing me any favors. When Knix tugged me aside and told me that we could give up the job, that he and the others would still help me, I had refused. My mind was a wreck, focusing it would help. Marv and I left for Sweratt Island Friday evening, not long after Texas had checked in for his new IT position.

"Sunshine." Marv's hand pressed to my cheek, his thumb rubbing up and down under my eye. I shifted in the seat of his BMW, groaning and reached up to wipe away the sleep. "We're here."

I yawned and got out of the car slowly. He grabbed our bags and shut the door for me. I offered to take one of the bags, but he caught my hand with his and tugged me after him. I looked around at the marina.

"Where is everyone?" I asked.

It was late in the evening. I had been up since early that morning and I was tired. That didn't halt my curiosity though, or my observations. The sun was almost set, light orange, yellow, and pink rays spanning across the horizon.

"Everyone is already there. We missed the ferry that left this afternoon," Marv said. The wood of the docks swayed under our feet, buoyed by the water.

"Then, how exactly are we getting there?"

He threw a grin over his shoulder, lighting the tornados in his eyes. "We're taking my boat."

We stopped in front of small, blue and white motor-boat with the inscription *Adventurer* over the back of it, the stern Marv told me. He tossed our bags in before jumping over the side and held his arms out to me. I reached for his hands, but he shook his head and slid his palms around my waist, lifting me into the boat. His biceps bunched and released and when he set me down, we were less than a breath away from each other. I looked up into his swirling, gray eyes.

His fingertips drifted up to touch my face again, and he pressed his lips to my temple before holding me close. "We don't have to do this," he said, his voice hoarse. "Just say the word and I'll take you back. We'll go to the hospital and stay with your mother. The others would understand."

Before he was even finished, I was shaking my head. "I don't want to do that," I said. "We've already agreed to this. We need to help." I needed the distraction.

He gazed down at me. "Your family is important."

"So is this," I argued. "I don't want to think about my

mom right now. I need to do this. I need to feel useful. Staying at the hospital watching her slip away isn't helpful. It's just going to make me feel worse. The doctor said that she has months left, not hours. Two days away will be okay. It'll give us a break."

He brushed aside a lock of hair hanging in my face. "Is that what you need? A break?"

I looked away. "I don't know, maybe." His fingers urged my face back and he lowered his head. His lips touched mine, soft, gentle, yet firm. He lifted his other hand to cup my head and hold me to him as his mouth opened and mine did too. Our lips met again and our tongues snuck out in search of each other. Marv moaned against my mouth, his hips nudging forward, something hard pushing against my stomach. I had to tilt my head back, and stand on tiptoe. Marv had to bend forward to meet me. His mouth was warm, comforting. He dragged his lips away from mine, trailing them up my face, over my cheek and temple into my hair. His breath fluttered over my scalp making me shiver.

"It's going to be okay, Harlow. I promise." He leaned back, his eyes boring into mine, holding me hostage. "You will never be alone again. You're with us now, with me."

He turned, releasing me, and began uncoiling the rope tied to the dock. I sat in the passenger seat as he readied us to go into open waters, feeling guiltier than I had ever felt before, and hating myself for watching him and craving him because the truth was, he wasn't the only one I felt safe around. He wasn't the only one I craved.

CHAPTER 17

The *Adventurer* rocked against the waves, cutting through the water quickly. Once the sun had set, the sky darkened and the air over the water was much cooler. I shivered against the wind whipping at our faces as Marv drove the boat. The roar of the motor was so loud, we didn't speak for the duration of the ride. Nearly a half-hour later, lights from Swerath Island came into view. Marv steered us toward a dock set up on the far side of the island. A light hung from the end, swaying back and forth. Two men dressed in white pants and blue dress shirts hurried forward as we docked. They secured the boat while Marv took my hand and helped me onto the docks.

"Ma'am, may I take your bags?" I looked up as a familiar voice spoke nearby. Texas' dark brown eyes met mine and he gently reached for the bags.

"Thank you," I said. He winked before he turned and strode away. I had no doubt that wherever Marv and I would end up tonight, we would have a way to contact Texas and the rest of the guys later.

Marv took my hand and we walked towards a narrow road behind the dock house where a six-person golf cart awaited us. We climbed into the backseat, his arm around my waist while the two men who had assisted us got into the front and set the cart in motion. I leaned my head against Marv's chest, and yawned. Marv toyed with the ends of my hair. I inhaled and he chuckled, rubbing a hand over my head.

"Are you smelling me?" he teased.

"Mmm hmm," I mumbled, inhaling again.

"What do I smell like?" he asked.

"Coffee," I said. "You always smell like coffee."

He laughed. "We all have our addictions. Just so happens that mine is caffeine and a smartass, little brunette." I blushed, but couldn't help the small smile that stretched across my mouth.

I looked in awe at the immense resort as the golf cart stopped in front of a lavish entrance. Marv stepped off the cart and held his hand out for me. I smirked, and took the offered hand, allowing him to help me step down. He kissed my knuckles, sending sparks jumping up my arms, before tucking my hand to his side.

"Welcome Mr. Carter." An older gentleman, with graying sideburns extending from dark brown hair, greeted us the moment we were through the doors. "My name is Jonathan. I will be your personal steward, and I will be on call for you for the entirety of your stay."

"This is my girlfriend, Harley," Marv introduced.

I blinked at the name, confused, but quickly recalled the pseudonym we had used at the hotel meet and greet. It would be odd to give my real name after I had already been introduced as 'Harley'.

"Pleased to meet you." I held out a hand for Jonathan to shake. He nodded firmly after dropping my hand and gestured towards a grand staircase just to the front of the lobby desk.

"Shall I take you to your quarters to dress and prepare for the meal this evening?"

"I thought we missed that," Marv said, his eyebrows rising.

"No sir," Jonathan replied. "Dinner will be served in another half-hour."

"I would like to change before then. Yes of course, please lead the way."

We followed Jonathan up the grand staircase and through a complex maze of hallways to a door with a gold plaque on the front. I memorized the number, knowing I would likely need it later when I would inevitably get lost.

"Thank you, Jonathan," Marv said.

I wandered into the room as Marv tipped the man. We had been given a suite of rooms instead of just one. There was a sitting area, larger than the living room in my duplex. There was a basket of apples on the counter. Plain shapes piled onto canvas masquerading as artwork on the walls. Otherwise, ocean themes layered every other inch of the space. I explored further. There was one bedroom with a light-blue and white duvet and an oak trunk at the foot of the four-poster bed. A grand bathroom was attached, larger than my bedroom at home, with a frosted-glass shower and a tub set into the side of a wall with small whirlpool holes along the sides, a Jacuzzi. It smelled like sand and water throughout every inch of the room. Marv followed me into the bathroom, his arms banding around me. My hands came up to hold onto him. Though it was cold in the room, I wondered if I trembled for other reasons.

"Our bags were just delivered. We have to get ready," he said.

"What's it going to be like?"

He rested his chin on the top of my head and looked at us in the mirror. "It'll be loud. There will be lots of drinking. Not everyone here is as kind as the people you met at the meet and greet. Some are more pompous."

"Snooty," I guessed. He nodded, his chin bumping against me. I laughed and turned, poking him in the ribs. "Get out, I'll change in here."

"No," he said, tugging me into the room. He grabbed a few things from his bag. "I'll change in there, you change here. I'll knock when I'm done so you know I'm coming out."

"Wait!" I called out as he headed back into the bathroom. He paused, glancing back. "What should I wear?"

He shrugged. "Whatever you want." The bathroom door closed behind him, locking him away from my sight. I sighed and looked towards my bag.

Ten minutes and three coats of mascara later, Marv knocked against the bathroom door before opening it slowly and peeking out. I stood at the white-wood vanity fixing my makeup in a black and white floral-patterned cocktail dress. My red heels were chafing at the skin of my ankles, but Texas and Bellamy had assured me that a few well-placed band aids would help with that. How they knew, I hadn't asked, but it made sense. I might not have worn heels in years, but that didn't mean I had forgotten the curse that they brought with them, especially new ones. Marv straightened his white dress shirt, rolling up the sleeves to his elbows. His checkered bow tie lay against his collar, undone.

"Do you need some help with that?" I nodded to the strip of fabric. He didn't seem to hear me. His eyes roved over the dress as he put a hand in his pocket and jangled the loose change there. "Marv?"

His head shot up. "What?"

I laughed, putting the eyeliner down next to the mascara and walked over to him. My fingers trailed around his collar, popping the white fabric as I quickly knotted and tied his bowtie. He watched me as I fixed it appropriately.

"You'd make a good wife," he mumbled.

"Hmm." I pretended to be absorbed in my task, not letting on just how that statement, coming from him, rattled me.

Any girl who could tie a tie or a bowtie correctly probably seemed like a good candidate for a wife, I assured myself. It was helpful that I managed to hold things together under certain situations such as spying on his peers. I folded his collar back down and smoothed it out. He looked dashing, his light-gray eyes a contrast with his dark hair. Stubble spread over his jaw line, giving him a little rougher edge than usual. It heated my blood all the same.

Marv took my hand as we exited our room. I was getting used to that. The hallways were empty and it wasn't until we descended the staircase again that we heard laughter and music down a long, navy-blue carpeted hallway.

The dining room was grand with globe chandeliers lighting the arched ceiling. Three candles, ranging from tall to nearly burnt out, sat in the middle of each table. The concierge gestured Marv and I to our table as I observed the room, the women in their dresses, the men ignoring the women in their dresses for other, prettier, younger women. My mouth grew dry. I clutched Marv's hand like a lifeline. If he noticed, he didn't show it.

A shadow fell over us and a waiter in black and white dropped off glasses of water and white wine. He paused behind Marv and me before setting our glasses down, knocking my napkin off the table with the flick of his hand. If I wasn't so high strung, I wouldn't have noticed that it was purposefully done. I looked at the waiter as he bent over and retrieved the scrap of fabric.

"I apologize, Miss," he mumbled setting the napkin on the table next to me. I memorized his face, the arc of his brows, the dull, doe-brown eyes and the sharp, slightly-too-large-for-his-face nose. He flicked a glance at the napkin once more before scurrying off. I reached for it as Marv leaned over and placed his lips in my hair, a hand on the back of my chair.

"Hand it to me," he whispered. It was then I realized that this was preplanned. The guys must have either paid the waiter or he was part of their team, part of Iris. I slipped the napkin into my lap and twisted my body towards him, scooting it to his knee. He opened the flap and retrieved something before passing it back. "Put it in your ear."

I waited a few moments as Marv stretched, groaned, and rubbed at his ear as he put in his own device before striking up a conversation with an older brunette across the table. She seemed flattered by his adoration of her jewelry. She fluttered her eyelashes and blushed, causing her husband to fawn over her and agree. Eyes turned to assess her necklace and earrings.

I slipped in the hearing device and Texas' voice came through, muted and hard to hear. It was as if he were far away maybe yelling across a long, crowded room. Thankfully, I could still make out the words without much concentration. I agreed with Marv about the other woman's jewelry as she told everyone where she purchased it and who the designer was.

"Space Man to Earth Princess, come in Earth Princess." I was reaching for a glass of water and snorted at Texas' teasing. Before I could draw every eye back to me, I jerked the water in front of my face to hide my reaction.

"Oh my god, Texas!" I hissed quietly. "Stop it."

"Just making sure I got you. I requested you, but Knix said I would get who I would get. I'm glad I got you."

"Tex–" I interrupted myself as the brunette's husband glanced my way and I put the glass to my lips and sipped.

"Alright, listen up, Princess. I've got some information for you. Marv is getting the run down from Knix now," Texas said. "Bellamy's been pulled." I bit my lip as I tried whispering through unmoving lips.

"Pulled?" I whispered. "Why?"

"Whoever's in charge of staffing wanted to change a lot, and a whole bunch of employees in non-essential positions were dropped last minute. Luckily, I'm way more than essential. I'm their king guru of tech. Guess that makes both of us royalty. The King of tech and the Earth Princess. Wanna get married?" I could picture Texas waggling his eyebrows. I smirked, coughed into my hand delicately interrupting him as he attempted to list the ways of kings and princesses.

"Right, right," he replied. "So, you've got me and whoever Knix and I manage to bribe to drop equipment with you and Marv. He should have a cell phone now, but you won't need it until later. Marv will explain the plan. For now, just sit tight, eat some good food and listen to everything." I hummed in agreement as our first course arrived and Texas grew quiet, only asking me embarrassing questions every now and then to make me blush. I hoped the others at our table just assumed I was shy and naturally pink.

"Planting drinks tonight?" I inquired lowly.

"Nope. Oh! And no drinking on the job, Knix's orders."

"I'm not old enough, yet," I argued. I could picture him shrugging at me, but he just repeated that it was under Knix's orders and went silent.

"So, Marvin dear," the brunette said. "Who is your lovely acquaintance?" My eyes widened as the attention at the table suddenly turned to me.

"Mrs. Foster, this young lady is more than just an acquaintance. This is Harley, my girlfriend." The older woman flapped a bony hand at him.

"Maya, darling. Call me Maya, and is she now?" Her eyes danced over me, analyzing me. "Harley, it's so very nice to see our boy Marvin with someone. He hasn't come out in ages!" She reached for the stem of her wine glass and brought it to her dark painted lips.

"I'm happy to be wherever he is." I smiled, reaching to grasp his hand in front of our audience. Marv's fingers intertwined with mine.

"So, what do you do?" she inquired.

"I'm sorry?" Panic edged along my nerve endings. Had the guys already put out a background on 'Harley'? Was this just a test from her? I looked at Marv, who merely raised an eyebrow at me expectantly. I took that to mean that he either didn't have any idea what she was talking about or he was more than willing to let me make it up as I went along.

"I mean what do you do with your time?" the woman asked. "I know that Marv here works with his parents when they request his assistance, but he's such a smart boy he was snapped up so quickly by another corporation. What was it called again? Islands? No, it was some flowery name…"

"Iris, Mrs. Foster," Marv supplied. "I work for Iris."

"Yes! That one." She didn't bother to correct him about her name again, and turned her focus back to me. "So, what do you do?"

"I'm going to school right now," I supplied. "Working towards a degree."

"Oh, how wonderful. What are you going for? Biology? Chemistry? There's so much available in those industries right now, especially in the research field. Isn't that right, Darling?" she asked her husband. Mr. Foster's face was lethargic, but he managed a nod at her insistence.

"Well," I began. "I'm interested in a few different subjects. So, I'm undecided at the moment."

"What subjects are you considering?" Her wine glass was half empty and she set it to the side as more waiters approached the table to set out the first course of clam chowder.

"I think architecture and technology are both interesting," I said. One reminded me of Knix and the other reminded me of Texas.

"Oh, those industries already have too many people. So many are pouring into the technology industry, they have an oversupply. You'll never get a job with that." She waved her hands as she leaned over and sipped from a small spoon resting in her chowder. I did the same, my muscles tightening. Mrs. Foster seemed a well-meaning person, but her interrogation was more stressful than easy going. "What else were you considering?"

I held my spoon above the bowl and looked at her. "All I want to do is help people," I admitted. "It honestly doesn't matter what industry I end up in or what company or job I end up with." I sat up straighter, feeling Marv's gaze on me. "I just want to make a difference in people's lives. If I can do that, then I'll be fine."

The old woman's eyes twinkled. "Good choice, Dear. Good choice."

~

I CAME AWAKE SLOWER THAN USUAL, MY EYES REFUSING TO open. I was encased in warmth and the wonderful smell of ocean and coffee. I flipped over and snuggled into a heated side before I realized what I was doing and my eyes popped open.

"Morning," Marv said, his gray eyes bright.

"How long have you been up?" I asked.

He shrugged, tossing the covers away as he sat up. "Few minutes." He stretched his arms over his head and I could see the veins just under his skin on the paler sides of his underarms. Marv reached over during my distraction and popped me lightly, teasingly, on the thigh. "Get up and get dressed. Texas will be here soon."

"What?" I reached over to slap him back, but he was already crawling out of the bed. I grunted as I rolled and almost fell off of the mattress. "Why?"

"You'll find out."

I groaned, but did as he asked. When we were in the common area and the smell of brewing coffee already scented the air, there was a brief knock on the door and with his cup in hand, Marv answered.

"Coffee?" Texas' voice perked up the room. "Do you have any cream or sugar?"

"Why ruin a good thing?" Marv sat back on the couch, lounging like the elegant, wealthy gentleman that he was.

"You mean make it better?" Texas shot back. "Knix, I think he means that I make everything better." My head turned as Knix walked into the room, taking up more than his fair share of space. Not that he could help it. Everything seemed so dainty when he was in the room. His dark-brown eyes scanned over me before he strode to the living area and plunked down on the seat across from me.

After Texas successfully found the cream and sugar, and joined Marv on the couch across from Knix and me, Knix sat forward and addressed the room.

"Here's the update," he announced. "Mr. and Mrs. Foster's room set off an alarm last night. Texas has set up a–"

A knock interrupted his sentence and all eyes turned to the door. As if they had choreographed their movements, Knix and Texas stood and ushered me into the bedroom while Marv went for the door. Knix pointed to me and then to the bed with a firm set to his mouth. I wanted to argue, but one look back at Texas' serious expression, I decided against it, doing as they wished, and sat.

The guys stood just behind the door, their ears close enough to eavesdrop. Even from the bed I could hear Marv's tone, first surprised, and then concerned. A few moments later and Marv opened the bedroom door. Texas scrambled back towards the bed to stand over me. Knix stood, like an unmoving mountain until whoever passed through the door with Marv was in sight. I watched his tense shoulders deflate.

Jonathan, the concierge who had first greeted Marv and I and shown us to our suite, came through with a younger woman. She had smooth, tan skin and a deep worried look in her brown eyes. The beauty mark below the side of her mouth trembled with her lips.

"We have a complication," Marv began.

Knix looked at the young woman and Jonathan and, with a sigh, nodded them towards the living room. After everyone was seated once more, Marv explained that the young woman with Jonathan, Beth, was his daughter-in-law. Jonathan had worked for Marv's parents at their charity events before, but he had never worked on Sweratt Island. Because he had recognized Marv and knew his family, he had thought it best to come here.

"It's begun," Marv said. "Jonathan, do you want to tell us what you know?"

Jonathan nodded, his weary eyes crinkling with stress as he explained that Mrs. Foster, the woman from dinner the night before, was missing some very expensive pieces of jewelry, and Beth was in charge of cleaning their suite.

"I knew something was wrong as soon as I entered the room," Beth said, her voice shaking. "I've met the Fosters. They seem like a put together couple. When I went in to clean, their room was a mess."

"I don't want them to blame her. She would never do this, sir." Jonathan's worried gaze flickered between us and Beth, who looked ready to cry.

"I don't think you will have to worry about that," Marv said reassuringly. "You're innocent."

"Begging your pardon, sir," Jonathan said. "But innocent people go to jail all the time."

"I can't go to jail!" Beth cried out, fat tears filling her eyes and streaking down her cheeks.

"That won't happen," Tex jumped in. "We're working on figuring out who is behind the thievery. We will figure it out before anyone leaves the island."

"What if you don't?" Beth sobbed. "I did not know of the stealing. Then I heard from some of the managers that this has happened before. I do not want to be blamed."

Beth put both of her hands to her face and leaned over, continuing to cry in her lap as her father-in-law attempted to soothe her. The guys shared a three-way look. Marv sighed before he stood up and clasped Jonathan on the shoulder.

"Do not worry, friend," he said. "We will make sure this is taken care of."

When Beth looked up, still teary eyed, I caught her attention and smiled. "Trust them," I said. "Trust *us*. We will help."

The guys all looked at me. Beth's whole body shook as she pulled in a nervous breath and nodded. Marv ushered Jonathan and Beth back out into the hallway and they were excused to go finish their duties. The front door closed, locking me in with the guys and a whole lot of pressure to find out who was stealing from the guests of Sweratt Island.

CHAPTER 18

I collapsed onto the couch in the living room, breathing out a sigh of frustration. Marv said something quiet to Knix and Texas who both glanced at me. I didn't hear what they said but I watched as Knix shook his head and ushered Texas and Marv out the door. As soon as the door was shut behind them, I steeled myself, but Knix didn't say anything as he strode back into the center of the room, his eyes trailing over me. He took a seat next to me, so close there was no way for me to move away without it being obvious that I didn't want to touch him. The problem wasn't that I didn't want to touch him, though. It was that I did. Very much.

I sat forward, edging my elbows close to my sides. "Why did Marv and Texas leave?"

"They have to set up for the next part of our plan," he said.

"Oh." I scratched a spot on my wrist. "Why aren't you with them? What's the next part of the plan?"

"Before I tell you that, can I ask you something?"

I paused before nodding. I didn't know why he felt the need to ask me if he could ask a question. Why he couldn't just outright ask me?

"What did you think of Jonathan and Beth?"

I frowned, confused. "I think they need our help."

He nodded as if he expected that answer. "And when you asked them to trust us, did you mean *us* as in you, Marv, Bellamy, Texas, and me or trust us as in me, Marv, Bellamy, and Texas?"

"Does it matter?" I asked, tilting my head to the side. "We're going to help them as a team, right? If you need me, I'm here to do whatever you need. Why am I here, if I'm not going to help them? I want to help."

Knix smiled, dark-blue eyes sharp. "I'm happy to hear you say that, but I needed to know because as of right now, most of your work is done. We can give you more to do, if you want to stay. But you were here to give a sufficient reason for Marv to be here as a guest. This is a couple's retreat after all. He needed a date to be here."

"If you didn't want me here, you could have just gotten an Iris girl," I said, recalling the strange conversation I had overheard between Bellamy and Texas. My eyes trailed to the lamp just beyond his head, trying to look away without truly doing so.

"Alex thought you would work well with us," Knix replied, shifting in his seat to lean closer. My gaze met his again.

"Alex isn't here," I reminded him.

Knix nodded. "You're right, he's not. I just needed to make sure that you knew if you wanted to leave, you could."

I remained quiet for several more moments. Did I want to leave? No, I wanted to stay. I wanted to help Beth and Jonathan. They needed us. It was then, with a jolt, I realized I wanted to be a part of their *us*. I wanted to be included so badly and, in a way, I felt like I already was. Looking back at Knix, I noticed him watching me, waiting patiently.

"Do you want me to stay?" I asked hesitantly.

He rubbed the underside of his jaw as a grin spread across his full lips. "I would like that very much, Little Bit," he said. "But it isn't about me right now. This is about what you want. What do you want, Harlow?"

I kept my eyes locked with his. "I want to know more about Iris," I said.

"That's the choice you have to make then," Knix replied. "Does your curiosity about Iris overrule your need to help others?"

My brows lowered until they formed a V between my eyes. "That doesn't seem fair," I said. "Holding information over my head to help people. Shouldn't you be jumping at the chance to get me on board? Don't you need my help?"

"We could use you, yes." Knix sucked back a breath, before releasing it in a huff. "But we could survive without you. If you're going to do this and go any further, you need to be doing it for the right reasons."

"And what reasons would those be?" I asked.

Knix sat up straighter. "You can't be doing this with the intent to get information. After this job, we may not feel like you're completely ready."

"You're saying that even if I finish this investigation with you," I began. "You still might not tell me about Iris?"

"That's right."

Knix waited as I turned that over in my mind. This whole time, they had been promising me things about Iris – information, jobs, connections, a network that would help me and my Mom. He was telling me that even if I risk myself in his investigation, I still might not get any reward. Though that thought made me wince, another thought was even more difficult to consider. If I didn't help, would Beth and Jonathan be okay? Would Mrs. Foster ever get her belongings back? Would whoever was doing this get away with it again? After several long moments of silence between us, I looked back at Knix with determination. He raised one brow.

"It doesn't matter," I said confidently. "You said this is about me, about if I want to continue, but it's not. It's about them – Jonathan and his daughter-in-law. It's about Mrs. Foster. They need help and I want to help them."

It shouldn't have been such a difficult decision and if I was honest with myself, once I got over the curiosity of Iris, it wasn't.

"Alright, then," Knix stood up and offered me his hand. "Let's go."

I took the offered hand, but frowned at him. "That's it?" I asked.

He nodded. "That's it." Knix tugged me towards the door. "Most of the guests are either in their rooms or downstairs at breakfast right now. We're going to meet with everyone in Texas' command center."

"Command center?"

My legs worked to keep up with Knix. He didn't release my hand as we moved down the hallway, passing several doors and Island Employees dressed in the same blue shirt and white pants uniform.

"It's the room they gave him to work on the security cameras and computer systems," Knix replied.

We headed towards what was obviously an employee hallway. The doors were plain with no gold ornamentation, and some were left open as if the occupants had left in a rush. From what I could discern, peeking into the rooms as we rushed by, there were two or three single beds smooshed together in each, with dressers and no other fancy décor that would have been basic for guests.

Stopping in front of a similar door at the very end of the hallway, Knix knocked twice before turning the handle. The darkened interior surprised me, but as I entered I saw that Texas was sitting like a king on his throne in front of a wall of monitors and boxes with wires peeking out and extending in every direction. He leaned back with rope candy hanging from his mouth.

"Everything good?" Texas asked, raising a brow. Knix and I both nodded in response.

"Tell us what you've found," Knix ordered, catching the back of a rolling chair, positioned on the other side of Texas, and pushed it towards me.

I looked down at it for a moment before tucking my skirt beneath my thighs and sitting down. Marv leaned against the wall behind me and Bellamy, dressed in an employee's uniform much like Knix and Texas, stood across the room from us.

"Okay, so here's the deal." Texas swung his chair back to the wall of monitors and to my left several of the dead screens lit up. One revealed a long empty hallway, the second two displayed a luxurious dining room filled with the guests, including Mr. and Mrs. Foster at different angles.

"Here are all of the guests and we've established that the thief or thieves – if there are multiples – aren't employees," Texas began.

"They can't be," Bellamy cut in. "Not if this has happened repeatedly over several different functions and there are new employees each time."

"But each time before, employees have been blamed, right?" Marv asked.

"Have any confessed?" Knix asked.

Texas shook his head.

I sat back and watched them, amazed by their keen intellects bouncing ideas off one another. Texas said that Knix was the boss, and I could understand that they followed his lead as a unit, but they were a team and like Marv had said before, none were a burden to the others. They worked surprisingly well together despite their differences.

"Harlow, what do you think?"

I was shocked out of my thoughts by Marv's question. I looked at him before turning to look at the rest. All eyes were on me. I bit my lip and contemplated. If employees were being blamed and none had confessed, but Sweratt had hired all new staff for each event, then it would make sense to consider that the thief or thieves were more than simple maids and butlers and waiters.

"What about the managers?" I asked. "There must be someone with the company that has to run every event."

Texas turned to a monitor on his other side, and after tapping on his keyboard for a few seconds, he pulled up a picture of a balding man with bright, cheery eyes. He scooted out of the way so that we could all see the image.

"This is Donald Carrigan," he said. "He's an accountant for Sweratt Inc. He's in charge of this event."

Texas leaned over and clicked a few more buttons causing several more faces to pop up alongside Donald. One was of a sharp looking woman with dull, brown eyes and flat blond hair in her thirties. The rest followed suit, all different, and all apparently connected with Sweratt.

"That's Marybeth Donnelly, Rodrick Redfield, Olivia

Briggs, and Roger O'Leary," Texas repeated each name while pointing to the corresponding picture. "Each of these people have managed events here and each hold a position within Sweratt's actual company."

"So, they don't have the same managers each time either," Knix said. He pinched the bridge of his nose between his eyes and sighed. "This is getting more and more complicated."

There was something else, though. There was a set of people we hadn't even considered yet. My eyes were drawn to the monitor of the luxurious dining room as the idea formed in my head.

"What if," I began hesitantly. Maybe it was ridiculous, but the longer I thought on it, the more the idea made sense. Who else could it be? Every employee for the event was new. There was no way it could be one of them.

"Harlow?" Bellamy prompted.

I turned back to the group. "What if we're looking at this all wrong," I said. "What if it's not the employees, but one of the guests?"

They all stared at me. The quiet made me nervous, but Bellamy blinked at me and then tilted his head. Slowly, a smile spread across his face and he let out a loud whoop. He took three long strides and whipped me out of my chair, spinning me around twice before planting my feet down once more and kissing my forehead.

"That's it!" He beamed down at me.

"Shh," Texas hissed. "The walls here aren't exactly soundproof."

Bellamy didn't seem to care. He continued smiling. "That's it," he repeated. "If we look through the guest log for this event and cross reference it with the old guest logs, we'll be able to find the link. If we don't have the thief now, then we will at least have a much smaller lead pool."

Marv stepped forward, clasping Bellamy on the shoulder and pulled him away from me. "How are we going to get those old event lists?"

Bellamy frowned. "Don't we have access to that online?"

All eyes turned to Texas.

Texas grimaced before scratching his chin uncertainly. "I can get it, but it might take some time."

"Go ahead and do it," Knix announced suddenly. All eyes flicked over to him. "Marv, take Harlow down to the dining room. You need to mingle with the guests. This time, instead of simply attending the activities, I want you to be actively searching for suspects. If Harlow is right, then we've missed something. Texas? Didn't we already check out the guests?"

"We ruled them out," Texas answered.

Knix's brows pinched down and his frown deepened. "And their plus one's?"

Texas' eyes widened like a deer caught in front of a blinding light. "I–" He glanced around, his eyes dazed as he tried to think. "Shit," he cursed lowly.

"I'll go ahead and head to the kitchens to see if they need any extra help," Bellamy volunteered.

"Good idea." Knix nodded. "I need to go discuss this with Mr. Carrigan. He needs to be made aware of the situation." He looked toward Texas. "We all make mistakes, don't worry," he assured him. "We'll fix this."

Texas frowned, but with grim lips he bent his head in acknowledgement.

Marv nodded and took my hand. Before he could direct me back into the hallway, Texas jumped up and offered each of us new earbud communicators with tiny speakers. He flushed as he helped me put it in this time.

"They're cheap," he explained. "And we don't want anyone suspecting anything, especially now that we're looking at the guests."

I nodded and adjusted my hair so that it covered the earbud. "It's all good." I smiled. He blinked at me for a split second, his hand hovering over the side of my face. "What?"

Texas shook his head. "Nothing," he mumbled, and turned away.

"You ready?" Marv asked.

I glanced back, wondering why Texas had looked at me so strangely, but nodded anyway. Marv pulled me into the hallway, towards the dining room. I hoped whoever the thief was, we would catch them sooner rather than later.

A STRING QUARTET SAT ON A RAISED DAIS IN THE CORNER of the extravagant Sweratt Island gardens. Marv and I, along with the rest of the guests of Sweratt Island, were dressed in light pastels and summer colors for the garden tea-party event. A much smaller number of couples had been invited and were seated at their own private tables. Sweratt employees circled them, pouring water and wine and offering bouquets of flowers for purchase. When an employee stopped by our table, Marv put a hand over his wine glass and politely shook his head.

"For you, ma'am?" the young man asked me.

I blinked up at him, shocked that I wasn't even being carded. "No thank you," I replied.

He smiled and poured each of us a glass of water before turning to the next table.

According to Texas, Bellamy was stocking wine in the kitchens. We likely wouldn't see him in the garden.

"Look for anyone acting out of the ordinary," Texas said in my ear. "Look for anyone paying special attention to one couple or another. They may still have their eyes on the Fosters, to see their reactions. If they think that the Fosters haven't noticed anything missing then they will likely find another target sooner rather than later."

I coughed and reached for my water glass, gulping down several mouthfuls as my eyes scanned the nearby tables. Like the night before, we were seated near the Fosters along with a few other familiar faces. All seemed to be focused on the event coordinator, Donald Carrigan, the man that Texas had explained was one of the many faces of Sweratt that had been placed in charge of the event. Not far from him, I recognized Mr. Daschund, one of the men Marv had introduced me to at the party in Charleston. Mr. Carrigan stood in front of the now silent quartet with a microphone in his hand, welcoming the guests.

"Thank you so much for coming everyone," he said pleasantly, wiping away sweat from his brow with a crisp linen square that he pulled from his pocket. "As you know, Sweratt loves to appreciate its partners and affiliates with these events and this retreat is no different. We want to offer you any choice menu item from the selections you have been given and please feel free to treat your ladies to bouquets and a dance."

I watched as some of the men at other tables rolled their eyes or watched with dull, uninterested gazes. A quick peek at Marv told me that while he was focused on Mr. Carrigan, he was still taking every opportunity to peer around at the couples surrounding us. I straightened the cream-lace edges of my floral dress and folded my hands in my lap once more after placing my water glass back in its original position.

"This garden party is simply a thank you from us to you. Please enjoy." Mr. Carrigan finished his speech, prompting several audience members to applaud politely.

"Would you like to dance?"

I jerked my gaze back to Marv.

"Now?" I asked, glancing out at the barren dance floor.

His lips quirked with humor. "Now is as good as any time," he replied, standing and holding out his hand.

"It's a good idea," Texas said in my ear. "It will give you guys a chance to scan the area."

Hesitantly, I took Marv's hand and stood. I wasn't scared to dance with him as much as I was scared to dance in the ridiculously tall, pastel-blue heels I had on. But Marv, ever the gentleman, put his hand around my waist and guided me gently onto the empty dance floor. The string quartet struck up a new song just as Marv pulled me into the length of his body and we began to move. I thought dancing in heels would have been harder, but with Marv it was as easy as breathing. I didn't even have to think, though I could count on one hand the number of times I had danced with a guy in a fancy dress.

Marv leaned down and whispered in my free ear. "What do you see?"

That's when I remembered, I wasn't there to play dress up. I was there to catch a thief. I took a breath and allowed my gaze to scan the crowd. Several more couples stepped onto the dance floor and began to sway alongside us. As Marv turned me in a circle, I caught sight of a shockingly familiar face. My eyes widened and I felt my mouth drop open.

"What?" he asked. "What is it?"

"Turn me back around," I ordered. "Slowly." If I was right, I didn't want to alert the man I had seen to our presence.

Marv did as I requested and stopped, allowing me to face the tables on the far side of the garden. Sitting next to an older blonde with graying roots, a young man, not much older than Marv, curled his fingers around the stem of a wine glass and grimaced as he took a drink. The man's face was lean and sallow like he had been sick recently or might be getting sick. His blue eyes and facial features were so familiar, I stared trying to place where I knew him.

It wasn't until a second man approached from somewhere behind a large rosebush that I realized why I felt I knew him. While I didn't know the man sitting down, I certainly did know the man at his side. Shock faded to irritation. It seemed no matter where I went, Grayson was always around. We had managed to avoid him at the party in Charleston, but now he was here on Sweratt Island. It made sense. His father was an executive director for the company after all.

"Marv," I said, throat working. "Grayson's here."

"What?!" The sharp question hadn't come from Marv's lips, rather from the earbud in my ear. I flinched as I heard a squealing of interference in the background and Knix's voice came across the line.

"Grayson Caruso?" Knix demanded. "What is he doing?"

"He's standing over that man – his brother – the one that was with him at the party," I replied quietly, leaning towards Marv's chest so that the other dancers around us wouldn't notice. "It just looks like they're talking."

I watched Grayson for several moments as Marv turned us and we swayed so that he, too, could observe. Dressed in light-khaki dress pants and a purple button-down dress shirt rolled up at his forearms, Grayson looked just like every other person there.

"Their father *does* work for the company," Texas muttered in my ear again.

I smiled because he had repeated my exact thoughts. Grayson frowned down at the man sitting at the table, obviously attempting to speak with him about something serious. His brother, on the other hand, didn't seem interested in conversation. His expression was impassive as he waved his hand in Grayson's face, dismissing him outright and stood. He offered the woman with him his palm. The woman vaguely resembled both brothers and, I thought, must have been either their mother or a close older female relative.

Grayson frowned at his brother, his lips curving down in frustration before his face turned and his eyes landed on me. I froze for a moment, and Marv cursed under his breath. Grayson didn't even glance at Marv. His eyes stayed on mine. I watched as he tilted his head backwards, nodding towards the gardens. Without thinking, I nodded back.

"Guys," I said as Grayson disappeared behind the rosebush once more. "I'm going to go talk to him."

Marv's hands tightened on mine. "No." Texas and Knix disagreed as well and I was sure, had Bellamy been there, his answer would have been just as immediate if not harsher.

I looked up at Marv's worried gaze. "I'll be fine," I

assured him. "I just think he wants to know why I'm here – as much as we want to know why he's here."

Grayson wasn't exactly known for being a selfless person, but I didn't think he would hurt me. Marv's expression could have been cut straight from stone. He walked me back to our table and pulled out my chair. When I remained standing he shook his head.

"It's not a good idea." Marv's eyebrows drew together in concern, lessening the rigidity of his expression.

"He's not going to hurt me," I replied.

Marv frowned. "I still don't trust him."

"Why?" None of the guys liked him. It made me wonder if there wasn't a deeper reason, if maybe they had a history.

"Why what?" Marv asked, confused.

"Why don't you trust him?" I asked. "You don't know him, do you?"

I watched as Marv's expression evened out completely from worried back to stone. "I know enough," was all he said.

"Well, I don't," I stated. "I'm going to talk to him."

"Then I'm going with you."

I placed a hand on his shoulder. "No, if you come with me then I won't learn anything."

Marv stiffened for a moment, listening to something on the other end of his earbud before, with a sigh, he nodded.

"Keep your earbud and speaker on you," Texas said. Obviously, he and Knix had been listening to our argument.

I didn't bother replying, but I didn't mind keeping the earbud and speaker. I knew they would want to listen in anyway. Moving further into the garden, the quartet's music slowly quieted in the background until I couldn't hear it at all anymore. Instead, the only thing I could hear was the bubbling and splashing of a nearby fountain. I followed the sound until I arrived at a three-tiered, stone fountain with beautiful, clear water streaming from the dips of shells into the bottom tier.

"What are you doing here?"

I spun to face Grayson, one hand over my chest. "Jesus," I snapped. "You scared me."

"Answer the question, Harlow. What are you doing here?" Grayson didn't move from his spot across from me on the other side of the fountain.

"I wanted to ask you the same," I said. "I'm here for a friend. Why are you here? Shouldn't you have a date? This is a *couple's* retreat."

I had never seen Grayson so serious. At school, he was playful, and generally uncaring about everything around him. But standing across from me, with dark circles under his eyes, and his hair in disarray, he looked tired. More than that, Grayson looked defeated.

"What's wrong?" I asked.

Rubbing a hand down his face, Grayson turned away. "Nothing. You should probably leave soon though. I didn't realize you'd be here with one of your boyfriends."

"They aren't my boyfriends," I replied with a huff. "Why do you always have to dodge what I'm asking? You never give me a straight answer." I moved around the fountain towards him. "It's a *couple's* retreat," he snapped, repeating my earlier words. "Why are *you* here?"

"None of your business." Grayson took a step away and I quickly reached out, stumbling a little in my heels and grabbed his shirt for balance. He turned back, hands automatically going out to catch me.

I slowly straightened. "I can tell something's bugging you, Grayson. You keep trying to get me to talk to you, well I'm talking to you now. Tell me what's wrong, maybe I can help."

"You can't," he snapped, jerking his hands away as soon as he realized that I was steady. "You can't fucking help someone who doesn't want it."

I blinked at the vehemence in his tone. I raised my hand slowly and laid it on his arm. He looked down and stared at my freshly polished nails. I had never gotten my nails done before, but I didn't mind them. I liked dressing up for this role I was playing. I liked the challenge of being Harley. Maybe it was because this job was distracting me from the disaster waiting for me back home. I liked to think it was because I was doing something that would help someone else. If Grayson let me, I could help him too.

"That sounds like something you might have said before," I said quietly.

Sharp, blue eyes meet mine. "Why are you here?" he repeated.

"I'm looking for someone," I replied, hinting. I had the feeling Grayson knew exactly what I was doing here, what the others were doing here. He had already admitted that he had seen Marv.

"Shit." Grayson cursed low, turning away from me, yanking his arm from my palm. I clenched my hand in a fist, but remained put. "Don't tell me you're looking for–" Grayson didn't finish his statement when he looked back at me. "You are, aren't you?"

"I'm what?" My mind was reeling. I had lost track of the conversation and I was confused by his outburst. Grayson turned fully towards me, hands gripping my arms.

"Don't tell them, Harlow," he said, eyes desperate. "Please don't tell them. I'm fixing it. I'll get him to stop, I swear I will. There's no other reason for you to be here. For *them* to be here. But please don't tell them. I'll get him to give it back and then we'll leave. I'll make sure he never comes back."

"Holy fuck," I heard Texas whisper in my ear. "He knows."

Texas continued to talk as Grayson tried to convince me to keep his secret, a secret that was already spilling out. "It's his brother," Texas said. "His brother has been to every event as someone's guest – Joshua Caruso. He's been the one stealing." Texas was no longer talking to me or himself. I was sure he was talking to Knix, who was likely alerting both Bellamy and Marv.

I kept my focus on Grayson. "Why?"

"My parents are cutting him off," Grayson admitted. "He's been trying to stockpile enough money for when they do. He's here with our Aunt Malinda. She has no idea."

I shook my head, confusion still whirling in my mind. "How do you know? How did you find out that he was stealing?"

Grayson released my arms, but didn't back away. His head lowered and he heaved a breath before looking away. "I found his stash," he admitted. "I paid someone to sneak it all back. He's furious with me. The only reason he hasn't taken a swing my way is because I haven't told our parents. If they knew, they would cut him off now instead of later."

"Why are they waiting?"

Grayson shook his head. "I don't know. I don't know what those people think. They do a lot of shit just because. Josh has a problem. It's not just the stealing."

Grayson's face was a mask of anguish and I couldn't

stop myself from reaching out to him. "Hey," I said, placing my hands on his cheeks. "It's going to be okay."

"No, Harlow. You don't understand. He won't listen to me. He won't listen to anyone. He doesn't care."

I bit my lip and made a split-second decision. Before I could second guess it, I voiced the idea aloud. "What if we got him to give back what he's stolen this time?" I asked. "Then we get him help."

"He won't give it back unless he gets caught," Grayson replied.

"He is caught," I said.

"No offense, Harlow. You're beautiful and not exactly intimidating."

I rolled my eyes and dropped my arms to cross them over my chest. "Yea, I'm not intimidating, but we both know that I'm not here alone."

Grayson's eyes nearly popped out of his skull as he realized what I was suggesting. "No, not just no, but hell no." He shook his head. "They would rather chuck me off the side of a cliff than help me with Josh."

"He's not wrong," Texas replied.

I had to stop myself from telling them both to shut up.

"Here's the deal," I said. "I'll talk to them about helping your brother as long as you continue to watch him and make sure he doesn't steal anything else. We'll figure out a plan. It should just be tonight. Tomorrow, we can get someone here to take him off the Island." Hopefully, Marv or one of the guys would have an idea of how to do that. "You said it yourself," I continued. "He has…other problems?"

Grayson stared past me at the bubbling fountain, his face concentrating on something further away. "If I can just get him into rehab, maybe that will help."

"Are your parents willing to pay for that?" I asked. It was a serious question to consider. There had been a waitress I had worked with, fresh out of rehab and in some serious debt because of it. Thankfully, she had received a much better job offer several months into working at Alex's Diner and gone off to better things. If Grayson's brother couldn't afford rehab, and his parents refused to pay for it, he might end up in her situation. But it was possible his situation wouldn't improve the way hers had.

"I'll pay for it," Grayson replied. "I don't care how much it costs. I just want him clean and stable."

"You can do that?" I didn't even think he had a job.

He smirked, returning his gaze to mine. "I can do a lot of things."

"Ugh. Fine. You're paying then." I paused. "What kind of rehab facility does he need to go to?"

Grayson rubbed a hand down his tired face. "Drugs," he said. "I'm not exactly sure what all he's been taking, I think it might be more than just pot. If it was just pot, that's not a big deal – it's getting legalized throughout the states anyway. But I'm pretty sure it's more than that."

I stepped forward, placing my hand on his shoulder. "It's going to be okay," I promised.

"Tell him to meet you in the room you and Marv are sharing tonight at seven," Texas said quickly.

I relayed the information and Grayson agreed. "I'll walk you back to the garden party," he suggested, moving so that his hand grazed my lower back.

My eyes followed his movements as we strolled back through the rosebushes. The sounds of music rose over the tops of the plants and we stepped around a gardenia bush to the back side of the dance floor. As we did, a woman paused and offered us a bouquet of white flowers with a sunny smile. Just as I was about to shake my head, Grayson passed her a twenty and took the bouquet, handing it to me.

I blinked down at the flowers, and he leaned over to kiss my cheek. Shocked, I jerked away from him and he turned with a ridiculously proud smirk.

"Tell your boyfriends I'll see them tonight," he said over his shoulder before striding away. My hand reached up and touched the spot on my cheek where he had kissed me.

"What did he say?" Marv asked, startling me.

I jerked my hand away from my face guiltily, though he had to have seen the kiss. "He said to tell you and the guys that he'll see you tonight."

Marv didn't reply, and instead directed me back across the dance floor to our original table. As I sat, I contemplated just what kind of history the guys might have with Grayson and why they might dislike him so much. As the string quartet struck up a new song, I figured I would find out soon enough.

CHAPTER 19

Electricity charged the air as Grayson stepped into the suite with his nonchalant mask pulled firmly back on with a smug smirk gracing his lips. Knix stood and crossed his arms as Marv and Bellamy both glared at him from the couch. I perched on the armchair next to Texas. It seemed out of all of the guys, Texas was less inclined to attack Grayson, though I knew none of them liked him. I had to wonder again if there wasn't some sort of history between them.

Grayson shut the door behind himself and took up a similar stance to Knix's except he kept his arms uncrossed. Awkward silence stretched between them all, and I rolled my eyes, standing up from my spot on the armchair. I moved towards Grayson and he raised an eyebrow at me as I grabbed the sleeve of his shirt, and dragged him further into the room. I pushed him into an empty seat against the back wall.

"Enough," I snapped. I directed my narrowed glare at each of them. "We have a problem here, and acting like children is not going to solve it."

Knix sighed, closing his eyes for a brief moment as he pinched the bridge of his nose before waving his hand at me to continue.

"We have a problem," I said, looking back at Grayson before letting my eyes roam to the rest of them. "I don't know why you have a problem with each other, but that's not what we're here for. *We* need to figure out a solution to getting Grayson's brother out without drawing attention. Then we need to convince him to let Grayson take him to rehab."

"Why should we protect his brother?" Bellamy demanded. "He's a thief. He's been stealing from people at these events for months now."

Grayson stood, narrowing his gaze across the room, and I watched as Bellamy straightened his shoulders, standing to meet Grayson's stare. I frowned, my brows furrowing as I debated how to keep them from attacking each other. When Knix stepped between them, relief coursed through me and I sighed.

"We need to keep this hidden because Sweratt asked us to," Knix replied. "They don't want it getting out that people coming to their events are being robbed. They've worked extra hard to keep it out of the rumor mill and we are not going to ruin that."

Bellamy sat back down with a huff and Grayson turned away, cursing under his breath. He whirled back to face Knix. "What do you suggest then?"

"I want you to ask your brother to meet you at the docks at—"

"He won't come," Grayson interrupted. "I've been trying to get him to stop for weeks. If I try to convince him, he'll just brush me off again."

"You'll just have to try harder then," Marv said.

Grayson flicked an irritated glance Marv's way but didn't respond to the slight.

"I want to take him to a rehabilitation facility in North Carolina. I have someone waiting to take him. As soon as I can get him off this island and back in Charleston, he'll meet us and we'll drive straight to the facility."

"You think that will help your brother?" Knix asked.

With a sigh, Grayson nodded. "If this doesn't work, he might as well go to prison. I want to do whatever I can to make sure that doesn't happen. If it fails then it fails, but no one can say I didn't try as hard as I fucking could."

The guys watched Grayson, all eyes analyzing, trying to determine his honesty. I could have told them he was serious. I could see it in his stance, in his hard, dangerous, blue eyes. Knix seemed to understand that as well. With a nod, Knix motioned for Texas, Bellamy, and Marv. They all stood.

"I want you to call your brother to the docks," Knix said.

"I said he wouldn't–"

"My men will go with you and make sure he comes. If you have to go directly to his room and drag him out, do it. Just make sure to keep a low profile."

"You want us to drag him out of here?!" Grayson snapped. "He will fight. There is no way that's going to be kept on the down low."

Texas smirked and reached to the side of the couch, lifting a small suitcase that I hadn't noticed before. It was barely the size of my forearm and obviously not meant for carrying clothes. Texas tapped his free hand against the side of the suitcase and winked at me before turning to Grayson.

"Don't worry about if he gets difficult. I got this."

"I don't want you to drug him," Grayson replied.

Texas widened his eyes and placed his hand – the one not holding the suitcase – over his chest in mock outrage. "I would never do such a thing as to drug a guest of this facility, sir," he huffed.

I didn't realize that I snorted until Grayson whirled on me and I raised a hand to my face, covering my smiling mouth. He narrowed his gaze before huffing at me and turning back to Texas.

"I mean it," he said sternly. "I don't know what kind of shit you have in that." Grayson paused to gesture to the suitcase absently before continuing. "Whatever it is, it can't be good."

"It's a last resort," Texas replied with an eye roll. "Don't worry. I doubt we'll need it. In case it has missed your notice, Bell and Marv don't exactly like you. They'll be more than happy to just knock your brother out."

It didn't escape my notice that Grayson didn't argue against that tactic. Knix glanced back at me. "Harlow, you'll come with me."

"Where are you going with her?" Grayson demanded.

Knix's glare was so potent even I almost took a step back. I had to hand it to Grayson, though, he didn't budge. If I were the one under Knix's death glare, I would have crawled beneath a piece of furniture. "You don't need to know that."

"The hell I don't!" Grayson took a step forward, interrupting my sight of Knix. Even though Grayson was a substantial guy for someone our age, he was nowhere near Knix's size or height. Hell, I thought, no one was.

"I would back off if I were you," Knix warned.

Bellamy and Marv moved closer and I half expected Grayson to explode and punch someone. Having had enough, I reached forward and grabbed a fistful of Grayson's shirt and yanked him back.

"Enough, guys," I said. I looked at Grayson. "It's fine. Knix would never hurt me. I'll be fine."

Grayson continued to glare at Knix, not even bothering to look at the rest of the guys. The tension between them was slow to dissolve, but when it finally did I released a pent-up breath that I didn't realize I had been holding.

"Alright, then," I said. "We're agreed?"

Bellamy and Marv continued to glare at Grayson. Texas looked like he was trying to contain his laughter, even though I knew he didn't care for Grayson either. Grayson and Knix were the only two sensible ones. Both looked away from each other and pretended that they hadn't been about to commit murder.

"Let's go then," Marv snapped.

I could tell that Grayson would have rather flung himself from the roof of the resort into the gardens below than go with them, but as Texas opened the suite's door with a flourish, and a wink in my direction, they all marched towards it.

"See ya on the other side, Princess," Texas said, closing the door behind him as I shook my head.

"They're gonna be the death of me," Knix groaned, taking two long strides to the couch and sagging into it. The springs creaked and screamed under his weight. I approached and sank into the cushion beside him. Knix dropped his head back, thumping it against the wall, watching me.

"Why didn't you want me to go with them?" I asked.

"Because I wanted to talk to you about the other day," he said. "I've been trying to find a way to talk to you about it, but after what happened with your mom...and then we needed to get on this job. I trust that in sending all three of them with Caruso that he will come back unscathed." He paused for a moment, frowning. "Well, mostly unscathed."

"Why do you dislike him so much?" I finally asked. It had been bothering me.

Knix grimaced, sitting up to rub the back of his neck. "It's complicated. Grayson and Marv know each other a bit. Their families are in the same social circles. I don't particularly have an issue with him, but I don't think he's a good influence on you. Bellamy and Marv are fairly close and Bell will back Marv no matter what."

Well, I guessed that explained Bellamy's extreme reaction to Grayson. He must have recognized him at the school when they met. "Oh." I thought about what he said before, about having me stay behind. "You wanted to talk about the other day?"

"When I kissed you," he clarified.

I froze, my heart thumping. Would he say that it had been a mistake? Would he apologize? I didn't understand why, but the thought of Knix apologizing for kissing me left a sour taste in my mouth and a burning in my stomach. Bellamy hadn't talked to me about *our* kiss. And Marv? What about Marv? I wasn't quite sure what to think about either of them. Did Knix know? Did he not like me anymore? I had to urge myself to calm down. I reminded myself that just because they had kissed me, and I had kissed them back didn't mean that they liked me in *that* way. Maybe it had just been a spur of the moment thing. It was completely understandable if Knix regretted it; even if I didn't want him to.

"I'm sure I surprised you with it," he said. I watched as his fingers scratched the underside of his chin, moving over his whiskers. Knix looked across the room, eyes focusing somewhere on the wall before he turned to face me. "I surprised myself, but I don't regret it, and I hope that you don't regret it either."

I shook my head. "I-I-" I had no clue what to say.

"I want to kiss you again," he said. "But I'm also aware that this could be a very dangerous thing if you were to agree to remain with us after the job."

"After the job?"

"I know you still aren't a hundred percent sure, even though I feel like you're leaning our way." His blue eyes pierced me through as he shifted to face me fully. "I want you to understand that even if..." I had never seen him look so unsure. Serious, yes. Amused, yes. But unsure? It was a new look for him, one that endeared him to me even more. "Even if there is nothing between us," he continued, "I want you to know that you're welcome in this group. If you decide to join Iris, you will be one of our own. You're eighteen and I'm twenty-three. We're adults. This-" he paused, gesturing to himself and then to me, "can come second if you need it to. We're a group, a team, and a family. If you let us, we'll be yours too."

I didn't know what to say. I knew I needed to tell him about Bellamy, but it really wasn't the right time. We needed to be with the guys. I needed to make sure they didn't kill Grayson. We needed to figure out what was going to happen with Grayson's brother, and then I really needed to figure out what I was going to do about my mom's medical options. There was really only so much I could do at once, and though I knew we needed to have a deeper conversation about the kiss, I knew that it would have to wait.

"I think you're right," I said, rising to my feet. "I am leaning towards this group. I'm not sure I understand Iris, but if it's important in helping people like Jonathan and Bethany and even Grayson's brother, then I think it's something that will help me too."

Knix stood as well, towering over me like he always did, the deep, blue pools of his irises swimming with pride and something else. It couldn't have been love, we still barely knew each other, but he definitely liked me, and I liked him too. Knix may have been quieter than the rest, but he was still the one that they all turned to, that I turned to. Despite his size or maybe, because of it, I felt protected. He was a good teacher, and a good kisser, and even though I would have loved to fall onto the couch and let him kiss me again and again, it needed to wait.

I held out my hand. "Let's go help the guys."

He smiled as he took it. "I don't think you're leaning towards us anymore," he said as I pulled him towards the door. "I think you're already with us."

I looked over my shoulder, confused, and as my hand reached the knob the door swung inward, sending me tumbling back into Knix's arms. Texas stood there, panting. His shirt was ripped on the side and there was a line of blood on his knuckles. A bruise was forming on the side of his face. Knix took the lead, pulling me back.

"What happened?" he demanded.

Texas' eyes were wild and there was still residual shock on his face, despite the fact that he must have run straight from wherever he had been with the others back here. They hadn't been gone that long, had they? My eyes trailed to the clock on the counter, it had only been about thirty minutes.

I turned back to Texas, worried about the blood and bruising. He looked at me and reached for me first, pulling me away from Knix. I frowned in confusion, but let him pull me into the hall. Knix followed.

~

WE ARRIVED AT A ROOM MUCH MORE SUBDUED THAN THE suite. It was a simple hotel-esque style with two queen beds and a small sitting area to the side of the bathroom. As Texas led Knix and I inside, with me sandwiched between them, I heard Grayson cursing. I took in the mess; a lamp laid on its side in the corner, the cover off and the bulb busted. One of the beds was pristine and unslept in while the other was nearly destroyed, with the sheets stripped away. I was certain there should have been more pillows, and the one that remained was ripped open.

"What happened?" Knix demanded. "Where are the others?"

"They–"

Just as Texas opened his mouth to answer, there was a loud thump and a cursing moan in the bathroom. We looked at each other for a moment before Knix stepped forward, reaching for the door knob. It opened and inside we found Grayson on the tiled floor between Bellamy and Marv.

"Damn it, hold still," Marv snapped, wiping at a cut on the top of his head.

"I'm fucking fine." Grayson waved Marv away and gripped the edge of the tub to pull himself up.

Marv cast an irritated look at Grayson before pushing past us to into the room. I glanced from Knix's confused expression to Texas' lightly bruised face. He was still breathing harder than normal, I noted.

"The brother was um..." Texas began as Grayson and Marv glared at each other. "Well, when we got here, he–"

"I was trying to help you, idiot," Marv snapped, interrupting.

"Stop," I said, huffing at him. Marv closed his mouth, but continued to glare silently. I approached Grayson, grabbed his hand, and snatched the cloth away from Marv.

Marv, Knix, and Texas watched as I tugged Grayson over to the unshredded bed, shoved him down to sit and began dabbing at the cut along his hairline. "You can't wipe at it," I said. "It just makes it sting more." I was no doctor, but I knew enough from old injuries during my mom's episodes to know that much.

"Where's Bell?" Knix asked.

"Josh took off," Grayson answered. "When we got here, we caught him…" He nodded his head towards the bedside table and I let my eyes roam that way. A wide rubber band sat next to a metal spoon and a dirty syringe.

"Meth?" I asked, shocked. When Grayson had suggested drugs, I never pictured anything so...hard.

"Heroin," Grayson corrected. "He just...he was..." Grayson took a deep breath, reaching up to still my hand. I pulled away as he took the cloth from me. "He was about to get high when we got here. He saw..." Grayson glanced at Marv and Texas out of the corner of his eye. "Them," he continued. "And he lost it."

"Punched Texas in the face," Marv said. "When he tried to run the first time, we tackled him."

"Is that how you got your cut?" I asked, turning back to Grayson.

He dabbed at his wound, but it was all but done bleeding. "Yea."

"He managed to throw us off and bolted," Marv finished.

"Bell?" Knix asked again.

"Took off after him," Texas supplied. "I came to get

you. There's no telling what security will do if they find out what's been going on. The upper management knows but no one else. It'll take for freaking ever to get this sorted if the cops get called and we get detained for questioning."

I crossed my arms and stared at Knix. "What do we do?"

He sighed and pinched the bridge of his nose. I noticed he was doing that more and more. Did he have a headache? Or was that just something he did when he was frustrated?

"Marv," he said. "Go find Bell. If he's caught up to the older Caruso, phone me. If not, get him to the docks. That's likely where he'll go next."

"You think he's going to leave?" I asked.

"He knows he's caught now," Texas answered. "And by more than just his brother. He knows it's serious. He's going to want to get as far from here as possible. That means getting back to the mainland."

"You think that will be easy for him?" I couldn't picture it: an obviously distraught man trying to leave in the middle of the day.

"My brother is very good at hiding his issues." Grayson stood and dropped the cloth to the bed. "Your boyfriends are right. He'll head for the docks, if he isn't already there."

I ignored the boyfriends comment. "You think they'll let him leave then?"

Grayson shrugged. "Yea, I do."

"What about your aunt?" I asked. "The woman who was with him."

"She's probably at a bar downstairs. She likely won't even notice the drug shit. She's not the brightest and she's mostly doped up on her own drug of choice." He looked at me with a tired expression. "Alcohol." Grayson sucked in a heavy breath and released it. "He's probably already on his way off the island."

"We can't lose him," Knix said. "Marv and Bell will head for the docks, if Bell doesn't already have him. Texas and I will take Harlow." He looked at me. "I'm sorry, Little Bit. I know you want to help, but if he's already off the island, I'd much rather have you out of it while we look for him."

I shrugged. I wasn't going to complain. I had no clue what I would do if they took me with them anyway. There was no way I wanted to be confined to a car and I knew that's what Knix would want.

"Let's head out then." I watched as Grayson went with Marv, his head low as they took off at a jog. I could only imagine what was going through his mind.

CHAPTER 20

I sighed as Knix pulled up to Erika's house. I understood them not wanting me along and I was okay with that, but somehow it also felt defeating to be dropped off while they all went on a man hunt for Grayson's brother.

Texas shifted around in the front passenger seat. "Sorry that we couldn't take you home, Princess."

"It's okay," I said, holding onto the bag I had grabbed before we all left the resort. The guys had been right. Grayson's brother had managed to get away from Bell and off the docks before we could even track him down. "I haven't talked to Erika in a while. She was excited that I asked to come over."

"We just don't want you going home right now. We doubt he'll connect you with us, but Grayson confirmed that his brother did see you with Marv and the older Caruso definitely got a look at Marv," Knix explained.

He didn't need to. I had already heard it from both him, Texas, and Marv. Bellamy hadn't had a chance to stay behind and talk to me much at all, but I was sure if he had, I would have heard the same from him. I smiled their way as I reached for the door handle.

"Hold on, let me get that for you," Texas said, popping his own door open.

"No, it's fine. I can–" His door slammed shut and I sighed as he reached the handle of mine and opened it from curb. "Thanks," I said, stepping onto the sidewalk in front of Erika's old, two-bedroom, brick house.

"Just text me if you need anything," he said, shutting my door after me.

"I'm sure I'll be fine."

He stuck his hands in the pockets of his pants and leaned back on his heels, appraising me. "I know this is kind of a shitty situation," he began. "We brought you in to catch a thief, but things have gotten a little out of hand."

I frowned. No, I realized, they hadn't brought me in to catch a thief. They had brought me in to act as a prop for Marv. A couple's resort would look odd if Marv had been alone. Grayson's brother had probably only brought his aunt because she was the type of woman who wasn't all there and didn't care what he did. She was the perfect prop for him. At least she hadn't been in the way, but I was...and that's why they were dropping me off with Erika.

Knix leaned over and spoke out of Texas' open window. "We'll call you when we're on our way back to pick you up."

I managed to nod my head as Texas popped his door and hopped back into the SUV. Knix shifted gears and eased away from the curb. I stepped back, holding my bag over my shoulder. I watched the SUV disappear down the street before turning and heading up Erika's walkway.

"Hey!" Erika answered the door a few seconds after my knock and welcomed me into the living room. I grimaced at the outdated floral wallpaper. It had been too long since I had seen Erika, but not long enough since the last time I saw the living room.

"Want to go to my room?" she asked as she fiddled with her phone. "My folks aren't home. Mom's gonna be on the West Coast for a few more nights. Dad has a late shift. If you want, you can stay over. We haven't talked in forever." She slid her phone into her pocket and looked back at me, expectantly.

"I'm not sure if I can stay over," I replied.

"Right." Her mouth tightened as she grimaced at me. "Sorry, I forgot...your mom. How's she doing?"

I didn't correct her. "She's fine," I assured her, "tough. She'll get through this."

"Do you want to sit then? We can hang out in here if you don't want to go to my room." Erika gestured to the couch that I had dropped my bag next to. "I'll grab some sweet tea and snacks."

"It doesn't matter where–" I began

Erika hurried out of the room, calling back over her shoulder. "No worries. Go ahead and sit. We can talk or watch TV, see if there's anything on."

I sighed and sank into the already sagging couch that had seen better days. I grabbed the remote and flipped the flat screen TV on before promptly flipping it back off as Erika walked back in with a tray. She set the tray down on the side table and handed me a glass before she took a cookie for herself.

"Okay, let's catch up," she said as she sat in the arm chair on the other side of the side table. "Did I tell you about my boyfriend?"

"I know you have one," I said absently. "But you haven't told me much."

"Oh, Harlow. He's amazing. He's honestly the best thing that's ever happened to me." She nibbled around the edges of her cookie before reaching for her own glass of sweet tea. "I was actually thinking about staying in the area because of him. He's talking about getting our own place when I'm ready."

I frowned, setting my glass to the side as I really listened. "Don't you think that's too soon?" I asked. "Moving in together? Did you just meet?"

"When you know, you *know*, Harlow." She sighed, taking a short sip. "It's like this. We understand each other, and it's not like this is the dark ages. We don't have to get married before we move in together."

"I wasn't thinking of marriage..." I said.

"There's nothing wrong with living with a guy." Erika laughed. "I mean, we're eighteen. It's time to move on. We're not kids anymore."

"What if..." I said. "It wasn't just one guy?"

She frowned, finishing off her cookie and reached for a second. "Like what?" she asked.

"What if you were living with multiple guys?"

"Like roommates?" She licked the crumbs off her lips.

"I guess." I stared at the floor, my head a whirlwind of activity.

There was no telling when my mom would get better, or if she would at all. Knix said he thought I was leaning their way and I guess, when we were on the job, I had been. But now that I was away from them, left behind while they searched for Grayson's brother, I wasn't so sure anymore.

"I think that would suck," Erika announced.

I blinked, drawn back to her. "Why's that?" I asked.

"Guys are messy. I really like JC, but one guy is enough for me to handle. You know what I mean?" Erika picked up her glass and gulped back half of its contents before continuing. "Roommates clean up after each other on the other hand. So, I don't know, maybe it could work. The only roommates I've ever had are my parents." She scoffed, setting her glass on the table. "And that's no experience at all, so I guess I'm not the expert. You want a cookie?" she asked, lifting the plate and leaning towards me.

I shook my head. "No, I'm fine." Something else was bothering me. If I *was* going to stay with the guys and I *was* going to be on their team – which there was no yes or no answer to just yet – we'd probably be roommates. It was more than that though. Bellamy had kissed me. So had Knix, and Marv. That complicated things.

"What if they're not all roommates?" I suggested.

Erika frowned, returning the plate to the table. "You mean like you're dating them?"

"Just um…" I began, "hypothetically. Maybe three?"

"Damn, girl, what have you been up to?" she grinned.

I rolled my eyes. "It's a hypothetical question, Erika."

"Sure, sure." She waved her hands. "Well, in that case, it would depend. Do they know about each other?"

"Maybe?" I winced and then sighed. "I would tell them," I decided.

"If they know about each other and they're okay with it, then things should be fine. But if they don't know and you're living together and they find out later, it might become a big deal. You could end up losing one or both or all of them. If you're actually dating them though, it would be pretty difficult to hide."

"You're right," I said. I wasn't dating any of them though. It had been just a kiss, three of them, with three different guys. Guilt rose up inside me as I slumped down further on the couch and thumped my head back on the cushions.

"I'm going to grab some more sweet tea," Erika said, shaking her nearly empty glass. "Be right back. You want anything else?"

I shook my head. "No, I'm just going to use your bathroom."

She shrugged. "You know where it is."

I stood up and moved to the hallway, ignoring the pictures on the wall that I had seen a thousand times before. Some were of Erika and me as children, others were of her parents and relatives I was unfamiliar with. I made it to the bathroom and shut the door behind me. I splashed my face with water and ran it through my frazzled hair. I sighed at my frayed ends, reminding myself to trim it the next time I managed to get some scissors. My back pocket buzzed. Dropping the lock of hair from between my fingertips, I fished out my phone and swiped across the screen to unlock it and read the message.

Knix: Coming back sooner than expected.

Harlow: Did something happen?

Knix: Caruso #2 got away. Probably left town. We're leaving it up to Alex.

I frowned. Did he mean my boss from the diner, Alex? I opened the bathroom door as I clicked down on the text box below to type a quick reply. I was halfway down the hallway when I realized Erika was talking to someone.

"She's in the bathroom right now, but I'm so glad you stopped by, Baby. I really wanted you to meet her."

"I can't stay, I have to go."

"What? Why? Can't you stay for some tea or something? Is it work?"

I was quiet as I moved down the hallway, my Keds quiet on the carpet. I glanced down at my phone and quickly muted it as I moved along the wall towards the living room. It was Erika's boyfriend, I knew that, but his voice was familiar. The cadence was low but more tenor than baritone.

"I'm gonna be out of town for a while," he said. "Some stuff came up. I just came to pick up that duffle bag I left over here last time."

"Oh, okay, sure." Erika sounded disappointed, but I was so focused on trying to figure out why I knew the man's voice that I didn't hear her coming around the corner until she was already there. "Oh! Jesus, Harlow, you scared me! But I'm glad you're done. JC is here to pick something up and I wanted you to meet him."

She grabbed my arm and dragged me into the living room and my eyes nearly bulged out of my head. I could tell the exact moment that Joshua Caruso recognized me. He had been standing in the doorway to the dining room, pacing. Once he saw me he edged towards the door, his eyes focused. I stepped further into the room, my eyes on him as I moved closer to the front door as well. My chest rose and fell as my heart raced. Grayson's brother was just like I remembered from the party and resort. He was handsome, his usually brushed-back, blond hair was shaggy though, hanging in strings around his face.

"Harlow, this is JC. JC this is my best friend." JC, for Joshua Caruso. If Erika noticed the tension, she didn't comment. "Why don't you guys talk while I go grab that bag? Be right back."

Erika left the room and Grayson's brother moved closer to the front door. A million thoughts raced through my mind. The guys were already on their way back. They hadn't been gone for very long so that meant they hadn't gone very far away before the search had been called off. If I could just keep him here until the guys came.

"We didn't expect you," I said quietly.

"I'm sure," he replied quietly, inching closer.

I shuffled on my feet, doing the same. If he tried to get out the door, there was no way I could stop him. He was easily twice my size, though still smaller than Grayson despite being the older brother. I hoped that if he saw me in his way, he wouldn't just bowl me over. I couldn't be sure. He *had* been violent towards the guys and Grayson, but they were all guys, and they had cornered him. He probably felt like a trapped animal. I crossed the room and propped myself against the table right next to the front door, letting my hands cup around the table edges and loosening my shoulders to appear nonthreatening.

"So, you're the mysterious boyfriend," I started, playing off that I didn't know who he was or who he was related to. "You look familiar, but I can't place you. Have you ever been to the school?"

"The high school?" he asked.

I smiled. "What other school would I be talking about?"

He shrugged, scratching his arm. I glanced down, noting that despite the hot, summertime air outside, he was wearing long sleeves. "Are you cold?" I asked.

"No," he said quickly.

"Sick?" I pushed.

"No."

I looked at the floor, crossing my feet and resting the entirety of my weight against the table. I slid my phone out of my hand onto the table. "Rash?" I guessed, nodding at the scratching. He stopped immediately.

"It's nothing."

"Are you sure?" I asked. "Do you want me to take a look?" I sat up.

"No," he snapped. "I said I'm fine."

Erika popped her head around the corner. "Hey, give me a few more minutes, Baby. I thought I put it in my closet but it's not there. Let me check the laundry room."

"It doesn't matter," he said, stepping towards the door. I stood up fully.

"No, no, I'll be real quick. If you need it, I don't want you to leave here without it and get in trouble." I could have hugged Erika. She didn't even know it, but she was helping.

Josh watched me as she disappeared into the kitchen, heading towards the laundry room by the back door. I tried to think of what else to say. It wasn't until I watched him glance towards Erika as she left that I had an idea. When she was out of hearing range, I relaxed back into position.

"So," I began. "How'd you and Erika meet?"

"What does it matter?" He was defensive. I understood that. He didn't know if I recognized him or not and he certainly didn't trust me.

"She and I met on a playground when we were kids," I said. "She was being bullied by this really snooty girl and my brother was too busy hanging out with his friends to notice that I had wandered away. The girl was being mean to her because she said that Erika wasn't good enough to play on the same playground as her." I let a short silence hang in the air before continuing, "Kids can be cruel."

"I don't care where she's from," he said. "She's just Erika to me. I care about her. There were other girls before..." he seemed to struggle with something for a moment.

"Other girls?" I pressed.

"When we were just starting out...just talking you know, I wasn't committed or anything."

"But?"

"Erika," he said. "She...ah...she doesn't judge people. She doesn't judge me."

I smiled. "You don't seem like such a bad guy," I said.

He straightened and looked me in the eyes. "Did you think I would be?"

I shrugged. "I didn't know what to think," I admitted. "She hasn't had someone she's been so enamored with. I would really hate to see her heart broken." I took a breath and let my gaze remain on his. "She was talking about you two moving in together in a couple of months. I told her it was too soon–"

"If that's what she wants, I'll do it," he said. "It's like I said, I care about her."

"Then you don't want to lose her over something stupid, do you?" He blinked, startled by the concept that he could.

"Let's say," I continued, "you had to go away and you couldn't tell her why. Would you lie to her and tell her you'd be back even though you didn't know if you ever would be? Would you want her to wait for you?"

"I don't know what you're talking about," he snapped, his eyes growing cold. "I think it's time for me to go."

His long legs ate up the space between him and the

front door. Without thinking, I stood up and pressed my back against it, putting a palm out to stop him.

"Wait!"

"What?" he snapped. I grabbed his arm, the one he had been scratching. Before he could stop me, I shoved his sleeve up to his elbow, revealing the track marks. He shoved away from me and jerked the sleeve back down over his arm. "What the fuck?! You know!" He took another step back as I reached for his arm.

"I know it might seem impossible, but if you really care about her, and you don't want to hurt her," I said, "stay."

He grimaced. "That's not possible anymore."

"It is." I clutched his sleeve. "What if you went to rehab? You could get better. It's like you said, she doesn't judge. I've known Erika my whole life. She's my best friend."

"Yea? Well, she's my–"

"JC?" Erika's shaky voice grabbed our attention. She stood in the doorway to the kitchen with a dark-gray, duffle bag slung over one shoulder. "What's going on?"

Josh pulled away from me, shaking me off. "Nothing, Baby. I gotta go." He strode towards her and accepted the duffle bag while leaning down to kiss her cheek.

She frowned, but let him. "When will I see you again?" she asked.

"I don't know," he replied. "Probably not for a while. I'll call when I can."

"Okay." I watched as Erika pulled into herself and moved away as Josh approached me.

"Move," he ordered. I sighed, but stepped aside.

The door swung open and Knix, Texas, Marv, Bellamy, and Grayson all stood there. Knix had his hand raised to knock.

"Josh!" Grayson stepped forward as his brother moved back, startled. He bumped into me and the duffle bag dropped. The zipper burst, revealing a collection of expensive jewelry and little objects. Stuff that someone might take with them on a short vacation – gold watches and money clips, leather shoes for men that probably cost a couple thousand dollars.

"JC?" Erika stepped forward. "What is all that stuff?"

Looking panicked, Josh looked at his brother before glancing at Erika. Almost as though he knew exactly what his brother was thinking, Grayson stepped forward.

"It's mine," he announced. "I asked my brother to hold onto some stuff I had while I moved out of our parents' house. I didn't realize my brother was dating you, Erika."

I had almost forgotten that Erika and Grayson had met. It felt like years since we had all been in school together, when in actuality, it had only been last week. Erika smiled, but seemed confused as to why there were so many guys outside her front door.

"Erika, these are some of my friends," Grayson's tone changed on the word 'friends', becoming more forced. I smirked as he introduced Knix and the guys. Knix stayed planted firmly in front of the door, not allowing Josh to bolt.

"It's nice to meet you," Erika said. "Would you like to come in for something to drink?"

"Actually," Knix announced, "we were just stopping by to pick up Josh and Harlow."

"Harlow?" Erika frowned as she glanced over at me. "Have you met JC before?"

I glanced at him, taking in his worried expression and the sweat dotting his brow. "Only briefly," I answered with a grimace.

"Your boss?" she asked. I nodded. "Oh...I was hoping you could have stayed longer."

I winced. "I'm sorry," I replied. "The guys were going to take me to the hospital later."

"I understand," she said. "I'd offer, but...my dad has the truck."

I hugged her. "It's no problem."

"Here let me get your bag." Erika hurried towards the couch and I elbowed Josh. He looked at me with eyes so wide, the whites were practically oozing from his eyeballs.

"Tell her goodbye and that you'll see her soon," I whispered.

"I-I..." he stuttered.

I sighed and grabbed his shirt, tugging him down so that I could whisper directly into his ear. "You're probably going to rehab," I assured him. "You don't have to tell her if you don't want to, but Grayson says that he'll pay for it. We're not the cops. If you give the stuff to Grayson to give back to the people you took it from, no one else has to know."

He slowly leaned away and I waited patiently. His expression didn't ease, but he nodded as Erika grabbed my bag and returned with it in her outstretched hand. I took it and thanked her, stepping back to give her privacy with her boyfriend.

"Baby," he said, taking her hand. "I'm...uh...gonna go away for a while."

"I know, silly, you already told me that," she chastised him.

"Right, yea, I did. But...ah...I didn't, I might not be able to call you very often. It's gonna be for a few weeks." He glanced at Grayson, who had lifted the duffel and held it under his arm. "Maybe a few months."

"Oh." Erika's gaze strayed to the floor. "That's...uh...a long time."

"I want you to wait for me," he said. "I don't want us to be over. I'll try to call as often as I can, but...I don't know when that might be."

Erika sighed and dropped his hand to cup his face. She lifted up on her tiptoes and kissed him soundly. "You're so stupid sometimes, Joshua Caruso," she said. "Of course, I'll wait for you."

Josh ripped her up from the floor and kissed her again, holding her close to his chest. I grimaced. It was gross watching my best friend make out with someone that looked way too much like Grayson. I turned away and stepped out the door, leaving the guys to sort the rest out. At least I knew Grayson would make sure his brother was taken care of and Erika was happy. The rest could be dealt with tomorrow.

Marv swooped in and threw an arm over my shoulder. "Ready to head home?" he asked.

"Aren't you going to stay behind and figure stuff out?" I asked.

He shrugged. "That's Knix's deal. I'm off for the rest of the day."

"I can see that," I said, smirking at his dress attire. His suit coat was gone, his sleeves rolled up to his elbows, and the top two buttons undone. He almost looked casual.

"What?" he asked as I shook my head.

"Nothing, Marv," I laughed, opening the back door to the SUV.

He stopped me before I could get in. "Let's take the BMW," he suggested, nodding toward the dark BMW I had first met him in. "I'll drive you over to the hospital to check on your mom. Knix and the rest can catch up."

I shrugged and followed Marv to the BMW. He opened my door for me, and it felt like old times, sliding into the interior and smelling the clean car scent. I relaxed into the headrest and drifted as Marv got in and turned the ignition. As we pulled away from the curb, I watched Knix and Grayson lead Josh out into the yard. Knix opened the back door and ushered him inside, while Grayson went for the hunter green convertible that must have been his brothers. He looked up and caught me looking as we pulled away. I could have sworn he winked at me.

What a cocky asshole.

EPILOGUE

Sometimes, it physically hurt to walk into a hospital. I hated them so much. When people were too sick to go to work or school, they stayed home. When you were too sick to stay home, you went to a hospital. Marv walked with me as we headed for my mom's room.

"You gonna be okay going in there alone?" he asked.

I nodded. "They probably have her medication figured out, and they have nurses to make sure she doesn't forget to take it," I said. "There probably won't be any bad episodes as long as someone is taking care of her." Better than I ever could, but I didn't say that.

"Okay, I'll be out here if you need anything," he offered, gesturing to the waiting room across the hall.

I smiled and nodded as he turned and walked away. For several moments, I stood in front of my mom's door and then, with a sigh, I knocked quietly and entered. Light spilled into the darkened interior of the room, casting beams across the end of her bed and over the floor. I stepped inside and quickly closed the door, needing to be close to her, but not wanting to wake her.

The railings on either side of my mom's hospital bed were pulled up and somehow, as I moved across the room to sit down on her far side, I felt like they made her even smaller. The large double-glass window at my back reflected the dim light of the evening. I grabbed the edge of one curtain and pulled it open to glance outside as I sat in my seat. I never understood why they gave patients windows, but no one ever opened the curtains.

"Hey, Baby." I jerked around at the sound of my mom's croaky and tired voice. Her weary eyes were open, though they appeared slightly sunken in.

"Mom." I quickly reached for her hand and took it in mine. I enjoyed these moments with my mom; the lucid moments when she loved me, and she really was my mom and not some woman who would change on me with no warning.

"What's wrong, Baby? You don't look so happy." Her wrinkled fingertips touched my cheek as I brought her hand to my face.

"How can I be happy when you're here?"

"No, Baby. I know that look. You've known I've been on my way here for a long time. It's something else." Pulling away from me, my mom scooted as far to the side as she could and then patted the bed next to her. There was barely room for an extra pillow, but I wanted my mom to hold me and I couldn't refuse her offer.

I crawled onto the bed next to her, lying on my side and squishing myself as far up against the bed railing as I could to give her room. She patted my face and smiled, waiting. I couldn't talk yet, so I just traced my hand over her arm. It wasn't until she laid her other hand over mine, stopping my motions, that I finally looked at her.

"Tell me," she urged.

The strange burning in my nose that made me feel like I was going to both sneeze and sob at once returned. I lowered my gaze, staring off somewhere else. For all I knew, I could have been staring at the darkened TV across the room, but I didn't know.

"Oh, Baby," mom said. "It's a boy isn't it?" I released a shuddering breath. "Two boys?" she asked. I laughed. "Three?"

She was just teasing. She had no idea just how close to the truth she was. "How many boys have you been hanging out with?" she whispered when I didn't reply right away. I snickered.

"It's been a wild couple of weeks, Mom," I finally admitted. She stroked my hair back from my face.

"What's got you all bothered?" I relished in the feel of her motherly attention, sinking further into the hard hospital mattress.

"I told you how I got that job," I started, hesitant, wondering if she would even remember. I could tell by the way she flinched that she wasn't sure what I was talking about.

"That's great, Baby," she replied anyway.

"It's um...well, I wouldn't be able to go to college right away, but they would help me pay for your medical bills and they said they would even help me get into and pay for college if I wanted to go later."

"Mmhmm," she hummed, continuing to run her long fingers through my hair, sifting the strands over my shoulder. "And is it something you want to do?"

"I-I think so," I said. "I'm not sure. They help people, but they would want me to work with a team and possibly move in with that team and I'm...scared."

Mom was quiet for a long time after my admission,

her hands curling through my hair, massaging my scalp. It felt so good that I almost fell asleep, but I couldn't. I needed to know what she would say.

"Do you remember," she began, "when you were a little girl and you watched the Olympics on that old, box television set we had?"

"Yea?" I leaned back to see her face, confused.

"You loved the girls on the beam." She smiled, reliving the memory in her head. "You thought they were superheroes. When you found out that almost anyone can practice gymnastics, you begged for classes. We started you out small, the free community classes, and you loved it. Do you remember your first competition?"

I hadn't thought about gymnastics in a long time, but I remembered the one she was talking about. My heart had been racing, my palms damp and sweaty. "I remember," I said.

"I was worried you were going to throw up on the matt," she whispered to me as if admitting a dark secret. I chuckled.

"Me too," I whispered back.

She smiled. "You were so scared, you begged me to take you home before it was even your turn. Do you remember what I told you?"

The memory was an old one. I tried to put gymnastics out of my mind since she had gotten sick. I had directed my focus to more important things like getting a job and paying bills. I didn't realize how much I had missed the feel of spandex on my stomach and brushing over my shoulders as I performed until now.

"I told you that life is full of big scary things, but most of those big scary things only look that way because we're so small. That when you walk up to the things that scare you, they aren't usually so big or scary," she whispered, sleepily. "You're so full of life, Baby. I would hate for you to give up something that makes you happy just because it scares you. I hated that you gave up gymnastics. Whatever it is that you're working on now, Baby, I can tell you love it already. If you didn't love it, you wouldn't be this torn. You can't be afraid of making tough choices, Baby." Mom yawned, resting her head back on the pillow. "Sometimes, you just have to do it. It's one of those now or never kinds of things. Jump in like you did with gymnastics. Fight for it if you want it, or else you'll spend the rest of your life wondering what could have been." I watched as her eyelids drooped and closed, spreading her lashes over the dark circles under her eyes.

I used to love gymnastics. I had been absolutely heartbroken when I realized we couldn't afford it anymore. Mom hadn't been that bad yet, but she had been exhibiting signs of deterioration. Even when she took her normal medication, her moods would fluctuate. I hadn't understood what was happening until the doctors explained it to me and even then, it was a very basic understanding.

She was right, though, about the memory. Gymnastics had been my safe place. Competition had turned it into a weapon that I didn't like. I had been so scared of falling and breaking my leg in front of the hundreds watching. But fear wasn't something that I could let myself fall victim to. Iris wasn't the same thing, but I was still scared because I didn't understand it. Yet, even beneath that fear, I trusted the guys. I knew they wouldn't hurt me, that they would help me if I let them. I wanted to let them. I wanted to grow with them.

The door opened and Bellamy stood there, lit from behind by the hallway. He took one look at my mom and quietly assessed me to see if I was okay. I gave him a shaky smile and slid off the bed. Almost immediately, she slid to the middle of the mattress. I tucked her hair away from her face and bit my lip to keep the tears from leaking out.

Bellamy took my hand as I approached him and pulled me in for a strong hug. My hands shook as I raised them and clutched his shirt, burying my face against his wide chest. I sniffed and rubbed my nose between his pecs. He chuckled and stroked my head.

"Ready to go?" he whispered.

I took a step back, wiping under my eyes to make sure I was still in the clear before I nodded. He took my hand and led me out into the hall. I stopped when I realized he wasn't the only one who had shown up. All of them had.

Knix was stretched out awkwardly in one of the uncomfortable waiting room chairs while Texas snoozed in the corner with a tablet on his chest. Marv paced back and forth in front of the nurse's station, drawing several curious and appreciative gazes. Knix sat up, taking in my face and my hand clutched in Bellamy's. He stood and approached as Marv strode to Texas and shook him awake. Texas' tablet slid to the floor with a soft thud and he stood up, looking around in concern.

"So," Knix said, as if he knew what I had been talking about with my mom. "What's the verdict?"

Now was the time to tell them if I was in or out. I took in their gazes and felt the rising of fear stab at my chest. It had been so easy to stay in the gray with them, yet it had been difficult too. I didn't like being left behind. Now, I had the choice to either step completely into their realm or remain in mine. I couldn't live in limbo forever.

"Harlow?" Bellamy prodded.

I looked at them. Knix. Marv. Bellamy. Texas. It felt like something was missing. Maybe that something was me.

"Harlow, you have to give us something," Marv said. "Don't just leave us waiting."

"Princess?"

"Little Bit?"

I laughed. They were all so nervous, just as nervous as me. It made me feel better, but they didn't need to be because I already knew my answer. I knew as soon as I said it, a new door would open and for the first time in my life, I was ready to fight for it.

"I want to know about Iris," I announced. They all stared at me.

"Are you sure?" Texas asked. "Because if we tell you, then that means that you're..."

"Yea," I said. "I'm in."

Knix smirked and drew me in for a hug. "Well, then, Little Bit," he said. "Welcome to Iris."

ABOUT THE AUTHOR

Lucy Smoke, also known as Lucinda Dark for her fantasy works, has a master's degree in English and is a self-proclaimed creative chihuahua. She enjoys feeding her wanderlust, cover addiction, as well as her face, and truly hopes people will stop giving her bath bombs as gifts. Bath's get cold too fast and it's just not as wonderful as the commercials make it out to be when the tub isn't a jacuzzi.

When she's not on a never-ending quest to find the perfect milkshake, she lives and works in the southern United States with her beloved fur-baby, Hiro, and her family and friends.

Want to be kept up to date? Think about joining the author's group or signing up for their newsletter below.

Facebook Group
Newsletter

ALSO BY LUCY SMOKE

Contemporary Series:

Sick Boys Series
Pretty Little Savage
Stone Cold Queen
Natural Born Killers
Wicked Dark Heathens
Bloody Cruel Psycho
Bloody Cruel Monster (coming soon)

Iris Boys Series (completed)
Now or Never
Power & Choice
Leap of Faith
Cross my Heart
Forever & Always
Iris Boys Series Boxset

The *Break* Series (completed)
Break Volume 1
Break Volume 2
Break Series Collection

Contemporary Standalones:

Poisoned Paradise

Expressionate

Wildest Dreams

Criminal Underground Series (Shared Universe Standalones)

Sweet Possession

Scarlett Thief

Sinister Engagement

Fantasy Series:

Twisted Fae Series (completed)

Court of Crimson

Court of Frost

Court of Midnight

Twisted Fae: Completed Series Boxset

Barbie: The Vampire Hunter Series (completed)

Rest in Pieces

Dead Girl Walking

Ashes to Ashes

Dark Maji Series (completed)

Fortune Favors the Cruel

Blessed Be the Wicked

Twisted is the Crown

For King and Corruption

Long Live the Soulless

Nerys Newblood Series (completed)

Daimon

Necrosis

Resurrection

Sky Cities Series (Dystopian)

Heart of Tartarus

Shadow of Deception

Sword of Damage

Dogs of War (coming soon)

www.ingramcontent.com/pod-product-compliance
Lightning Source LLC
Chambersburg PA
CBHW021939120726
47992CB00001B/60